MOLLY THYNNE
HE DIES AND MAKES NO SIGN

MARY 'MOLLY' THYNNE was born in 1881, a member of the aristocracy, and related, on her mother's side, to the painter James McNeil Whistler. She grew up in Kensington and at a young age met literary figures like Rudyard Kipling and Henry James.

Her first novel, *An Uncertain Glory*, was published in 1914, but she did not turn to crime fiction until *The Draycott Murder Mystery*, the first of six golden age mysteries she wrote and published in as many years, between 1928 and 1933. The last three of these featured Dr. Constantine, chess master and amateur sleuth *par excellence*.

Molly Thynne never married. She enjoyed travelling abroad, but spent most of her life in the village of Bovey Tracey, Devon, where she was finally laid to rest in 1950.

BY MOLLY THYNNE

The Draycott Murder Mystery

The Murder on the Enriqueta

The Case of Sir Adam Braid

The Crime at the 'Noah's Ark': A Christmas Mystery

Death in the Dentist's Chair

He Dies and Makes no Sign

MOLLY THYNNE

HE DIES AND MAKES NO SIGN

With an introduction by
Curtis Evans

DEAN STREET PRESS

"He dies and makes no sign."

—*Henry VI*, Part II

INTRODUCTION

Although British Golden Age detective novels are known for their depictions of between-the-wars aristocratic life, few British mystery writers of the era could have claimed (had they been so inclined) aristocratic lineage. There is no doubt, however, about the gilded ancestry of Mary "Molly" Harriet Thynne (1881-1950), author of a half-dozen detective novels published between 1928 and 1933. Through her father Molly Thynne was descended from a panoply of titled ancestors, including Thomas Thynne, 2nd Marquess of Bath; William Bagot, 1st Baron Bagot; George Villiers, 4th Earl of Jersey; and William Bentinck, 2nd Duke of Portland. In 1923, five years before Molly Thynne published her first detective novel, the future crime writer's lovely second cousin (once removed), Lady Mary Thynne, a daughter of the fifth Marquess of Bath and habitué of society pages in both the United Kingdom and the United States, served as one of the bridesmaids at the wedding of the Duke of York and his bride (the future King George VI and Queen Elizabeth). Longleat, the grand ancestral estate of the marquesses of Bath, remains under the ownership of the Thynne family today, although the estate has long been open to the public, complete with its famed safari park, which likely was the inspiration for the setting of *A Pride of Heroes* (1969) (in the US, *The Old English Peep-Show*), an acclaimed, whimsical detective novel by the late British author Peter Dickinson.

Molly Thynne's matrilineal descent is of note as well, for through her mother, Anne "Annie" Harriet Haden, she possessed blood ties to the English etcher Sir Francis Seymour Haden (1818-1910), her maternal grandfather, and the American artist James McNeill Whistler (1834-1903), a great-uncle, who is still renowned today for his enduringly evocative *Arrangement in Grey and Black no. 1* (aka "Whistler's Mother"). As a child Annie Haden, fourteen years younger than her brilliant Uncle James, was the subject of some of the artist's earliest etchings. Whistler's relationship with the Hadens later ruptured when his brother-in-law Seymour Haden became critical of what he deemed the younger artist's dissolute lifestyle. (Among other things Whistler had taken an artists' model as his mistress.) The conflict between the two men culminated in Whistler knocking Haden through a plate glass window during an altercation in Paris, after which the two men never spoke to one another again.

Molly Thynne grew up in privileged circumstances in Kensington, London, where her father, Charles Edward Thynne, a grandson of the second Marquess of Bath, held the position of Assistant Solicitor to His Majesty's Customs. According to the 1901 English census the needs of the Thynne family of four-- consisting of Molly, her parents and her younger brother, Roger- -were attended to by a staff of five domestics: a cook, parlourmaid, housemaid, under-housemaid and lady's maid. As an adolescent Molly spent much of her time visiting her Grandfather Haden's workroom, where she met a menagerie of artistic and literary lions, including authors Rudyard Kipling and Henry James.

Molly Thynne--the current Marquess has dropped the "e" from the surname to emphasize that it is pronounced "thin"-- exhibited literary leanings of her own, publishing journal articles in her twenties and a novel, *The Uncertain Glory* (1914), when she was 33. *Glory*, described in one notice as concerning the "vicissitudes and love affairs of a young artist" in London and Munich, clearly must have drawn on Molly's family background, though one reviewer reassured potentially censorious middle-class readers that the author had "not over-accentuated Bohemian atmosphere" and in fact had "very cleverly diverted" sympathy away from "the brilliant-hued coquette who holds the stage at the commencement" of the novel toward "the plain-featured girl of noble character."

Despite good reviews for *The Uncertain Glory*, Molly Thynne appears not to have published another novel until she commenced her brief crime fiction career fourteen years later in 1928. Then for a short time she followed in the footsteps of such earlier heralded British women crime writers as Agatha Christie, Dorothy L. Sayers, Margaret Cole, Annie Haynes (also reprinted by Dean Street Press), Anthony Gilbert and A. Fielding. Between 1928 and 1933 there appeared from Thynne's hand six detective novels: *The Red Dwarf* (1928: in the US, *The Draycott Murder Mystery*), *The Murder on the "Enriqueta"* (1929: in the US, *The Strangler*), *The Case of Sir Adam Braid* (1930), *The Crime at the "Noah's Ark"* (1931), *Murder in the Dentist's Chair* (1932: in the US, *Murder in the Dentist Chair*) and *He Dies and Makes No Sign* (1933).

Three of Thynne's half-dozen mystery novels were published in the United States as well as in the United Kingdom, but none of them were reprinted in paperback in either country and the books rapidly fell out of public memory after Thynne ceased writing detective fiction in 1933, despite the fact that a 1930 notice speculated that "[Molly Thynne] is perhaps the best woman-writer of detective stories we know." The highly discerning author and crime fiction reviewer Charles Williams, a friend of C.S. Lewis and J.R.R. Tolkien and editor of Oxford University Press, also held Thynne in high regard, opining that Dr. Constantine, the "chess-playing amateur detective" in the author's *Murder in the Dentist's Chair,* "deserves to be known with the Frenches and the Fortunes" (this a reference to the series detectives of two of the then most highly-esteemed British mystery writers, Freeman Wills Crofts and H.C. Bailey). For its part the magazine *Punch* drolly cast its praise for Thynne's *The Murder on the "Enriqueta"* in poetic form.

> *The Murder on the "Enriqueta"* is a recent thriller by
>   Miss Molly Thynne,
> A book I don't advise you, if you're busy, to begin.
> It opens very nicely with a strangling on a liner
> Of a shady sort of passenger, an out-bound
>   Argentiner.
> And, unless I'm much mistaken, you will find
>   yourself unwilling
> To lay aside a yarn so crammed with situations
>   thrilling.

(To say nothing of a villain with a gruesome taste
in killing.)

There are seven more lines, but readers will get the amusing gist of the piece from the quoted excerpt. More prosaic yet no less praiseful was a review of *Enriqueta* in *The Outlook*, an American journal, which promised "excitement for the reader in this very well written detective story ... with an unusual twist to the plot which adds to the thrills."

Despite such praise, the independently wealthy Molly Thynne in 1933 published her last known detective novel (the third of three consecutive novels concerning the cases of Dr. Constantine) and appears thereupon to have retired from authorship. Having proudly dubbed herself a "spinster" in print as early as 1905, when she was but 24, Thynne never married. When not traveling in Europe (she seems to have particularly enjoyed Rome, where her brother for two decades after the First World War served as Secretary of His Majesty's Legation to the Holy See), Thynne resided at Crewys House, located in the small Devon town of Bovey Tracey, the so-called "Gateway to the Moor." She passed away in 1950 at the age of 68 and was laid to rest after services at Bovey Tracey's Catholic Church of the Holy Spirit. Now, over sixty-five years later, Molly Thynne's literary legacy happily can be enjoyed by a new generation of vintage mystery fans.

Curtis Evans

CHAPTER I

RAIN, BLURRING THE white outline of the cliffs at Dover; rain, playing with needle-pointed fingers on the Customs House roof; rain, sweeping slantwise across the fair green fields of Kent; the dreary, monotonous patter of rain on the carriage windows, and then respite as the train drew in under the shelter of the echoing roof of Victoria Station.

Dr. Constantine, watching the blank faces of the waiting porters as they slid, like the numbers on a tape-machine, across his vision, relapsed still further into despondency. He was returning from a chess tournament on the Continent and was in the grip of one of his rare moods of depression, engendered partly by a vile crossing and partly by the humiliating conviction that he, who prided himself on finding food for entertainment in the most unlikely places, had been hopelessly and utterly bored.

That he had been defeated at the tournament annoyed rather than depressed him. What he did resent acutely was the cause of his downfall, a lady from the Balkans whose name he could neither pronounce or remember, who had been all that a woman should not be, pug-nosed, dough-faced, and monstrously fat. The only word she knew outside her own language appeared to be "sheck", and she used it with a monotonous regularity that drove him to a frenzy of dislike and impatience and caused him to make an exhibition of himself, as a chess player, that even now he grew hot to think of. No, he had not enjoyed the Continent, and it seemed from the look of things as though he were going to enjoy England even less.

London, he reflected savagely, as he picked out the imperturbable face of Manners and signed to it, would be empty and dreary to a degree, while the thought of a wet Easter in the country filled him with unutterable depression.

"Has it been raining long, Manners?" he asked, as he alighted.

"The best part of a week, sir. Very pessimistic, they are, on the wireless, I regret to say. I hope you have had a satisfactory time abroad, sir?"

Constantine, who was perfectly well aware of the fact that Manners followed his progress assiduously in the chess columns of the daily Press, glowered at him, and then, for very shame, tried to shake off his black mood.

"I came to an inglorious end and I deserved it," he said with an attempt at cheerfulness. "Everything all right at the flat?"

"Perfectly, sir. I engaged a taxi, thinking you would wish to go."

Constantine left Manners to deal with the luggage, and, as his cab slithered and splashed its way through the drowned streets gave his mind to the task of circumventing the Easter holiday. He had thrown his hat on the seat beside him, and, as he sat swaying with the motion of the taxi, he not only felt, but looked, his age. The dark eyes beneath the heavy lids were dull and lifeless. Only the magnificent crop of thick white hair that crowned the fine-drawn, olive-skinned face seemed to have retained its magnificent virility.

He had arrived at no conclusion as to his plans when later, fortified by a hot bath and an excellent dinner, he gave his mind to the correspondence that had accumulated during his absence.

"Three telephone messages from the Duchess of Steynes! Did you tell her when I was coming back?"

"Yes, sir."

Manners placed a last knob of coal on the fire, surveyed the result with the air of a connoisseur, and straightened himself.

"If I may say so, sir," he vouchsafed, "Her Grace seemed greatly annoyed to hear you were abroad. She desired to be informed immediately on your return."

Constantine looked up.

"What did she say exactly?" he demanded with interest.

"'Bother the man,' were her exact words, sir," Manners informed him, his manner slightly more pontifical than usual. "She also alluded to your absence as 'abominably inconvenient'."

"In fact, '"Hell," said the Duchess'," murmured Constantine, pulling himself wearily to his feet.

"I beg your pardon, sir?"

"I was quoting an author who might almost have been a personal friend of the Duchess of Steynes," answered his master as he made his way to the telephone.

The Duchess was dining out. Would she ring him up immediately on her return?

He returned to his letters, his mind straying whimsically at intervals to the Duchess and her desire to see him. In spite of his genuine affection for that lady, and, indeed, for her whole family, he was ruefully aware of her shortcomings. One of these, which was apt to react forcibly on Constantine himself, was her delusion that the Duke—the simplest, sanest and most reasonable of men—was one of those people who had to be managed. Coupled with this otherwise harmless mania was a conviction that the collusion of Constantine, one of her husband's oldest friends, was indispensable to the process.

The three-cornered comedy that was apt to ensue, the Duchess painstakingly leading her husband to the water which he had had every intention from the beginning of drinking, the Duke, with a mildly satirical eye on his wife's unwilling confederate, jibbing just enough to lend zest to the leading, was one which, though it exasperated Constantine, never failed to amuse him. Here, at any rate, should be entertainment enough to tide him over Easter.

Tired with his journey, he had begun to undress when the Duchess rang him up. Her opening was characteristic.

"Thank heavens you're back! I've been out of my mind with worry. You've heard about Marlowe, of course?"

"I've heard nothing. You must remember I'm only just back and haven't seen an English paper for two days."

"Oh, it's not in the papers yet. Not that that makes much difference, considering that People are Talking already."

Even over the telephone the capital letters were apparent. Constantine realized that the Duchess must have real cause for perturbation.

"I'm so sorry. I hope it's nothing serious."

"We may save the situation yet if we get together at once. I rely on you. Utterly. Bertie's taking the most absurd attitude. You must talk to him. You're my one hope!"

"But, Duchess, what am I to talk to him about?"

"I can't tell you now. Goodness knows who may be listening. Luncheon to-morrow. Please! Come at half past twelve and we can make a plan."

"Of course. Delighted. Anything I can do . . ." murmured Constantine vaguely.

He rang off, feeling distinctly ruffled. That something serious had happened was obvious, for the Duchess did not as a rule deal in superlatives, and it was irritating to feel that he had been jockeyed into blindly taking sides against the most level-headed member of the family before he had even discovered what the argument was about. He felt sorely tempted to sound Manners, whom he knew to be far more *au fait* than himself with the gossip appertaining to the best society, but he conquered the impulse and went to bed that night his curiosity still unassuaged.

The Duchess was waiting for him next morning in her own special sanctum, a room Constantine loathed. The door had hardly closed behind the butler when she launched her bombshell.

"Marlowe has involved himself with a girl," she announced tragically.

Constantine could only stare at her, for once bereft of speech.

Marlowe, the Duke's only son, and, as regards birth, the best *parti* in England, who had reached his thirty-fifth year still unscathed, owing, apparently, to a total inability to distinguish one girl from another, had been the despair of half the mothers in the country, not excluding his own. "He must realize that he has got to marry some day," she had wailed to Constantine not so very long ago.

"You're not pleased?" he asked fatuously.

"Pleased!" She was a fine woman, though she had just missed being a beautiful one, and was magnificently built for moments like these. "Considering his extraordinary propensity for picking out the plainest and least eligible girl in the room to dance with, do you imagine he has shown any sense in this? Pleased!"

Constantine wilted.

"Who is she?" he asked feebly.

"An actress of sorts. She has been playing very small parts at one of the London theatres. Marlowe met her at one of these clubs that give Sunday performances."

"Any family?"

"A grandfather, I believe. Nobody has seen him," answered the Duchess, dismissing him with a magnificent, if careless, gesture.

"How far has it gone?"

"What are Marlowe's intentions, you mean? My dear Doctor Constantine, being Marlowe, of course, they are strictly honourable. That's why the whole thing is so serious. Do sit down and we can settle what's to be done about it."

Constantine seated himself obediently, still intent on eliciting information.

"He intends to marry her?"

The Duchess groaned.

"He's only waiting till he has brought her here to announce the engagement."

"And Bertie?"

It was characteristic of this couple that, whereas the Duke was "Bertie" to all his friends and a large number of acquaintances, very few people outside her immediate relatives called the Duchess by her Christian name.

"Bertie is being simply impossible. Marlowe introduced him to the girl at the Trastevere, and she seems to have got round him entirely. When I try to get him to do something about it, he goes off at a tangent on the subject of effete old families and fresh stock. He might be the father of a racehorse from the way he talks. But you know what Bertie can be!"

Constantine's eyes twinkled.

"'I think nobly of the soul, and no way approve his opinion,'" he quoted softly.

For a moment the Duchess looked suspicious, then: "Oh, Shakespeare, I suppose. I've the greatest respect for Bertie's opinion about some things. It's when he gets one of these contrary fits that he's so difficult. However, thank goodness, he can always be managed. That's where you come in, dear Doctor Constantine."

"And where, if Bertie hadn't the patience of an archangel, I should go out," said Constantine. "After all, Duchess, he's seen the girl and you haven't."

The Duchess turned on him.

"Doctor Constantine, you know better than that. He's seen a girl who's probably quite pretty, well dressed and skillfully made up, who has deliberately set herself out to charm him. He wasn't with her for more than an hour in a crowded restaurant. He hasn't seen her home or her people; he hasn't seen her in the morning, slopping about in a soiled dressing-gown, among dirty champagne glasses…."

She stopped, suddenly conscious that the picture was possibly too suggestive of an American film to be convincing. Constantine was openly smiling.

"He probably wouldn't notice the dressing-gown, and he'd make an effort to wash the glasses," he said. "In that respect, you know, he and Marlowe are very much alike. Seriously, why not see the girl before you make yourself perhaps unnecessarily unhappy?"

"You're not going to pretend that it's a good match, I suppose?"

"From a worldly point of view it's deplorable, but Marlowe, charming though he is, is not an easy proposition. The War caught him at an age when most men are sowing their wild oats; perhaps that's why he never seems to have gone through that phase. Certainly it was beginning to look as if he were never going to marry. Isn't it possible that he has found the woman best calculated to make him happy?"

The Duchess glared at him in silence for the space of several electric sounds. This was rank heresy on the part of one she had grown to consider her staunchest ally. Then a great light broke on her.

"You've been talking to Bertie," she announced decisively.

"I assure you I haven't. What I said was based entirely on my knowledge of Marlowe. You must admit that he was always known his own mind, and that, having made it up, he very rarely changes it."

"That's just what makes it so imperative that *we* should do something, instead of wasting precious time in arguing. If you knew how I've been depending on you!"

"I hope I shall never fail you," he assured her, "but I can be more useful when I have had time to look round and see how matters stand."

"If by looking round you mean shutting yourself up with Bertie and being talked over by him, I shall deeply regret having asked your advice," said the Duchess with a dignity that degenerated suddenly to mere crossness as the luncheon bell pealed through the house.

Constantine rose and faced her. His smile was disarming.

"Do you know, I've never really been talked over by either of you yet," he said gently. "I've managed, so far, to preserve my integrity while supporting you to the best of my ability."

Her face softened.

"And we've all used you unmercifully," she admitted. "Come and eat, and do what you can with my tiresome family."

The tiresome family was represented on this occasion by the Duke, looking, if anything, taller, leaner, greyer and milder than usual. He greeted Constantine warmly, and kept the conversation drifting through pleasant channels during the meal. He seemed entirely at peace with himself and the world at large. Only once did he mention the topic that had brought Constantine to the house.

"You have heard our news already from Violet, I expect," he said with a whimsical gleam in his eye.

The Duchess glanced hastily round her. The room, for the moment, was empty of servants.

"My dear Bertie," she protested, "is it necessary to take Portland into your confidence?"

The Duke inclined his head in a gesture that was almost a bow. He treated his family with a kind of absent-minded courtesy that never failed to fascinate Constantine. It was so punctilious and yet so curiously sincere, as opposed to the more florid variety he had just left on the other side of the Channel.

"Portland, if you asked him, would probably give you a far more detailed and circumstantial account of Marlowe's movements during the last few days than either you or I could provide," he said quietly. "And, incidentally, the servants' hall is quite sure to be more bitterly opposed to the whole affair than ourselves."

The return of Portland and his minions made it impossible for the Duchess to say what was in her mind, and Constantine hastened to bridge an awkward gap in the conversation.

"What news of Trastevere?" he asked. "Still a howling success?"

"Howling is an excellent word for it," said the Duchess. "Fortunately our bedrooms are on the other side of the house."

Constantine glanced at her in surprise. The Duchess had sponsored the opening night of the Trastevere Restaurant, and had been largely responsible for its immediate popularity.

The Duke supplied the explanation.

"The Trastevere has got into the hands of the opposition," he said with a gleam of humour in his eye. "Personally I find it rather amusing, though I have a suspicion that the Bright Young People are more entertaining to others than themselves."

"I'm afraid that the Trastevere is going to turn out one of our mistakes," sighed his wife plaintively.

Constantine's lips twitched. The last appeal from the Duchess, six months ago, which had brought him post-haste to her aid, had been on the subject of the Trastevere Restaurant.

When, in seventeen eighty-three, the eighth Duke had built Steynes House, that huge barrack overlooking the Park, he had followed in the footsteps of his crony, the Prince Regent, and equipped it with stables out of all proportion to its size. Even in the days of horses these had proved to be as unwieldy as they were inconvenient, situated as they were at the far end of the garden that lay behind the house. When the motor-car came into being they became little less than a white elephant, and the present Duke, soon after his marriage, converted part of the equally inconvenient and rambling servants' quarters of Steynes House into a garage, and left the stables to their fate.

It was the Duchess who, on hearing that the manager of a well-known restaurant in London was looking for a site, conceived the brilliant idea of offering him the stables. The project had hardly taken form in her mind before she was at the telephone invoking Constantine's aid. Constantine, who had a far clearer perception than herself of the condition of the ducal finances, was privately of the opinion that the Duke would require very little persuasion. The restaurant would be too far from the house to encroach on its privacy, the entrance need not even be in the same street, and the Duke, as Constantine knew, was not nearly so conservative as he looked. But the Duchess, having made up her mind that her husband was going to be "difficult", laid her plans accordingly and proceeded to put them into execution, dragging the alternately amused and exasperated Constantine in her wake.

The result had been the Trastevere Restaurant, which owing partly to the organizing capacity of Angelo Civita, the proprietor, and the determined patronage of the Duchess, had prospered increasingly from the day it was opened.

Looking back on the events that had attended its birth, it was amusing, to say the least of it, to hear it stigmatized by the Duchess as "one of our mistakes".

Constantine rashly looked up, met the Duke's eye, and turned away.

"Do you still use the private door?" he asked hastily.

The Duchess stiffened.

"Bertie and Marlowe use it," she said frigidly. "The whole tone of the place has changed so much that I never go there. Civita is making a fortune out of it, I understand."

In accordance with his agreement, Civita, in remodeling the stables, had made the palm court, which ran along the entire back of the restaurant, windowless, so that the garden of Steynes House was at no point overlooked. The court was furnished with a glass roof and opened directly on to the restaurant, leading down to which was a short, broad flight of steps. But behind a towering bank of palms in the back wall of the palm court was a small door furnished with a Yale lock, and at the culminating point in the opening ceremony at the Trastevere the key to this door had been handed to the Duchess by Civita with an apt, if somewhat florid, little speech. Parties from Steynes House were thereby enabled to reach the restaurant by way of the garden, and, as a result, the Duchess's dinner-parties, which had erred somewhat on the side of dullness, had suddenly become un-wontedly popular with the younger set.

Constantine, who had the restaurant habit in his blood, felt his heart sink at the news that the Trastevere had fallen under her ban. His mind went back to the apparently inordinate length of some of the functions at Steynes House in pre-Trastevere days, and he decided that the Victorian tradition was becoming a little moth-eaten even in her capable hands.

He was as nearly out of patience with her as he had ever been when, over the coffee, she unmasked her batteries.

"Doctor Constantine and I have been discussing this absurd infatuation of Marlowe's," she announced, as Constantine, with the pessimism born of long experience, took his first tentative sip of the worst coffee in London.

The Duke crossed one long thin leg over the other and said nothing.

"If you can call it a discussion," amended Constantine, "seeing that it is a subject about which, up to the present, I know precisely nothing."

The Duke inclined his head.

"Sheer waste of time," he agreed. "Far better to see the girl, then you'll have something definite to go on. She's a very nice girl, you know, my dear."

The Duchess's voice was full of compassion.

"How like you, Bertie dear! Can't you see that the only way to deal with the situation is to take a firm line from the beginning? It's just because you consented to meet her that you're so useless to me now. Now I've simply got to act alone!"

"Marlowe's of age, you know," the Duke reminded her mildly.

"Marlowe will get over this foolish infatuation if only he's given time," she retorted with magnificent finality.

The Duke rose to his feet.

"Constantine," he said, "have you ever met a more obstinate beggar than my son?"

Constantine's laughter was so unexpected and infectious that the veiled amusement in the Duke's eyes deepened and the Duchess stared at him in pained surprise.

"I'm sorry," he said, as soon as he could speak, "but your father asked me that very question in practically the same words not so many years ago. The answer is in the affirmative."

For the first time since the beginning of their interview, the Duchess permitted herself a somewhat wry smile.

"Marlowe takes after his father," she said, "and I couldn't tell you, Doctor Constantine, what they can both be like when they deliberately set out to be annoying. If I hadn't thought Bertie was lunching at his stupid club I should never have asked you to come to-day."

The Duke, who realized that, truly earnest herself, she had never really succeeded in understanding flippancy, looked genuinely apologetic.

"Spiked your guns, my dear," he said. "I'm sorry. But Constantine's got to hear my side of the argument some time, and it may as well be now as later. Coming, Constantine?"

And, evading his wife's wrathful eye, he snatched her guest from under her very nose and bore him off to the library.

Once there, he proceeded to deal with the whole business with his customary clearness and brevity.

"Marlowe's old enough to know his own mind. He wants to marry the girl and, though I cannot make my wife see it, there's no reason why he shouldn't marry her. She's been brought up as carefully, in fact more so, than some of the girls my wife looks upon as suitable. According to Marlowe, there's an old martinet of a grandfather in the background who has looked after her since she was a baby, and whose hair would stand on end at the sight of some of the diversions of our bright young people. She's a charming girl and perfectly presentable. I believe her to be genuinely fond of the boy and I like her, and I'm not going to stand in their way."

He bent over the fire and kicked a log into position with the toe of his shoe, then, with a glance, half whimsical, half shy, over his shoulder at Constantine:

"The truth is, I want to see my grandchildren before I die, and it was beginning to look as if there was deuced little chance of my wish ever being gratified. If you can talk my wife round, Constantine, I shall be grateful."

Constantine nodded. He understood.

"I'll do my best," he said. "It would be easier if I knew the lady's name. Neither of you have seen fit to enlighten me so far!"

The Duke laughed.

"Ridiculous situation, really," he agreed. "Betty Anthony is the name, and her grandfather plays the fiddle or something in the Parthenon orchestra. Now you know the worst, and it is the worst, I assure you."

Before he left Steynes House Constantine had definitely made up his mind that this time, at least, he would not be co-erced by the Duchess into any line of conduct but his own, and, by token of his independence, had arranged to meet the young couple at dinner at the Trastevere on the following night.

The Duchess rang him up twice next morning, but drew a blank each time. The respectful Manners who shared with the staff at Steynes House a comprehensive grasp of the whole situation, could only assure her that his master was out and that he could not say when he would be back. She gave instructions which he dutifully imparted to Constantine on his return soon after lunch.

"Her Grace requested that you would ring her up immediately on your return, sir," he said, as he helped his master off with his coat.

"In that case I think we will assume, for the time being, that I have not yet come back," replied Constantine firmly.

Half an hour later Manners entered the study, discreetly closing the door behind him.

"I understood you to say that you were not at home, sir," he began, in a somewhat hushed voice.

Constantine's mind flew to the Duchess of Steynes. She must indeed be hard pressed if she had gone so far as to come to the flat.

"Who wishes to see me?" he asked.

"Lord Marlowe is in the drawing-room. I said that I would ascertain whether you had returned, sir."

Constantine threw the book he had been reading on the table.

"Of course I'm in!" he exclaimed.

There was a conspiratorial flavour about Manners's stately withdrawal which suggested that, Duchess or no Duchess, interruptions would not mar the coming interview.

"This is a pleasant surprise . . ." began Constantine as his visitor entered the room, then broke off at the sight of his face. "My dear boy, is anything the matter?"

Lord Marlowe, a more sturdy, loose-knit, bronzed edition of his father, obviously had no time for preliminaries.

"Doctor Constantine," he said, "is it true that you've got a pull with the fellows at Scotland Yard?"

"I know one or two fairly influential people there," admitted Constantine.

A smile flickered for an instant on Marlowe's lips.

"You've heard my news from my mother, I know," he went on, "and I'm afraid her description of Betty may have been a bit biased. It's on her account that I'm here. She's worrying herself sick, and we can't get the local police to move. They seem to think the matter isn't serious. Personally, I'm inclined to believe that it is. You see, I know old Anthony."

"Is that Miss Anthony's grandfather? Surely he hasn't got on the wrong side of the law?"

"Good heavens, no! But he went out last night to play quartettes with some friends as usual, and he hasn't been seen since."

"You mean that he's actually disappeared?"

Marlowe nodded.

"Utterly and entirely. He's simply vanished," he said.

CHAPTER II

CONSTANTINE ADMITTED afterwards that his first thought was of the Duchess. She had been in his mind when Lord Marlowe was announced, and, as the full meaning of the news he had brought dawned on him, he realized that, from her son's point of view, a more unfortunate thing could hardly have happened. Whatever might be the cause of this old man's disappearance, were it an accident or a stroke or only loss of memory, it would find its way into the Press, and Marlowe was in no mood to keep his own connection with the affair from the reporters. The premature announcement of the engagement, and the inevitable publicity attendant on the whole business, would prejudice his mother even more hopelessly against the girl and her belongings.

"You say you've been to the police?" he asked.

"Betty went to the local police-station early this morning. They were decent to her, but when they found that Mr. Anthony had only been missing since last night they seemed to think there was no real need for anxiety."

"Did they take any steps about it?"

"I don't think so. They told her to go home and let them know if she heard nothing from him in the course of the day. Betty's hard at it rehearsing just now, so, as they live in rooms and there's a very decent landlady, she went off to the theatre, leaving directions that she was to be sent for if he came home or if any news came through. I knew nothing till I picked her up for lunch. We went back afterwards to her rooms, only to find that there had been no news. Then I went to the police-station.

"I did manage to persuade them that old gentlemen of seventy don't go off on the burst without some very adequate reason, and they undertook to get on to the hospitals and see if they could trace him to one of them. I rang up half an hour ago, feeling convinced that they'd have found that the poor old chap had been run over or something, only to be told that they'd drawn a complete blank. They say it's probably a case of loss of memory, and that, if we don't hear something soon, they'll arrange for a wireless SOS. That's what I've got to go back and tell Betty, unless you can suggest anything."

"I could get on to Scotland Yard, I suppose," said Constantine thoughtfully, "but, if I did, I don't see quite what they could do. They were quite definite about the hospitals, I suppose?"

"Quite. As a matter of fact, I was standing by, expecting to have to go and identify anyone that seemed likely, but, so far as I could gather, every case that had been admitted since yesterday evening has been neatly labeled with a name and address and some of the other police-stations have anything to report either. If I didn't know Betty's grandfather, I should say it was loss of memory. As it is, I refuse to believe it."

"It's quite a common occurrence, you know."

"Common occurrence be damned! I'm sorry, sir, but those sheep at the stations have been bleating those very words at me every time I've got on to them to-day. Look here, I'm sorry to be personal, but do you see yourself walking out of this flat any time this evening and knowing no more about anything until you're picked up by Manners on the pier at Blackpool, having forgotten who you are and where you live or how you got there? Do you?"

Their eyes met, Constantine's so dark as to appear black, Marlowe's blue and deceptively sleepy-looking, both steady and controlled, with the glint of humour behind them.

"I don't," said Constantine; "but I might do it. So might you."

"You don't really believe that any more than I do. I didn't do it in nineteen sixteen, and I'm not likely to now. Old Julius Anthony is as normal as we are and as utterly incapable of going off the deep end in that way. You don't know him. I do. I haven't said so to Betty, but he's either ill or has had an accident. That's why I want to get Scotland Yard on the job. The local people are doing their best, but they're only half-hearted about it. They've got loss of memory on the brain."

"He may be staying away of his own accord and have sent some message that hasn't reached you," suggested Constantine.

"Is there any possible reason why a respectable old gentleman should hare off at ten o'clock at night, without any luggage, to parts unknown, when he's got a perfectly good home of his own?" demanded Marlowe. "And there's another thing I haven't told Betty. I got this yesterday morning. He must have posted it on Sunday night."

He took a letter from his pocket and handed it to Constantine. It was brief and rather disconcertingly to the point, and as Constantine read it he realized that Miss Anthony's grandfather was by no means such a nonentity as the Duchess had suggested.

DEAR LORD MARLOWE (it ran).

I understand from my grand-daughter that she has consented to marry you. I do not know what the attitude of your family may be towards your engagement, but I imagine that they must share my views as to the utter un-suitability of such a match. In any case I must ask you to postpone the announcement of your engagement until I have had an opportunity to place certain facts before you. I should be obliged if you would tell me when and where I can find you, and grateful if you would refrain from mentioning the subject to Betty until you have seen me.

I remain, yours sincerely.

JULIUS ANTHONY.

The letter, written in a firm, angular hand in keeping with its stilted and uncompromising phraseology, brought Constantine to a clearer understanding of the writer than any attempt at de-scription on Marlowe's part would have done, and he handed it back with a new feeling of respect for the old man.

"It certainly doesn't look as if he had any intention of going away," he admitted. "You've no idea, I suppose, what he wished to say?"

Marlowe shook his head.

"Not the foggiest, and I can't ask Betty without showing her the letter. I don't want to do that till we've found the old man. She's got the wind up enough about him already. So have I, for the matter of that. If he's been knocked down in the street, surely Scotland Yard ought to be able to trace him."

"When was he last seen?" asked Constantine.

"About nine-fifteen, when he left the friends with whom he always spends Tuesday evening. Betty rang them up and they said he left a little earlier than usual, but said nothing about going on anywhere, and they thought he was going home. He seems to have been quite fit when he left them, and they hadn't noticed anything unusual in his manner, but he's a funny, reserved old chap, a bit crabbed till you know him, but very human at bottom. Betty's devoted to him and he's been very decent to me. So much so that I never dreamed he'd take this line about our engagement."

Constantine's mind went back to the letter.

"He may object on general principles," he said, "or, of course, there may be something definite against Miss Anthony's marriage. The letter looks a little ominous. However, that's not the main point at the moment. Frankly, I doubt if Scotland Yard will do more than is being done already. If he doesn't turn up soon the Press and the wireless will be enlisted as a matter of course."

Marlowe hesitated for a moment, then:

"I wish you'd see Betty, sir," he suggested, rather shyly. "I know you're meeting her to-night if I can persuade her to come along, but she hates leaving, even for half an hour, in case he should come back. If it wasn't for her job she wouldn't have gone out at all to-day. But if you'd see her quietly first, you might be able to reassure her and persuade her that everything possible is being done. I believe I could get her to come here if you can spare the time to see her."

Constantine glanced at his watch.

"I'll go to her," he said decisively. "She'll only be on tenterhooks if she comes here, and, if I do rope in my friend Arkwright, I'd like to have a clear array of facts to put before him."

Marlowe's face cleared. This was what he had hoped for from the beginning.

"I've got my car outside," he said. "We shall be there in no time."

The Anthonys lived in rooms at the top of a house in a small street off the Fulham Road. The girl had been on the watch and opened the door to them herself. At the sight of her Constantine realized that her day had been one long vigil, and he felt certain that every footstep that sounded in the unfrequented little street had brought her rushing to the window.

He had not exchanged a dozen words with her before he went over, unreservedly, to the Duke's side. Not only was she charming to look at, and that stood for a good deal with Constantine, whose Greek blood never failed to respond to sheer beauty, but there was intelligence in the frank grey eyes that met his with a trust and friendliness that went far to undermine any prejudice he had felt against her. She looked worn and strained, and her first words were about her grandfather.

"You've heard nothing, I suppose?" she asked with a desperate effort at hope.

Marlowe took both her hands in his.

"Nothing yet," he said gently, "but Doctor Constantine's got Scotland Yard in his pocket, and he's going to make things hum."

"Doctor Constantine's got a certain amount of influence with one detective-inspector," Constantine amended. "But if anybody can help, he will. Meanwhile, I've come to bother you with a few questions, I'm afraid."

"I'll tell you anything I can," She answered, "only I seem to know nothing. But my grandfather never would have stayed away like this of his own accord. Of that I'm certain."

Constantine, climbing the narrow stairs behind them, watched Marlowe's arm go around her shoulders, saw the sudden shudder that ran through her as she pressed closer to his side, heard his voice, deep and very even, in her ear, "Steady, old thing," and became, even more definitely, a spoke in the wheel of the Duchess.

By the time they reached the long, low room, looking out over the chimney-pots, she was herself again and pathetically anxious to give him any information that might be helpful.

"He went round to supper with our friends, the Hahns, just as he always does on Tuesdays," she said. "It's the one holiday he allows himself in the week, the one night he doesn't play in the orchestra, and he always spends the evening playing quartettes with the Hahns. You see, it's the only chance he gets nowadays of playing or hearing decent music, and he loves it. I rang them up, and they say that they broke off as usual at about nine. Grand-father had a cup of coffee and left at about a quarter past nine. They thought he was coming home. That was the last anybody has heard of him."

"It seems absurd to ask if you've any idea where he may have gone," probed Constantine gently.

She started at him, wide-eyed.

"There is nowhere. He is old, you know, and rather set in his ways. When he's not at the Parthenon I can always tell, almost to the minute, what he's likely to be doing at any time of the day."

"He's never gone off like this before?"

"Never."

"Was he at all secretive about his affairs? Is there anything, I mean, in connection with his work, or his life outside his work, that he might not have told you?"

She shook her head.

"Nothing. Our life here is so simple, really. He has his work and I have mine, and we neither of us have much time for any-thing else. Music is the only thing he cares for, and his only trou-ble is that he cannot afford to give up the cinema and enjoy it."

"There's nothing you can think of that he might have delib-erately kept from you?" persisted Constantine, remembering the letter Marlowe had shown him.

She was about to repeat her denial when a sudden thought made her hesitate.

"There *was* something I've never quite understood," she said at last. "Mrs. Berry, the landlady, told me once, when I'd been away, that he'd gone off unexpectedly. But that was quite different. He told Mrs. Berry beforehand that he was going, and practically how long he'd be away. And he had luggage with him then."

"When was this?"

"About three months ago. I can look it up and tell you the exact date if you like."

"Where did he go?"

The girl's frank eyes clouded.

"That's what made me think of it. It was odd. He never said where he was going. He told Mrs. Berry that if he wasn't back in three days he would write. But he came back after supper two days later, and never said a word to Mrs. Berry about where he'd been. That wasn't so queer, because, though he was always pleasant to her, he never talked much to her. I was away on tour at the time, and she told me about it when I came back."

"Did your grandfather never speak to you about it?"

"Never. It bothered me at the time because, though he was funny and reserved in some ways, he always spoke quite openly about his affairs. I remember I said something about his having been away, and he just looked at me for a moment and said, 'Yes.' There was something in his manner that made me feel I'd better not say any more."

"You had a distinct impression that he did not wish to be questioned?"

"Yes." Her colour deepened. "I know it sounds as if we aren't on very good terms with each other, but it isn't that. I've lived with him ever since I can remember, and we're the greatest friends really. But I think he still looks upon me as a child, and though he's the kindest person on earth at bottom, he can be forbidding sometimes. He's not a person anyone would dream of taking liberties with. When he shut me up like that I knew it wouldn't do to persist. But I couldn't help wondering what he'd been up to," she finished, with a little uncertain smile.

"Was there anything in his manner, apart from that, that struck you as unusual?"

She frowned.

"He did seem quieter, a little more unapproachable, perhaps, for a time, but that may have been my imagination. He's always been a rather silent person. But Mrs. Berry told me that when he came back he looked so white and tired that she was anxious about him and very nearly wrote to ask me to come home. But after he'd been back at work a couple of days he seemed quite himself again, and she was glad she hadn't bothered me. He may simply have over-tired himself with the journey. Anyway, he's never alluded to it since, and I'd almost forgotten it till you asked me."

"Is there nobody you can think of who might have sent for him? Any friend or relation?"

She shook her head.

"We've got extraordinarily few relations, and I know all his friends. You see, my father was his only child, and he and my mother died soon after I was born. My grandfather lived in Paris for a time, and he may have made friends there that I've never heard of. Certainly he never alluded to them. I thought at first he might have gone away on business. He hates the cinema work and would jump at a good orchestral engagement, but he wouldn't have been so reticent about that. He always discussed that sort of thing quite openly."

"You did have a definite impression that he didn't wish to talk of it?" persisted Constantine.

She agreed emphatically.

"Ordinarily I should have gone on asking him about it," she admitted, "but I knew at once from his manner that it wouldn't do to persist. Grandfather is quick-tempered, but he is never really angry with me for long. I have to be careful, though."

Constantine hesitated. He did not know what to say. Privately he was coming round to Marlowe's opinion that the old man must have met with an accident. On the earlier occasion his departure had been a perfectly normal one, and it did not look as if there could be any connection between it and his present disappearance.

A sudden movement from the girl made him turn to her, to find a look in her eyes he did not like to see.

"I keep imagining him," she gasped, as though she could hardly find breath for the words, "laying in some hospital, trying to tell them who he is. Wanting me and not able to say so. He'd hate it all so, the strange nurses and being helpless. If only I knew!"

She was obviously very near breaking point. Constantine rose to his feet, but Marlowe was before him, standing over the girl.

"Look here, old thing," he said, "this won't do. If he's lost his memory or anything of that sort, he'll want you when he comes back. If you let yourself go to pieces, what good will you be to him? You've got to be there when he needs you, that's what you've got to remember. If you let your imagination rip like this, you'll be no more use than a sick headache. The thing is not to think until you've got something definite to think about. Isn't that true, sir?"

He had given Constantine time to perfect the merciful lie that was all he could find to meet the situation.

"Marlowe's right," he said "This other journey of your grandfather's, mysterious as it is, sheds a new light on the situation. If he went away at a moment's notice before he may very well have done so again. I'll get in touch with New Scotland Yard and put the facts before them. After that you can comfort yourself with the thought that everything possible is being done. The moment there's any news I'll see that you get it, if you let me know exactly where you are to be found at stated intervals."

By the time he had finished his little speech she had rallied, and when she answered her voice was carefully under control.

"I'm sorry I was a goose," she said with a swift, shy glance that Constantine found very bewitching, "but sitting here waiting makes one imagine all sorts of things. And yet I don't know what else to do. I ought to be rehearsing now, but I simply couldn't face it."

"I should carry on as usual, if I were you," Constantine advised her. "Provided we know where to find you, we can always get you at a moment's notice."

"There's my job to think of," she admitted, "and, if my grandfather's ill, we shall need all the money we can get."

At the sound of a muttered exclamation from Marlowe she paused, and her eyes met Constantine's frankly.

"He thinks I'm mercenary," she went on, "but, when you've always had to count your pennies as we have, you learn to look ahead. To people like us illness always means expense, and I can't afford to lose my job."

"Once we're married, Mr. Anthony's my affair," got in Marlowe. "We've had this out before, and I thought we'd done with it."

"When you know him a little better you'll realize that Mr. Anthony's very much his own affair," she retorted. "Whatever may happen eventually to you and me, I don't believe you'll persuade Grandfather to take a penny. Besides, he's done everything for me for years, and it's up to me to look after him now."

"Of all the arrant nonsense!" began Marlowe heatedly, only to subside, muttering, as she turned to him.

"Don't let's start all that again now, please," she begged. "When all this trouble's over we can straighten things out."

She rose, and Constantine realized her slender beauty for the first time.

"I'm going to work," she said. "It's stupid to sit here worrying. You know the address if anything turns up. I don't know what Doctor Constantine thinks about the dinner to-night?"

"Let it stand," advised Constantine firmly. "We can get here in ten minutes in a car, and, after all, you must eat somewhere."

She turned again to Marlowe.

"Will you come back and pick me up here then?" she said, adding, with a directness that seemed characteristics of her, "I'd like to talk to Doctor Constantine, if he can spare the time."

Marlowe picked himself out of his chair and stood staring at her. There was suspicion as well as a gleam of humour in his eye.

"Can I trust you both?" he demanded, then challenged Constantine directly. "Whose side are you on, sir?"

Constantine's glance rested for a moment on the girl at his side.

"I can answer that now," he said "You go about your business with a quiet mind and leave us to ours. If you see your father, tell him that I congratulate him on his wisdom."

With a grin that took ten years off his age Marlowe removed himself. A moment later they heard the front door slam behind him.

Constantine turned to the girl.

"I think I know what you're going to say," he told her. "My advice to you is, don't say it."

Her colour deepened, but she was not to be diverted from her object.

"But I must," she said. "I need someone to talk to so badly. Grandfather's been no good; he's hopelessly prejudiced against the whole thing for reasons that sometimes seem utterly futile and at others terrifically important. At bottom I know he's right, and then I wonder whether this isn't the one case to which his objections don't apply. But you're outside it all, and you've known Alex and his people for years. You *can* help me. Please!"

"Of course—if you need any help from outside," said Constantine slowly. "But I think you will do well to trust to your own instinct in the matter. I won't insult you by asking whether you care for Marlowe."

It was impossible to doubt the sincerity of her reply.

"I care for him enough to send him away and never see him again rather than injure him," she said.

"Then will you believe me when I tell you that that would be not only the stupidest, but the cruellest thing you could possibly do to him? Not every woman could make Marlowe happy. You could, and I think you know it. Isn't that so?"

She hesitated, then, with a little hopeless gesture, capitulated.

"I suppose I do. But perhaps every woman feels like that about a man she cares for. It's so easy to persuade oneself one's right. Sometimes I tell myself that Alex's position is so assured that marriage, even with me, cannot hurt it. If he was just no-body, just beginning to work out a career for himself, it would be different. I might really drag him back. But Alex isn't ambitious. The sort of things he wants I can give him. But it's so difficult to see things straight when he takes it all for granted. He won't try to see the other side, and meanwhile I do nothing but flounder," she finished with a rueful laugh.

"Why not adopt his point of view and have done with it?" suggested Constantine, watching her curiously.

"Because, all the time I know there is another side to it and I try to see it!" she exclaimed, with a flash of impatience. "I don't *want* to be a duchess, you know!"

Constantine nodded.

"I can believe it," he said comfortably. "I should hate to be a duke myself. But you can't have it both ways," he finished with a whimsical smile.

She laughed in spite of herself.

"I know. But if only he was on the stage, or a pianist, or some-thing sensible, don't you see how much easier it would be? The Duke's been a dear, and Alex wraps up things in neat little sugar pills before he gives them to me, but do you suppose I don't know what the Duchess feels about it? He had to admit that she wouldn't see me, and, honestly, I don't blame her. And I've said from the beginning, I won't come between him and his mother."

"Is that the only snag?" asked Constantine.

She looked at him uncertainly.

"I—I think so. That is, if you're not against it too. You see, I know so little about his world. It's difficult for me to judge."

"His world is like any other, my dear," Constantine assured her, "though it may strike you as a little vulgar till you're used to it. You see, it's very busy aping its conception of your world at the moment and it doesn't know much about it. But you'll soon get used to that. As regards the Duchess, when she surrenders she will surrender completely. You've probably got a pretty shrewd idea of the kind of person she imagines you to be! The mere fact that you don't in the least resemble the bugbear she has created will go far towards helping the good work. I can assure you that you won't come between her and Marlowe for long. Does that satisfy you?"

She nodded.

"If you really mean it. After all, you're persuading me to do the one thing I want, you know!"

Constantine rose.

"Then that's settled and we can both go our ways. Don't think any more about it, you've enough to worry you already. You need Alex at a time like this, so make the most of him. I'll get on to the Yard and tell you this evening what steps they are taking, unless, of course, something turns up before then."

Before he left her she scribbled a number on a piece of paper that would find her should he want to ring her up. She was in the act of giving it to him when the jangle of the telephone sent her flying to the instrument, and Constantine, watching her, saw the hope flicker and die in her eyes as she answered the call.

"Yes. It's Betty speaking. No, we've heard nothing. Not a sign. Did the Hahns tell you? You what? Where was he going? You left him there? At the door? Didn't he say why? No, I can't imagine. Did he seem all right? Yes, I'll tell them. Oh, I'm all right, only worried to death. I know. Thank you."

She turned to Constantine, amazement in her eyes.

"I can't understand it!" she exclaimed. "That was Sidney Howells, an old friend of Grandfather's. He's a violinist, and he was playing with them that night at the Hahns'. He says that Grandfather had an appointment with someone after he left the Hahns and that he went with him as far as the door and left him there. He's only just heard that he didn't come home or he'd have let me know before."

"Who was he going to see?" demanded Constantine.

"Mr. Howells doesn't know. Grandfather simply spoke of an appointment, and Mr. Howells parted from him at the door."

"Where was it?"

She stared at him in utter bewilderment.

"The Trastevere Restaurant," she said. "It's the last place he would be likely to go to, and I can't imagine what could have taken him there."

CHAPTER III

ON LEAVING Betty Anthony, Constantine went straight to New Scotland Yard. There he met with his first setback. Detective-Inspector Arkwright, who had every reason to be grateful to him for his help in at least two cases in the past, and on whom he had intended to exercise his powers of persuasion, had gone to Paris on an extradition case and was not expected back until next day.

Constantine interviewed the officer who had taken over his work during his absence, and put the case before him, but, in spite of the copious notes and hearty reassurances his story evoked, he made up his mind to get in touch with Arkwright as soon as he returned to London.

When he rejoined Betty and Marlowe that evening at dinner he could at least assure them that all hospitals were being notified, and that if Mr. Anthony had met with an accident they would undoubtedly get news of him before morning.

"I suppose you've had no luck at this end?" he said, glancing round the crowded restaurant.

Marlowe shrugged his shoulders hopelessly.

"The same old blind alley," he said. "Betty rang me up this afternoon and told me what this chap Howells had said. I came round here at once and interviewed everybody I could get hold of. There's no doubt he was speaking the truth. When I described Mr. Anthony, the man on the door recognized him at once, said he had noticed him, as he was carrying a violin-case. When he first saw him he was standing on the pavement outside the door talking to another man. That would be Howells, I suppose. Some people came out who wanted a taxi, and he lost sight of him. He does not know whether he came into the lounge then, but he certainly saw him leave later. There's one odd thing. He's practically certain that he was not carrying the violin-case when he came out, and I've ascertained that he did not leave it in the cloak-room. He passed the porter on the way out, and that's the last anyone seems to know about him."

"Did anyone else see him while he was here?"

"A waiter and one of the cloak-room attendants remember an old man sitting on one of the couches in the lounge apparently waiting for someone, but they are vague about his appearance. The cloak-room attendant has an idea that he saw him talking to one of the pages, but, if he did, the boy must have gone off duty, as I haven't been able to find him. The night staff is only just coming on duty now, and I haven't been able to get hold of Civita himself yet, though I don't suppose he's likely to be of much help. He doesn't show himself in the lounge much as a rule."

"When did the porter see Mr. Anthony leave?" asked Constantine.

"He's a bit vague, says it was before ten when he saw him outside, which tallies with what Howells told Betty on the telephone. He thinks the second time he saw him was about half an hour later, but it might have been more. The cloak-room attendant says that the old man he saw was in the lounge for at least half an hour, so that the various accounts we have got seem to fit in with each other pretty well. Anyway, there seems no doubt that he did come here."

"It looks like it," agreed Constantine.

An uncomfortable silence fell on the little party. There seemed nothing to say, and yet none of them cared to be left for long with his own thoughts.

"I wish Civita would turn up," said Betty suddenly. "He can't know anything, but there's something so amazingly capable about him."

Constantine turned to her with a smile.

"Fergusson, of the *Banner*, christened him 'Il Duce' when the place first opened, and, if the clientele here had had even a bowing acquaintance with Italian politics, the name would have stuck. He's a very distinct personality."

"It's extraordinary the way in which he managed my mother," said Marlowe. "If Father hadn't kept his head we should have lost half the garden. As it was, the foundations of the lounge had been dug before we discovered that she'd given him permission to shift the wall at this end. As things have turned out, it's been rather a convenience."

"Especially during the last fortnight," suggested Constantine gently.

Marlowe laughed.

"It's been a godsend," he admitted. "Betty slips in at the front, and I stroll across the garden from the house and there we are. Saves complications!"

Constantine nodded absently.

"How many keys are there to that door into the garden?" he asked abruptly.

Marlowe looked doubtful.

"So far as I know, only the one Civita gave my mother on the opening day, but, if there is another, we could hardly take exception to his keeping one himself, provided he saw to it that it wasn't used indiscriminately. You're not suggesting . . ."

He pulled himself up sharply. Constantine knew what was in his mind: the letter Betty's grandfather had written to him asking for an appointment, and of which the girl knew nothing. Constantine had not alluded to it on his visit to Scotland Yard, but he had every intention of putting his friend Arkwright in full possession of the facts as soon as he could get hold of him. In the absence of any other motive, there seemed a faint possibility that Mr. Anthony might have called at the restaurant in the hope of seeing Marlowe, though why he should go there rather than to Steynes House was a mystery.

"You didn't use the door yourself last night, I suppose?" he asked.

"No," answered Marlowe, in a tone that showed that he fully realized the trend of Constantine's thoughts. "My mother had a bridge-party, and I was on duty all the evening."

"Where is the key kept?"

"In a box on the writing-table in the library. Anyone who knew about it could borrow it, I suppose. As a matter of fact, my father may have used it himself. He was at some public dinner or other last night and got back too late for the first rubber. He's fond of strolling over here and watching the dancing. He may have come over last night."

"Would he know Mr. Anthony if he saw him?"

Betty answered him.

"I'm sure they've never met," she said decisively. "My grandfather disapproved of our engagement and wouldn't have anything to do with it, in spite of the fact that he's always liked Alex. So far as I know, he'd never been inside this place in his life."

"Forgive me, Miss Anthony, but were you speaking of your grandfather?"

Betty looked up with a start, to meet the eyes of the man who stood over her, his whole attitude a lesson in friendly subservience. One of the secrets of Angelo Civita's success lay in his ability to gauge the exact degree of familiarity he might safely indulge in with his various patrons, and Betty had already noted with some amusement the very subtle but unmistakable alteration in his attitude towards her since her elevation to the rank of a potential duchess. In events of social importance Civita was invariably a day ahead even of the Press, not because the man was in any sense a snob, but because such knowledge formed an essential part of his professional equipment.

She answered him eagerly.

"You've heard that he was seen here, M. Civita?"

He bowed.

"I know he came here," he answered in his precise but fluent English, "but I did not see him myself. I wish now that I had."

"Have you any idea why he came here?" asked Marlowe.

"He came to see me," answered Civita with a little deprecatory gesture.

If he had dropped a bombshell on the table he could hardly have produced a more effective sensation. Before the obvious question had time to leap to Betty's lips he hastened to explain himself.

"When you first came here, Miss Anthony," he said, "I did not know you were the grandchild of an old friend. I knew your grandfather years ago in Paris and I can remember you as a little girl. When I ran into Julius Anthony in the street only a few days ago and learned that he had a grand-daughter on the stage I was astonished, I can tell you. I guessed then that the Miss Anthony on whose patronage I had congratulated myself so often was the little girl I used to see playing in Julius Anthony's flat in Paris."

He paused, his keen, observant eyes on Betty's expectant face. Constantine, watching him with the interest that this man never failed to evoke in him, reflected for the hundredth time that the Roman Church had lost an imposing prelate when little Angelo Civita left his village on the Campagna to take up his job as piccolo in a café at Nice.

He knew something of the man's history, for Civita, under the spell of Constantine's almost perfect Italian, had told him frankly of his earlier struggles. The village priest had destined him for the Church, and, if his mother had had her way, he would, in Constantine's opinion, have been well on the path to advancement by now. His face now, broad, bland, clean-shaven and inscrutable, the thin, straight lips with their tucked-in corners, relaxed in a smile so sympathetic and, at the same time, so deferential as to be void of all offence, belonged to the cassock rather than to the faultlessly cut evening clothes that were almost his livery.

He had taken up his tale again.

"Your name was not mentioned, Miss Anthony," he continued, the smile deepening, "by either of us. In my business one learns discretion, and I remembered your grandfather as being on the puritanical side in the years when I knew him. We are all that is most respectable here, but I was careful, and so our talk was all of business."

He hesitated for a second, then:

"I asked him to call upon me when he had time. In view of what I understand has happened, I could wish he had not chosen last night when I was most busy. I was obliged to send him a message, making an appointment for to-morrow. They tell me that he left soon after he received it, and I can get no clue as to where he was going. I am sorry."

His distress was no doubt genuine, but Constantine had the impression that he had skated adroitly over a treacherous gap in the early part of his speech. From the way in which his eyes had shifted for a moment to Marlowe's, he had an idea that, unhampered by the presence of Betty, he might prove more communicative.

"He came here definitely to see you?" demanded Marlowe.

"But certainly. We had named no special date in our conversation, and he chanced finding me disengaged. There is, however, one thing I have discovered. Someone, a man, was with him when he arrived here, and someone joined him outside the restaurant when he left. It may have been the same person; I do not know."

"Who saw them?" asked Constantine sharply.

"The man on the door saw the first one, though, like most of his kind, he seems incapable of an intelligent description. Somers, the cloak-room attendant, saw someone that, from his description, I take to be Mr. Anthony, leave the lounge and go through the swing doors. Now there is a window to the cloak-room, and the attendant glanced through it a minute later and saw a man come up and speak to an old gentleman, who seemed to be coming from the restaurant. He declares that the two men went away together."

"Was my grandfather carrying his violin-case?" asked Betty.

"According to the doorman he was carrying it when he first saw him, but neither he nor the two cloak-room attendants can remember to have seen it again. He certainly did not leave it here. It is curious, but I can get no information that is more exact. I am afraid you are anxious, Miss Anthony. It is only natural, but you are sure to hear news of him soon. I myself have known such cases of loss of memory. They are not uncommon, especially among the old, and, if this man was with him, it should be easy to trace him."

The last words, spoken with the quiet conviction of one stating an established truth, did more to reassure Betty than the rather half-hearted encouragement that had been meted out to her all through that long day. There was something impressive in Civita's calm air of authority, and when he withdrew, after a few well-chosen words of sympathy, he left a more cheerful atmosphere behind him.

They sat for a time over their coffee and then parted.

Constantine had a few words with the cloak-room attendant on his way out, but beyond the fact that the man he had seen with the old gentleman had been dark and not very tall, he gleaned nothing.

It was not till nearly five o'clock on the following day that he was able to get in touch with Arkwright, who, tired though he was with his journey from Paris, and secretly convinced that the old man would turn up in the course of the next few hours, had too much regard for Constantine to disappoint him. He promised to give the matter his personal attention, and Constantine, having passed on the news to Betty that, so far as accident or illness was concerned, the police had drawn a blank, returned to his flat.

Once there he dealt summarily with two alternative invitations for Easter with which he had been mildly dallying since his return to England. Apart from the fact that the weather showed little sign of improving, he felt no desire to leave London at this juncture. Added to his growing interest in the fate of the elusive Mr. Anthony was an impish delight in the contemplation of the Duchess's reactions to this unexpected complication of her son's affairs. That she would eventually yield to Betty's quite exceptional charms he had no doubt, but it would be after a manner peculiarly her own.

He had just handed the letters to Manners for the post when the telephone-bell rang. Marlowe was at the other end, talking rapidly in a voice very unlike his usual lazy drawl.

"I'm with Betty," he said. "Someone's ransacked her rooms while she was rehearsing. She came back and found the place in the dickens of a mess. Drawers turned upside down and the floor covered with papers and things. She rang me up, and I've only just got here. Shall I get on to the local police or will you tell your friend at Scotland Yard?"

"How much has been taken?" asked Constantine. "Did Betty keep any jewellery in her room?"

"As far as we can see there's nothing of hers missing, though we haven't had time to make a thorough search. The thief seems to have given her room a miss. There was about five pounds odd in her grandfather's bedroom, and that hasn't been touched. And none of her trinkets are gone. I don't believe it's an ordinary burglary."

"Stay where you are," said Constantine decisively. "I'll try to get Arkwright and then come round myself."

When he and Arkwright drove up to the house half an hour later, Marlowe opened the door to them himself.

"We've left things as they were when Betty found them," he said, "but we've gone through them pretty thoroughly and there's nothing missing apparently. Certainly nothing of any value has been taken. And Mrs. Berry, here, has seen the thief."

He stood aside and revealed a stout, comfortable-looking woman in a state of breathless indignation.

"Let him in myself, I did," she panted. "Never suspected a thing, I didn't. Said he'd come to tune the piano, same as usual; and tune it he did, at least I heard him myself a-runnin' up and down it the way they do. And he was carryin' a little black bag and all."

Betty's voice reached them from where she stood on the landing.

"The piano was tuned less than three weeks ago, and I've just rung up the people who have always done it for us and they say they sent no one."

"What did the man look like?" demanded Arkwright.

"Well, I didn't look at him very close," admitted Mrs. Berry. "I was expecting me husband back early and wanted to get on with his tea. He was shortish, and he'd got a little dark moustache and spoke like a foreigner. That didn't surprise me because they generally send someone foreign for the piano—a Belgian I think he is. One of those refugees that have stayed over. Isn't that right, Miss Anthony?"

"Yes," agreed Betty. "But Duval, the man they generally send, hasn't got a moustache. He's tall and fair. You know him quite well, Mrs. Berry."

"That's right," agreed Mrs. Berry cordially. "But this one bein' foreign too made me think it was all right, if you understand me. He spoke just like a piano-tuner, too."

Arkwright, with an amused glance at Constantine, refrained from further research into the language of piano-tuners and brought her firmly back to the point.

"You say he did tune the piano?" he said. "Were you within hearing all the time?"

"He certainly started on it," she answered doubtfully. "I could hear him ripplin' up and down. But I was in a hurry to get on with the tea, and down in the kitchen you can't hear much, and anyway, I wasn't listenin'."

"Did you see him out?"

"No, He let himself out, the way the other tuner does. I didn't see him again."

"Looks as if that was our man all right. Would you know him again if you saw him?"

Mrs. Berry shook her head hopelessly.

"I might, and then again I mightn't," she said, with an agonized glance at Betty. "I wouldn't have had this happen for anything, and you in such trouble already!"

Betty ran down the stairs and propelled her with comforting words towards the basement while Marlowe led the way to the scene of the crime.

The sitting-room was in a state of hopeless disorder. Every drawer of a massive bureau that stood in the window had been wrenched out and the contents emptied on to the floor, and, from the look of it, the accumulated epistolary litter of years was piled on the carpet.

Arkwright, his massive figure almost filling the doorway, ran a quick, seeing eye over the room.

"Any real valuables kept in here, Miss Anthony?" he asked.

She pointed to a table near the piano.

"There are a couple of snuff-boxes, one silver and one gold, in the drawer there," she answered. "My grandfather takes snuff and these were given to him. I believe they're worth a lot. And the violin in the case on the piano would be worth taking. But the thief probably wouldn't know that, I suppose."

Arkwright took the room in a couple of strides and opened the drawer of the table. The snuff-boxes were revealed, lying among a litter of smaller objects.

"Not been touched," he said. "Did Mr. Anthony go in for autographs or etchings, or anything of that sort?"

Betty shook her head.

"I'm sure he had nothing of the kind of any value. I'm not certain what he kept in the drawers of the bureau, but I'm pretty sure that it was the usual collection of business papers and letters. I glanced over this mess without touching it, and it looks a perfectly ordinary jumble of receipts and things."

Arkwright bent over the piano.

"He opened this and 'rippled up and down it' all right, and that's about all he did. Doesn't seem to have left any marks, but I'll have it tested. It might be one of our old friends, but I doubt it. May I see your room, Miss Anthony?"

Betty led the way across the passage, and Constantine and Marlowe were left together.

"They'll surely take the old man's disappearance seriously after this," said Marlowe in a low voice.

"You think there's some connection?"

Marlowe stared at him.

"I don't see how else to account for it. The chap who did this wasn't after loot. I've seen Betty's bits of jewellery. They aren't worth much, but they haven't been touched."

They were interrupted by the return of Arkwright.

"Suppose we try to get some order into all this?" he said genially, squatting on his heels in front of the most formidable heap of papers. "It oughtn't to take long if we all lend a hand."

In a shorter time than seemed possible they had everything sorted and back in the drawers of the bureau. Arkwright stood in front of it, rubbing his chin thoughtfully.

"Just as Miss Anthony said," he murmured. "Not a valuable or even confidential document among them, with the exception of a few private letters. Will you glance through them, Miss Anthony?"

Betty went through the contents of the packet he handed her.

"There's nothing here," she said at last. "They almost all deal with professional matters, and couldn't possibly be of any interest to anyone. There are some letters of mine here too. I didn't know he had kept them."

She bent over the packet, her face hidden, and busied herself with stacking the envelopes together. But her fingers fumbled at their task, and Marlowe, with a side-glance at Arkwright, went over and squatted on the floor beside her.

But Arkwright had not noticed her emotion. He was turning over the pages of a cheap commercial diary in which Mr. Anthony had apparently been in the habit of jotting down the events of each day. Constantine, looking over his shoulder, saw that it contained only the barest statement of the old man's movements. Evidently he kept it merely for the sake of possible reference. He was turning away when a low exclamation from Arkwright caught his ear.

"Miss Anthony," he said, "do you know whether your grandfather made regular entries in this diary? I mean, did he keep it up to date or just write it up every now and then from memory?"

Betty's voice came, husky but emphatic.

"He wrote it up every evening before he went to bed. He was extraordinarily methodical about things like that. When he didn't come home on Tuesday I looked in it to see if he'd mentioned anything that might give me some clue as to his plans, but there was nothing."

"It was up to date when you looked at it?"

Betty turned to him in surprise.

"The last entry was on Monday night," she said "Can't you find it?"

For answer Arkwright held the book towards her, the covers bent back so that she could see the jagged ridges of paper where the leaves had been torn out. She sprang to her feet.

"Why, half the book's gone!" she exclaimed. "It wasn't like that when I looked at it on Tuesday!"

Arkwright put the book down on the flap of the bureau, hooked his foot round the leg of a chair, drew it towards him and sat down.

"Now," he said with grim satisfaction, "we know where we are and what all this mess is about. Let's see what's missing."

He turned over the pages.

"A day to a page. All right up to January the eighteenth. That's missing, and so is every page up to March the twenty-second. Torn out in a hurry too. If the chap had had more time I'll wager he'd have been more selective in his choice, and we probably shouldn't have noticed anything. Now do these dates mean anything to you?"

Betty hesitated.

"I'm a fool about dates. Give me a moment."

She stood drooping, one slim hand over her eyes, then suddenly:

"January! I was away in January. Let me have the diary."

She flipped back half a dozen pages immediately before the cut.

"Here it is. I knew Grandfather would have made a note of it."

She pointed to the entry. It ran:

"Betty left for Manchester by the nine-thirty."

"I didn't come back for three weeks," she went on breathlessly. "Wait, I believe I know!"

Before Arkwright could open his lips she had thrust the book back into his hands and was out of the room. They could hear her footsteps on the stairs and her voice calling Mrs. Berry. Arkwright turned an enquiring eye on Marlowe, only to realize that there was no help to be got from that quarter.

Constantine sat waiting, his mind going back to a conversation he had had in his very room only the day before.

It was to him she turned when she came back.

"I was right!" she cried. "Mrs. Berry remembers the date quite well. He went away on January the eighteenth."

"Your grandfather?"

The question was Arkwright's, and it was Constantine who answered him.

"A pretty little problem, Arkwright. On January the eighteenth Mr. Anthony took a journey. Except that he went of his own volition and evidently expected to be away for several days, his whereabouts seem to have been as ambiguous as they are at present. He came back, when?"

"On the evening of the twentieth, Mrs. Berry says," answered Betty.

"It looks as if the missing pages in that diary are those containing any reference to his journey," continued Constantine.

Betty turned to him, dismay in her eyes.

"Then if I'd only had the sense to look up those dates on Tuesday night, we might have had some idea where he's gone!"

"You can hardly blame yourself," said Constantine. "But these missing pages shed a rather interesting light on that sudden journey of his. Whoever took them was content to leave the entries up to the very day of his departure untouched."

"Knowing, apparently, that they contained nothing danger-ous," cut in Arkwright. "I see your point. Until the actual day on which he left his house Mr. Anthony himself was unaware that he was about to be called away. It looks as if history had repeated itself."

He stopped at the sight of Betty's stricken face.

"But why should there be danger in the diary now?" she cried. "What can anybody have to hide?"

None of the three men could find words in which to an-swer her.

CHAPTER IV

CONSTANTINE WAITED while Arkwright interviewed Mrs. Ber-ry, and then suggested that he should join him in a hasty meal before returning to the Yard. Arrived at the club, Arkwright plunged into the telephone-box. Constantine was already in the dining-room when he came out.

"Do you realize how late it is?" he asked. "Close on nine o'clock. Knowing you'd got to get back to the Yard, I thought I'd better hurry things up here. No news of the old man, I suppose?"

"None. We shall have to put out an SOS if we don't get something soon. I must admit, this business to-day makes the whole thing look a bit fishy. How much do you really know about these Anthonys, sir?"

"Nothing," said Constantine frankly; "but it seems to me that, judging by the daughter and her surroundings, they speak for themselves. Apart from the fact that the girl is exceptionally charming, she appears to be a perfectly normal example of the intelligent professional class. There's a dash of Latin blood in her, I should imagine. Certainly the grandfather has lived abroad. From her description I should say that he belongs to the old-fashioned type of musician, such as one used to find by the hundred in Germany. Wrapped up in his art, probably intolerant of modern standards and quite impervious to social or monetary distinc-tions. Intellectual snobbery he might be guilty of, but he sounds a singularly independent and strong-minded old person. Whatever may be behind these mysterious departures of his, I should be surprised if it was anything he has cause to be ashamed of."

"Where, precisely, does Lord Marlowe come in?"

"Unofficially he and Miss Anthony are engaged, and, I fancy, it will not be long before the announcement will be made. The grandfather is opposing the match. That will give you a clue as his character."

"On what grounds?"

"Social, I should say, but there may be more behind it."

Constantine told Arkwright of Mr. Anthony's letter to Lord Marlowe.

"That doesn't look as if he had been contemplating a journey of any kind," said Arkwright.

"I'm convinced that he wasn't. On the last occasion he went off at a moment's notice, and that's no doubt what happened this time. Miss Anthony's comment this afternoon on the destruction of the diary was disconcertingly to the point. I don't like it, Arkwright!"

"I shan't be sorry when he's found," agreed the inspector. "If this diary business is an attempt to cover up his traces it looks a bit ominous. You've built up a pretty good portrait of him from hearsay, sir; can you think of any reason why a respectable elderly musician should go traipsing off into the void like this?"

"I can't. Frankly, he's the last person I should suspect of such a thing. He may have been decoyed away by the offer of some professional engagement. I understand that he was dissatisfied with his job at the cinema. More than a cut above it, I imagine. But that wouldn't account for the secrecy."

"I've been having a dig round at the Trastevere," said Arkwright. "You know what he went there for?"

Constantine's eyes lit up with interest.

"For some reason that Civita didn't care to reveal before Miss Anthony," he said. "What was it?"

"According to the proprietor, he was in search of funds. Something to do with a quartette he was keen on. Mr. Civita was interested, and had offered to put up some of the money. The idea seems to have been for Anthony to give up his present job and go on tour with some other musicians. Does that fit in with what you know of him, sir?"

"Perfectly. But I don't understand why he didn't discuss it with his grand-daughter. I think she'd have mentioned it if he had."

"Apparently Civita was to share the proceeds till the loan had been paid back. He thought it a sound financial proposition, and, if he'd had the money ready, would have handed it over on Tuesday night, but he hadn't expected Anthony so soon and hadn't had time to make arrangements with his bank, so, when he heard that Anthony was there, he sent a waiter with a written message asking him to call on the following day for the cheque. Anthony sent a verbal assent. I've verified all this, seen the waiter and the page to whom he handed the envelope. The page gave it to Anthony. So that's that."

"That's the boy Marlowe tried to run to earth and couldn't get hold of?"

"He was off duty last night. According to his account he was standing by the porter outside when Anthony arrived. Anthony asked him if Mr. Civita was disengaged. The boy spoke to a waiter, who ran Civita to earth in his office. Civita, who was very busy, scribbled a few words on a card, shoved it in an envelope and sent it to Anthony, with a verbal message to the effect that he was engaged. The waiter passed it on to the page, who, finding Anthony still outside the restaurant, talking, so he says, to another man, delivered it and took the answer. He declares that he could identify this man, but he went straight back into the restaurant and has no idea what Anthony did after that."

"Howells says they parted, so presumably Anthony went into the restaurant. Certainly the door-keeper saw him leave over half an hour later."

Arkwright raised his eyebrows.

"Without his violin-case?"

Constantine frowned.

"That's not the only queer feature of the case. Why did he go back into the restaurant at all? The appointment with Civita had fallen through. Have you found anyone who served him with coffee or drinks? I think we can take it that he didn't go into the supper-room. The place would be far beyond his means."

"He didn't. I've ascertained that. And he ordered nothing. There's every indication that he remained in the lounge until he was seen to leave the place for good. When we've traced that blessed violin-case we may be nearer to knowing what he did. If it wasn't for that business to-day and that other journey of his, I should be inclined to think that he'd just wandered off and forgotten where he lived. He was getting old, and if he'd been worrying about this scheme of his and the shortage of money he might have had a lapse."

"His brain was clear enough when he went away before. There's no doubt that he made all his arrangements, gave instructions to the landlady and so forth, in the most normal manner. If, as we think, there's some connection between this absence and the last, he's probably in full possession of his faculties now."

Arkwright rose to his feet.

"Well, I've done my best," he said. "And I've started the machinery working. It'll sweep the old gentleman in automatically in the course of the next few days. Meanwhile, I've got a nice little pile of stuff waiting for me at the Yard and I've got to tackle it. They'll report to me if anything transpires and I'll let you know."

"I'm really grateful," Constantine assured him. "I know you've gone out of your way to take a hand in this. If I wasn't personally interested in the affair I wouldn't have put the extra load on your shoulders just now."

Arkwright beamed affectionately on him from his great height.

"That's all right. You've given me a pretty hefty shove in the right direction twice, you know, though I hate your secretive methods! If you find old Anthony for yourself to-night, I suppose you'll lock him in a drawer and hand him to me on a salver with my breakfast to-morrow morning!"

Constantine shook his head.

"I'm going home to bed. All I ask is that you don't treat me to a dose of my own medicine! If anything crops up I want to know about it, no matter what hour of the day or night. I'm very sorry for that girl."

"Right. Only don't blame me if I spoil your beauty sleep. And I count on you to protect me from Manners. I'd rather face a Chicago gunman than Manners in his dignified wrath!"

Arkwright was only half serious, but it was a significant fact that the voice that strove with Manners over the telephone in the small hours of the morning was that of an unsuspecting subordinate, despatched by the inspector to the nearest call-box.

Constantine, roused by the insistent bell, emerged from his bedroom to the sound of an imperturbably reiterated: "Doctor Constantine has retired for the night," and brushed Manners's portly pyjama-clad form away from the mouthpiece with a decision that quelled the protest on his lips.

He listened; then, with a brisk affirmative, hung up the receiver.

"A taxi and my heavy overcoat," he said, "then you'd better get back to bed. No, I don't know when I shall be back. I'm perfectly aware of the fact that it's past one o'clock. It was raining when I went to bed, and I'll take your word for it that it's raining still. Good heavens, Manners, I'm not an octogenarian!"

He beat an inglorious retreat, thereby missing the spectacle of Manners, for once crudely human, apostrophizing the closed bedroom door.

When his taxi deposited him at the main entrance of the Parthenon Picture Theatre he found the doors closed and locked and the vast frontage in darkness. There was no sign of life anywhere, but, making his way down the narrow side-street, he saw a gleam of light at the end and a dark figure in uniform standing within its radius.

Following the constable's directions, he went through a door, down a short passage ending in a steep flight of steps, and found himself in a low-ceilinged, dimly-lit structure that, from the untidy conglomeration of theatrical properties stacked against the walls, he realized must be the cavity under the stage built for the cabaret shows with which the management interspersed the cinema performance.

A long table ran down the centre, littered with the instrument-cases and coats of the orchestra. Behind it gleamed the pale faces of a little group of men talking excitedly among themselves.

To his right as he entered was another table, at which Arkwright, a couple of officers of the C.I.D. and the police surgeon, were standing.

As his eyes grew more accustomed to the dim light he realized the grim significance of the table, at the foot of which a photographer was packing up his paraphernalia preparatory to departure.

Arkwright turned and saw him.

"We've got him, sir," he said, as he came forward. "I'm afraid it's worse than you suspected."

"Dead?" asked Constantine, his eyes on the table.

Arkwright nodded.

"Been dead about eight hours according to the surgeon. At least, he puts the time at between six and nine hours ago."

For a moment Constantine stood silent, his mind on the girl with whom he had been dining not so many hours before, then he wrenched his mind back to the present.

"What was it? Heart failure?" he asked.

"It'll take an autopsy to decide that," was the abrupt answer. "From the look of things he died quite peacefully, and, except for a superficial wound at the back of the neck, there's no sign of violence, but . . ."

He paused, then:

"Come and look at this," he said, swinging round on his heel.

Constantine followed him as he skirted the table and led the way to a low cavity, a little over a foot in height, that ran the whole length of the end of the room. Constantine, though a small man, had to stoop to peer into it.

Arkwright snapped on a light and revealed a litter of musical scores piled on the floor.

"This runs under the orchestra," he said, "and it's used as a kind of storeroom by the members. It's here that they found the body."

He pointed to an empty space at the extreme end of the cupboardlike structure. A couple of music-stands and a broken chair stood in front of it.

Constantine indicated them.

"How did he manage to get behind these?" he asked. "Or have they been moved?"

"We moved them to get the body out, but they have been put back. The place was pretty much as you see it. The body was literally jammed behind them. If it hadn't been for a change in the programme to-morrow that necessitated fresh music, it might have been here for days. As it was, a couple of chaps from the orchestra came here after the performance to-night to sort out the new music, and, of course, they spotted it."

Constantine bent forward and examined the cramped space behind the chair. He was met by a faint odour that made him retreat abruptly.

"He never got there by himself," he said. "Apart from the unlikelihood of his attempting such a thing, it's an almost impossible feat for an old and probably sick man."

"He was put there," agreed Arkwright grimly. "And when I said 'jammed' I meant it. The legs haven't stiffened yet, but we couldn't straighten out of the body, and you'll see for yourself that the position's unnatural."

"In fact, whether he died of heart failure or not, the body was deliberately hidden? It's no good asking if you've any clue as to how it got here?"

"None. We were called in less than an hour ago, and, as you see, the routine work's only just finished, but I've detained everybody who was on the premises at the time and we may get something from them. The audience had already dispersed. Apparently the members of the orchestra hung about chatting and discussing to-morrow's programme for a bit, with the result that it was nearly midnight before they started to look out the scores and unearthed the body. I've established one rather significant fact, however. There are only two ways of getting into this place: one through the orchestra and the other by the door you came in at. Now the orchestra has never been unoccupied for a moment since the place opened at one o'clock to-day, and the stage door you used has a spring lock and can only be opened from inside. Also, the members of the orchestra are in the habit of slipping out into the passage for an occasional cigarette, and they declare that, in consequence, the passage and this place are continually occupied. They are unanimous in declaring that it would have been next to impossible to smuggle a body in during the last eight hours."

"What about the organist? I suppose they have one of those jack-in-the-box affairs that rises out of the bowels of the earth and subsides again when the solos are over?"

Arkwright shook his head.

"I see what you're driving at," he said; "but the organ here is a fixed one and the organist sits actually in the orchestra."

"Even then he would hardly be likely to notice anyone who passed behind him when he was playing."

"I quite agree, but I've just been speaking to a man who states that he was sitting in the orchestra all through the organ solos. He's a non-smoker, and was reading a book in a chair close to the door all the time. He declares that no one could have passed him without his knowledge. And you must remember that anyone wishing to reach the orchestra, unless he came through this room, would have to go through the auditorium."

"The old man may have died in here."

"We can't afford to ignore that possibility," agreed Arkwright, "but, owing to the interest his absence had already aroused, he would certainly have been noticed if he'd been seen at all. It is a fact, however, that he was one of the few people who possessed a key to the side-door from the street. He *could* have got in."

"In which case, assuming that he did come in and die from natural causes, why hide the body?"

"Exactly. And the key's missing."

"Missing?"

"We've been through his pockets. His key-ring's there, but the key has been removed. According to various members of the orchestra he always kept it on the ring, and had often been seen to use it. And there's the wound in the neck. The doctor states that it is too slight to have been the cause of death, and, though I've only made a cursory examination, there seems nothing in this room that could have caused it if he got it in falling. At the same time, it's sufficiently deep to be painful, and it's unlikely that he would have walked in here with a hole in his neck and made no effort to get it attended to."

"He might have been knocked down or injured in the street and made his way here only to die of shock or heart failure."

"He might. But it seems improbable that he should have concealed himself first in a place that would be awkward even for an able-bodied man to get into. We shall know more, of course, after the post-mortem. What about Miss Anthony?"

"Let her sleep in peace to-night, at any rate," said Constantine decisively. "I should suggest that you allow me to get in touch with Lord Marlowe at once and let him break the news to her to-morrow."

"Right," agreed Arkwright with relief. "Of all a policeman's jobs, that's the one I hate the most. Meanwhile, I must get on with this one. Are you too tired to stay for a bit?"

Constantine glowered at him.

"Between you and Manners it's a wonder I'm alive at all," he snapped. "There's no objection, I suppose, to my having a chat with the crowd over there?"

He indicated the little group on the other side of the long table.

Arkwright grinned.

"Not the slightest. No doubt you'll worm more out of them in five minutes than an unfortunate policeman could in an hour. Good luck to you, sir!"

He joined the doctor, who was waiting for him in the doorway.

Constantine, seeing that the little group round the smaller table had evaporated, strolled over to it and turned back the edge of the green baize tablecloth that had been spread over the body of the old man. The face he revealed was so like the one he had reconstructed from the data he had gathered concerning Betty's grandfather that he was startled. Sensitive and intelligent in the stillness of death, it bore lines only to be found on the faces of those whose bodies are a prey to their emotions. In life he could picture the old man as impetuous, irascible, and, withal, lovable. A good friend and a bad enemy.

With a sigh he replaced the cloth, stood for a moment contemplating the contents of the dead man's pockets, now piled in a little heap on a chair, then joined the group of musicians at the other end of the room.

Constantine, when he set out to please, was difficult to withstand. Something of a jack-of-all-trades himself, he could talk shop with most men, and even those members of the orchestra who had begun to chafe at their detention by Arkwright thawed under the spell of his quiet friendliness. The saxophone player, who had been the first to discover the body, was only too glad of a fresh audience, and took full advantage of his opportunity.

Constantine listened patiently, putting in a question here and there that drew the information he needed. He gathered that Julius Anthony, in spite of his intolerance and rabid contempt for the type of music he was required to play, was both liked and respected by his colleagues. The conductor spoke of him as the best first violin he had ever had the luck to secure.

"He hadn't the knack for the sort of stuff we play here," he said, "but he was a sounder musician than I am, and I don't mind admitting it."

"I know the type," agreed Constantine. "It's commoner in Germany than here. Music is, literally, life to people of that sort."

"That just about expresses it. I don't believe he had any other interests at all except music. If he had I never heard him speak of them. Now I'm fond enough of my job, but billiards is my hobby."

"I'd give something to know how he got here," said another of the men. "I've been in and out of this place myself at intervals all through the afternoon and evening, and I'm ready to swear there's been one or other of us about most of the time."

The conductor nodded.

"The thing's a mystery," he agreed. "It's a long job, ours, and, provided everybody's present during the orchestral selection, I don't make a fuss if the fellows slip off now and again. If Mr. Anthony didn't want to be seen, I suppose, knowing the ways of the place, he could have managed it, but what would he want to hide for?"

"He didn't get behind those props of his own accord," declared the saxophone player emphatically. "I saw him and the way he was lying, and I'm certain of it."

"There are other exits, I suppose, besides the one in front?" said Constantine.

"Two, one on each side of the auditorium, not far from the orchestra, but there's a pretty sharp eye kept on them. You see, boys are apt to hang round them, and the little beggars slip in when they're opened to let the various houses out. As a result they're never opened except between the houses when there's an attendant on duty. The rest of the time they're closed with a bar and can't be opened from outside. Besides, anyone coming in that way would have to go through the orchestra to get here, and I'll wager no one could do that without being seen. What time do they think he died, sir?"

Constantine made a rapid calculation.

"Some time between four-thirty and six-thirty, according to the doctor. It's only a rough estimate, of course, and he may alter his mind after a further examination."

"Then he didn't come through the orchestra. One or other of us was there all the time, even during the organ solos."

"Is the stage door at the end of the passage here always kept locked?"

"Always. As a matter of fact, we don't use it much. It's easier to slip through the barrier and out at the emergency exit. And you may take it that whichever door we do use we shut after us. It's the one thing the management's fussy about, owing to the boys. They're always on the look-out for a chance to slip in, and, for our own sakes, we don't want them round here messing about with the things."

"How do you get back if you do get out?"

"Through the main entrance. Mr. Anthony was the only one of us who had a key to the stage door. He used to come here and play the organ in the mornings sometimes, for his own amusement. It's electric run, and, as there was no objection, Mr. Raleigh here arranged for him to have a key."

The conductor nodded.

"He was a fine organist. I've come down more than once in the mornings to listen to him."

The little knot of men in the doorway stepped aside to make way for the ambulance men with a stretcher, and the conductor instinctively moved in their direction. Constantine followed him, and, waiting till they were out of hearing of the others, said:

"I suppose there's no chance that anyone did leave any of the doors open to-day?"

"It's extraordinarily unlikely. The truth is there's been a hell of a fuss over those doors. A short time ago one of the doormen here was discovered letting in boys through the emergency exit at twopence a head. He was making quite a nice little profit out of it too. Since then they've been doubly strict. Besides which, as Campion said, we don't want the little beggars monkeying with our things. As a matter of fact, it was Mr. Anthony who prevented the man from getting the sack. He got round the manager, and that and his war record saved him."

Constantine looked surprised.

"What made him interest himself in the man?" he asked.

"It wasn't like him, it's true. He never took much interest in what was going on here, but, in this instance, I suppose he felt responsible. It was he who spotted what was going on. Actually saw the boy handing over the money to Binns. The whole thing was characteristic of old Anthony. Instead of reporting it at once he went straight to Binns and told him what he'd seen and what he was going to do. Then he went to the management."

"How did Binns take it?" asked Constantine, his eyes on the departing stretcher.

"Oh, the usual thing. Swore he'd get even with Mr. Anthony, and then went to him with tears in his eyes and asked him to speak for him."

Constantine waited until the ambulance had gone, and then passed on what he had learned to Arkwright.

"I don't suppose there's anything in it," he said. "This man, Binns, may have had a grudge against Anthony at one time, but he's every reason to be grateful to him now."

"He may have been present when the old man died," suggested Arkwright, "and, remembering his own threats in the past, have got into a panic and tried to hide the body. It sounds pretty futile, but people have done queerer things than that in an emergency. No harm is having a look at it from that point of view. If you're going now I'll get a man to call you a cab."

"I can pick one up for myself. There's bound to be a rank near by," said Constantine with suspicious mildness.

"If there is I'll see you into it," insisted Arkwright. "I owe that much, at least, to Manners."

As soon as he got home Constantine made a ruthless assault on Steynes House. It was some time before he could get an answer, and there was another delay while Marlowe was being fetched. He told him what had happened and asked him to break the news to Betty.

As he hung up the receiver he was conscious of the hovering figure of Manners bearing a glass that steamed, and realized that it contained the one thing he needed.

It was some time before sleep came to him. Lying in the darkness he visualized the scene he had just left. He could see again the table bearing the curiously humped form under the baize cloth, and, on a chair next it, the contents of the dead man's pockets. Aided by the retentive memory of a chess player he went through them, with the result that his mind leaped suddenly into wakefulness just as it was beginning to drift comfortably towards slumber.

Arkwright was barely out of bed next morning before he was summoned to the telephone. Constantine was at the other end.

"Can you give me a list of the contents of Anthony's pockets?" he said. "Unless my memory's woefully at fault, that key is not the only thing that's missing."

"Give me time to get my notebook," was Arkwright's answer. He fetched it and reeled off the list.

"As I thought," was Constantine's comment. "According to Miss Anthony her grandfather was a confirmed snuff-taker. She'll be able to tell us whether his snuff-box is missing, but I should be very much surprised if he went out without it."

Arkwright chuckled as he rang off. Anybody but Constantine would have asked whether there was a snuff-box among the dead man's effects and left it at that, but the old man's sense of drama had, as usual, been too strong for him. He had been unable to resist taking a circuitous route to his little climax, and Arkwright knew how thoroughly he had enjoyed doing it.

CHAPTER V

CONSTANTINE'S FIRST VISITOR the following morning was Marlowe. He had seen Betty and broken the news to her of her grandfather's death.

"She's taking it wonderfully," was his report. "I think in a way she was prepared for it, though she's quite at sea as to what has happened. She's terribly cut up, of course, but it was the suspense that was telling on her. Going by your account, I was able to say that, judging by appearances, he had died quite peacefully. That old Mrs. Berry's a treasure. I've left Betty with her."

"Did you get my note this morning?"

"It came just as I was leaving. Betty wasn't fit for much, poor little soul, but I managed to get the information you wanted.

She's quite definite about the snuff-box. Her grandfather never moved without it, she says, and must have had it on him. She described it, and it sounds so unusual that it ought to be easy to trace. He bought it from a Russian in Paris years ago, and it's made of silver inlaid with strips of steel."

Constantine nodded.

"I know the type. Tula work, I believe it's called. You don't often see it in England. Had he ever spoken to her about this man Binns?"

"Not a word. But I gather he seldom discussed affairs at the Parthenon. He hated it, and, I suppose preferred to forget it when he was at home. Betty scoffs at the idea of his having any enemies, says he would argue hotly about music and even refuse to speak to people for days who didn't see eye to eye with him, but she's certain he never did anyone an injury in his life, and I'm ready to swear that he had no interests outside his profession."

"It looks as if Arkwright's theory is correct," said Constantine thoughtfully, "and that he died by accident or from natural causes in the presence of someone who lost his head and hid the body. The theft of the snuff-box may have had something to do with it. Those things look more valuable than they are. On the other hand, his gold watch was not taken, and gold's fetching a good price just now."

Marlowe rose.

"I must get back," he said. "If the police need Betty for identification purposes I'd like to be there. By the way, she had an idea that her grandfather's violin-case might be at the Hahns'. She rang them up yesterday and they say that he took it with him as usual when he left. Do you think he did leave it, after all, at the Trastevere and someone pinched it?"

"I don't think anything at the moment," confessed Constantine. "The whole thing seems so lacking in motive as to be insane. There's only one thing I do feel sure of, and you can pass it on to Betty. Whatever may have been the cause of her grandfather's death, it was quick and merciful."

His next visitor was Arkwright, to whom he had offered lunch if he could find time to take it.

"If anything, the fog's getting a bit thicker," was his cheerful report. "That chap Howells turned up at the Yard this morning. He'd heard the news from one of the people at the Parthenon and had something he thought might be of interest to us. As a matter of fact, it merely confirms Civita's statement. He says that, while he was talking to Anthony outside the Trastevere, a page to whom Anthony had spoken when he first arrived came up to him and gave him an envelope. It contained a card, which Anthony read. It slipped from his hand on to the pavement and Howells picked it up and returned it to him, but, beyond the fact that it had a message in pencil scribbled on it, he cannot describe it. We found a plain card with a message answering to the description Civita gave us in Anthony's note-case, a pencil note asking him to call for the money next day. I showed this to Howells, but he could only say that it looked very like the one he had picked up. It undoubtedly is the one; Civita has identified it. Howells made one curious point. He says Anthony was going away from the Trastevere when he left him."

"Away? That's interesting. Was he carrying his violin-case?"

"Yes. Howells is emphatic on that point. It looks as if he'd left it somewhere and then returned to the Trastevere, though why he should go back there is a mystery. There was nothing on Civita's card to warrant his doing so."

"Perhaps he decided to make another attempt to see Civita."

"He may have," agreed Arkwright doubtfully, "but he doesn't seem to have been in urgent need of the money, and there was no reason why he shouldn't have waited till next day for it. Another thing, the man he was seen talking to later outside the restaurant wasn't Howells, if his account is to be believed. He declares that he went straight home after leaving Anthony, but, as he lives alone in a flat with no servant, we can't check his statement. We've looked up his charwoman. He was still in bed when she arrived next morning, and she is certain there was no one else in the flat, so Anthony did not spend the intervening hours there."

"What about yesterday?" asked Constantine. "Wherever Anthony may have been on the nights of Tuesday and Wednesday, he was undoubtedly killed on Thursday."

Arkwright nodded.

"Howells says he was at home, giving music lessons, last night. I've a list of the pupils and it will be easy enough to verify his statement, but I don't suppose he'd have risked making it if it wasn't true. He got rid of his last pupil at ten-thirty and went to bed. Yesterday afternoon he lunched with a friend, going on with him to a concert at the Queen's Hall. This alibi's not so complete as it sounds, as Howells admits frankly that their seats were not together, though they met in the interval at about four o'clock. Says he cannot remember the number of his seat and has lost the counterfoil, but he can tell us approximately where he was sitting. He could have done the job at the Parthenon and got back in time to leave with his friend at five-thirty."

"Has he ever been employed at the Parthenon? Whoever concealed the body must have known his way about the place pretty well."

"Says he has only been there once to see Anthony. As a musician, I fancy he's a cut above that sort of thing. So far as the stage door is concerned, he could have used Anthony's key. By the way, there was a receipted bill in Anthony's pocket which may give us a lead. The date's illegible, but the shop, curiously enough, is only about three minutes' walk from the Trastevere. He may have gone there that night."

"After nine o' clock?"

"It's possible. The bill's for the resoling of some shoes, and these small cobblers stay open till all hours. I'm going up there now. Like to come along?"

"I should. As a matter of fact, I'd meant to go up to the Trastevere and have a chat with Civita. He knows what's happened, I suppose?"

"I told him this morning. He's genuinely cut up about it; seems to have had a real regard for the old man."

"He knew him in Paris years ago. There's just a chance that he may remember something that may shed a light on those mysterious journeys of Anthony's. Apart from which I should like to get his angle on the whole affair. Civita's one of the most astute people in London, and his opinion's always worth having."

The shop was in a narrow cul-de-sac hardly a stone's throw from the Trastevere, and, as Arkwright had predicted, was the kind of little one-man concern that opens and closes with a fine disregard for County Council regulations. The owner, a wizened, dusty-looking individual, put down the shoe he was resoling and came forward to serve them.

"This your receipt?" asked Arkwright, handing him the scrap of paper.

The cobbler peered at it through his old-fashioned, steel-rimmed glasses.

"That's right," he said. "Mr. Anthony's not ill, is he?"

"What makes you think that?" countered Arkwright.

"Well, it seemed queer him not comin'. Said he'd be in first thing Wednesday mornin'."

"When did he say that? Tuesday night?"

The little man peered more closely at Arkwright, a suspicious gleam in his dim eyes.

"I ain't 'ere to answer questions," he snapped. "I got me work to do. If you've come from Mr. Anthony, say so, but I'll want more authority than that bit o' paper. You might 'ave pinched it off 'im for all I know."

If Arkwright was taken aback he did not show it. He thrust his warrant card under the man's nose.

"When did you last see Mr. Anthony?" he demanded.

The cobbler's feeble attempt at truculence collapsed with surprising suddenness.

"Tuesday night, when he come in and paid that there bill," he answered obediently, watching Arkwright with eyes that were both anxious and guarded.

"Sure he hasn't been here since then?"

"Certain sure. Fact is, when you give me that there bill I thought as 'e'd sent you. Then when you started askin' them questions I begun to think there might be something' fishy. I didn't want to make no error."

"Why should he send anyone? He'd paid your bill, hadn't he?"

Without answering, the cobbler turned and went through a door at the back of the shop. He returned carrying a canvas-covered violin-case and placed it carefully on the counter in front of the two men.

"I know the store he sets by that there violin," he said, "and I thought maybe you might be after it. Said 'e'd fetch it 'imself, 'e did, on the Wednesday mornin'. When 'e didn't come I thought 'e must be ill."

"How did he come to leave it here?"

"Said 'e'd got an appointment and didn't want to be 'ampered with it like. I've known Mr. Anthony a long time. Very good friend 'e's been to me. Used to give my son 'Erb lessons on the fiddle. Took a lot of interest in the lad."

The flow of information dried up suddenly. Constantine saw the anxious lines on the man's forehead deepen and the guarded look come back into his eyes.

"Can you remember what time Mr. Anthony came in?" asked Arkwright.

The man answered readily enough.

"Just before I closed down, it was. When I've got a lot on 'and I goes on till ten o'clock. Never work later if I can 'elp it. I wasn't at it more than ten minutes after 'e left. Then the church clock struck. I always goes by that."

"Any idea where he was going?"

The man shook his head.

"Not me. Didn't even notice which way 'e went when 'e left. There ain't been nothin' 'appened to 'im, 'as there?"

"He died suddenly yesterday, and we're anxious to trace his movements during the last few days. That's the best you can do for us, I suppose?"

The little cobbler's anxiety had given place to genuine consternation.

"Mr. Anthony dead," he muttered. "I'm sorry, that I am. 'E was a good friend to me."

Arkwright picked up the violin-case.

"I'll see that his daughter gets this," he said. "If there's anything further you can tell us, let me know at the yard."

Outside in the street he glanced up at the lettering over the shop.

"G. Plaskett, hand-sewn bootmaker, seems to have something on his mind," he remarked thoughtfully.

Constantine nodded.

"He was on the defensive from the moment he saw your card," he said, "but I don't believe his anxiety had anything to do with Anthony or the violin. He was ready enough to talk about him. We're beginning to get his movements straightened out at last. He must have gone straight to Plaskett's after parting from Howells."

"Then back to the Trastevere. Why?"

"Civita may have some theory about that. If I get anything out of him I'll let you know."

Ten minutes later Constantine was sitting in Civita's office sampling a sherry that seldom found its way into the restaurant.

"It is all right, yes?"

Constantine yielded himself with a sigh of sheer satisfaction to the comfort of the luxurious leather-covered armchair.

"Perfect, like everything else in this room. Where do you get these chairs?"

Civita shrugged his massive shoulders.

"I look round till I find what I want. I can give you the address if you like, Doctor Constantine, but this suite was made specially for an American, whose money went suddenly, pouf, like the flame of a candle, in the slump. Another man would say, 'Furnish me an office. I will pay so much,' and then wonder that he is uncomfortable. But me, I have a theory. It is the little things in life that matter, and so I give as much thought to them as to the big business. And I am comfortable!"

Constantine's eyes twinkled. Civita was big in brain as well as in body, but the Latin in him would out. Give him a lead and he would boast like an overgrown schoolboy.

"Fifty-guinea suites are not little things, at least to people like me, but then I don't think in hotels and restaurants."

He paused for a moment, then dropped into Italian, the language he generally used with Civita.

"Tell me," he said, "why did Mr. Anthony come back here on Tuesday night?"

Civita swung round in his swivel-chair, his intelligent face alight with interest.

"Did he come back? From what my man said I thought he had been here all the time until he was seen to leave."

"He went away after he had received your note. But he came back again. Why?"

Civita started at him in amazement.

"He went away and came back? And I have been asking myself why he came in at all! But this is more extraordinary. If he had come to see me he would have asked for me and I should have heard of it. My people are well disciplined, they do not neglect messages like that. But why should he want to see me after he had read my note?"

"You can think of nothing that would bring him back?"

"Nothing. And more, I can think of nothing that would bring him here at all, after my message. You knew Mr. Anthony?"

"No. I only met his grand-daughter for the first time on Wednesday."

"Well, I have known him well in the past, and I tell you that, even if he had become a rich man in the interval, I should have been astonished to find him in a place like this. You would say that everybody in London knows Civita, *non e vero?*"

He tapped his chest with an emphatic finger, and Constantine, with an inward smile, said gravely:

"Everybody who matters."

"*Ma che!* Julius Anthony mattered more, in a finer sense, than half the *pesce cane* who come to my restaurant, but, I tell you, until the day I met him in the street here in London, if you had asked him, 'Who is the proprietor of the Trastevere Restaurant?' or even, 'Where is the Trastevere?' he would not have been able to answer you. That he should come here, except to speak to me, is extraordinary!"

Constantine nodded.

"It's a curious business," he said. "There's nothing in his past that seems in any way significant, I suppose? Nothing associated with his life in Paris?"

Civita made a sweeping gesture.

"What was his life in Paris? His pupils all the morning; in the afternoon, his quartette; in the evening, sometimes an engagement, sometimes a concert—but music, nothing but music all the time. What could there be?"

"He had his enemies, I suppose? He seems to have been downright to a fault."

"Disputes, you mean? Over the merits of Puccini and Wagner, Strauss and Verdi! But people do not entice an old man from his home many years afterwards to avenge Wagner or Puccini!"

Constantine sighed.

"If only the spirit had moved you to go into the lounge on Tuesday night, we mightn't be puzzling our brains now," he said.

"And I was here in my office all the time. Tuesday was a busy night for me, and I did not get away till nearly two in the morning. I remember that night, because my car was stolen."

Constantine looked up quickly.

"Did you get it back?"

Civita nodded.

"The police found it in a street in Kensington. It was none the worse, but it robbed me of an hour's sleep when I needed it most. And Wednesday was another heavy day, but last night I slept—oh, how I slept! I am like Napoleon, you know. I can always sleep."

Constantine laughed.

"Went to bed early, did you?" he asked innocently.

Civita leaned forward impressively.

"Listen. At seven o'clock yesterday morning I went to Mass. Always, every morning, I do that. That surprises you, yes? But I promised *la Mama*, years ago, and I never forget. Then I came here and I worked. But at five in the afternoon I went home and at six o'clock I was in bed. And I did not wake till six o'clock next morning. The affairs here managed themselves last night. Civita was asleep!"

He laughed, a huge, boyish laugh that filled the room. Constantine rose to his feet.

"I wonder whether you'll say the same when you're my age," he said ruefully. "Where do you keep your car?"

Civita cast a shrewd look at him.

"You think there is some connection between the theft and the affair of Anthony? I do not believe it. I keep the car in a lock-up garage near my flat. When I got home on Tuesday I went upstairs to fetch the key of the garage to put my car away, and by the time I got downstairs again the car was gone. I go to bed, but in the morning I get up early and ring up the police before I go to Mass. Later I hear that when I telephoned to them they had already found the car."

"I can't see any connection, unless Anthony stole it himself," admitted Constantine with a smile; "but the whole business is so fantastic that I'm prepared to accept any explanation."

"You will express my sympathy to Miss Anthony if you see her?" said Civita as they parted. "I was so sure myself that her grandfather would return. It is a tragic ending."

Constantine repeated the conversation to Arkwright when he dropped in late that afternoon.

"It doesn't amount to much," he said, "though, if you want to add him to your list, his alibi for yesterday evening is even poorer than that of Howells. I don't know whether Civita's servant sleeps in or not, but he can hardly have had his eye on him all the time."

"We shall have to take him into account as a matter of course," answered Arkwright, "but, for the life of me, I can't see why he should have had anything to do with the affair. If he'd had any designs on Anthony he'd hardly have fixed on the Trastevere as his jumping-off place. His own restaurant, teeming with witnesses! I've got one bit of news for you, by the way. Stolen cars seem to be our strong suit just now! Anyway, I think Plaskett's queer manner is accounted for."

"The cobbler? He's been at the back of my mind all day."

"His son was arrested at Esher yesterday evening for pinching a car. The father's record's all right, but the boy's been in bad company for some time, and I fancy Plaskett's been expecting something of the sort. When he saw my card he thought the worst had happened. The boy was with two other lads, and there's no reason to think they were doing more than joy-riding. There's no evidence that the car had been used for nefarious purposes. As it is, he'll come under the First Offenders Act."

"I suppose Anthony couldn't have interfered with him in any way? He was interested in the boy, remember."

"The idea's far-fetched, but possible. He seems to have been a determined old gentleman. I called young Plaskett a lad, but he's nineteen and would probably be more than a match for an old man. Anyway, I'm seeing him to-morrow."

"Has the doctor's report come in yet?"

Arkwright shook his head.

"The Flying Squad had a nasty smash-up in our division this morning and he's been busy. I'm expecting the report every minute now. I'll let you know what he says."

"What about Howells?"

"We've verified everything he told us, but, so far, we've no means of tracing his movements during the concert. We've questioned the attendants and struck a blank there, which is hardly surprising. Of course, he may have been in his seat all the time."

He hesitated for a moment, then:

"You'll be glad to hear that Lord Marlowe's definitely out of it. He was with us, as you know, at Miss Anthony's till nearly nine yesterday, and spent the evening at Steynes House, where the Duchess was holding a reception."

He shot a rather nervous glance at the old man, remembering the time when another of Constantine's friends, Lord Richard Pomfrey, had fallen foul of Scotland Yard, but Constantine did not rise to the bait.

"In view of that letter from Anthony, you could hardly leave him out of your calculations," he said mildly. "As a matter of fact, I'm still wondering whether Anthony didn't go back to the Trastevere on the chance of catching him there. He was evidently very anxious to see him, and may have known that he was in the habit of meeting Betty there."

"Drawing a blank there, he may have gone on to Steynes House," suggested Arkwright with a wicked twinkle in his eye.

"And been slain by the Duchess. After all, she is the only person who may be said to have had a motive. Oh, you may laugh, but I've heard you propound an even more preposterous theory than that in my day," retorted Constantine pointedly.

"Give me some facts to work on and I'll undertake to leave your friends alone, sir," Arkwright assured him, as he took his departure.

An hour later he rang up to say that the doctor's report had come in.

"As we thought, the wound in the neck was superficial, and undoubtedly caused after death," he said. "And he didn't die of heart failure. The cause of death was morphia poisoning. The marks of the injection are plainly visible on his arm."

"Surely Anthony wasn't a drug addict?"

"Macbane's convinced that he wasn't. For one thing, there are no other punctures on the body; for another, there is every indication that he was a remarkably well-preserved man for his age. Must have had a thoroughly sound constitution, according to Macbane. Besides, we searched that room pretty thoroughly, and there was no sign of a hypodermic syringe."

"He might have administered the drug to himself outside somewhere, and had time to get rid of the syringe."

"We considered that possibility, but, unfortunately, there's further complication. About fifty grains of chloral hydrate have been found in the stomach. Macbane's opinion is that it was taken by the mouth and not in sufficient quantity to cause death. The implication is obvious."

"That he was drugged in the first instance, you mean?"

"Exactly. If he were given butyl chloride, say, in coffee or beer, it would have been easy to administer the injection while he was unconscious. Of course, there is still the possibility of suicide, but, in that case, why chloral?"

"Taking into account the position of the body when found, I think we can knock out suicide," said Constantine.

"Just so. Julius Anthony was murdered right enough."

CHAPTER VI

THE DUCHESS CHOSE the precise moment at which Constantine was sitting down to dinner to make her final and triumphant effort to get him on the telephone.

Manners' expression, as he silently removed the soup and bore it back to the kitchen, expressed his master's feelings admirably.

Constantine, realizing that "The Parthenon Mystery", as it had already been christened in the evening papers, would hammer the last nail into the coffin of Marlowe's hopes, made a hasty endeavour to formulate some sort of plan of campaign as he answered the imperious "Hullos" that were booming across the line.

To his surprise the lion was roaring as gently as any sucking-dove, and his conscience-stricken apologies for having proved so inaccessible passed almost unnoticed.

"Of course, I quite understand! I know how splendid you've been all through this terrible affair. Marlowe is full of gratitude, and that nice Inspector Arkwright can't say enough about you. You know I've got the poor child here?"

For a moment Constantine was puzzled. Even the most besotted admirer could hardly relegate Arkwright's six feet of brawn to the nursery. But the Duchess's next words enlightened him.

"Of course I went to her the moment Bertie told me what had happened, and found the poor little soul alone in those dreadful lodgings, with a crowd of the most horrible young men with cameras on the doorstep. I got her away and into the car before they realized what I was doing, but they've no reverence for anything, even grief. I've just found Bertie giggling over the most appalling photograph of me, looking exactly like old Lady Caradoc, only worse, in one of those abominable evening papers. It's a comfort to feel that poor little Betty is at least protected from that sort of thing now she's with me."

"I'm so very glad you've taken her under your wing," was all the bewildered Constantine could find to say.

"It's a pleasure to have her. Why didn't you tell me how charming she was? And just the person for Marlowe, who, you must admit, isn't easy. When one thinks of what he might have chosen!"

Constantine swallowed the reproof meekly. After all, knowing the Duchess, he ought to have expected this. He contented himself with enquiring after Betty.

"She's worrying terribly, poor child, about that report Civita's circulating about her grandfather. The man's insufferable! I only wish we'd never been persuaded to have any dealings with him!"

"This is news to me," answered Constantine, completely puzzled. "What has he been saying?"

"Some absurd story about Mr. Anthony's having borrowed money from him. Betty says he wouldn't have dreamed of such a thing."

A light broke on Constantine.

"I'm so sorry that's been troubling her. There was no question of a loan in the ordinary sense. Civita had agreed to help him in a purely business venture. I don't know what the arrangement was between them, but I've no doubt he would have had his share in the profits. Tell Betty not to worry her head about it."

"But she is worrying! She says her grandfather had a horror of debt and would never have lent himself to such a thing. Apparently other people have offered to finance him in the same way, and he never would even discuss it. She feels very hotly about it on his account. She says he would have been furious at the mere report of such a thing."

"I expect she's overwrought and probably exaggerating the whole thing. As it was, owing to her grandfather's death the scheme never came to anything. I'd no I'd no idea she felt like that about it, but I'm afraid it's true. Civita was quite definite in his account of the transaction. No doubt he persuaded Mr. Anthony. He'd be difficult to resist, once he gave his mind to it."

He had forgotten for the moment that Civita was in the Duchess's black books.

"I've no doubt he took advantage of the poor old man!" she retorted bitterly. "All the same, I wish you'd see Betty. She's taking it more seriously than is good for her."

"I'll call on her to-morrow," Constantine assured her.

He sent Manners out for all the evening papers, and was amply rewarded by the snapshot of the Duchess, apparently in the act of delivering a running kick at her own car, dragging a cowering Betty behind her.

It was the first opportunity he had had of reading the reports of the tragedy. Arkwright had handled the press artfully. The accounts, lurid though they were, did not mention any wound on the body, and, having gone to press before the autopsy, were written on the assumption that Anthony had died a natural death.

Constantine heaved a sigh of relief. Not only was Betty in good hands, but, for one night at least, she would be spared the knowledge that her grandfather had been murdered.

In the meantime, while Constantine was talking to the Duchess, Arkwright sat in his room at the Yard listening to the report of a police constable.

"I'm morally certain it's the same, sir," the man as saying, "but the bench was between two street lamps and he was lying in the shadow. The name and address are identical. I only saw the circular this evening."

"What time was this?"

"Just on three-thirty by Big Ben on Wednesday morning, sir. He was lying full length on a bench on Westminster Embankment and appeared to be asleep. I roused him and told him to move on. He objected on the grounds that he wasn't destitute, in proof of which he produced some silver and coppers from his pocket. He then gave his name as Julius Anthony. I took down that and his address, and, seeing that he'd complied with the regulations, continued on my beat. When I passed again, half an hour later, he had gone."

"How was he dressed?"

"In a dark overcoat, with the collar turned up against the cold, and a black felt hat with an unusually broad brim. I put him down as an artist, judging from his clothes."

"What about his face?"

"Pale and clean-shaven, that's as much as I can say, owing to the light being bad. He spoke like an educated man, rather stilted like, and his voice was the voice of an old man. I've been to the mortuary and inspected the corpse, and I've no doubt in my own mind about its being the same, sir."

Left to himself, Arkwright stretched a long arm across his table, picked up the report on Binns, the door-keeper at the Parthenon, and apostrophized it moodily.

"Sleeping on the Embankment when he'd got a perfectly good bed of his own waiting for him. What the devil for? Last seen talking with a man unknown outside the Trastevere Restaurant at approximately ten-thirty. No further trace of him till a constable finds him asleep on the Embankment at three-thirty. It's got me beat!"

The door opened to admit Macbane, the police surgeon.

"Any developments in the Anthony case?" he asked.

"Seen on the Embankment at three-thirty on Wednesday morning. That doesn't help us much at present. Unless someone comes forward who saw him yesterday we're at a deadlock."

"Well, you won't love me any better when I'm through," announced Macbane imperturbably.

Arkwright waited while he ran his matches to earth in his trouser pocket and busied himself with the relighting of his pipe. He had a feeling that doctor was in no hurry to make his announcement.

"I should have embodied it in my report," he said at last, with true Scottish deliberation, "but, to tell you the truth, the thing had escaped my memory. Since writing it I've had a look at my text-books."

He leaned forward, emphasizing his words with the stem of his pipe.

"In the case of almost any other form of death my estimate as to time would have been correct, but this man died of morphia poisoning. Now here's the snag. Whereas in the case of poisoning by strychnine, or after death from convulsions, rigor mortis may persist for months, in the case of narcotic poisoning the effects are reversed. Rigor mortis is not only delayed, but may be absent altogether. The same rule applies to coagulation of the blood. Oxyhæmoglobin is almost entirely absent and clotting very feebly developed. Taking into account the fact that the body was that of an old man and would, therefore, cool more rapidly than that of a person in the prime of life, I placed the time of death at about five to seven hours previous to the finding of the body, but in view of the quantity of morphia present in the body we may now extend this period almost indefinitely."

Macbane's little lecture, delivered in a voice even more precise and deliberate than usual, ceased. He sat puffing stolidly at his pipe, and awaited the outburst he knew was coming.

Arkwright glared at him in silence for a moment, then:

"We've been going on the assumption that the death occurred any time between four-thirty and six-thirty yesterday afternoon. Are you trying to tell me that it may have taken place any time before then?"

Macbane nodded.

"Owing to the action of the morphia I cannot undertake to give any opinion as to the time of death," he announced sententiously.

Arkwright exploded.

"Confound it!" he exclaimed. "Do you realize where this lands us?"

But Macbane was already at the door.

"All the pretty little alibis gone west, eh?" he said, as he backed neatly through it. "Man, I'm sorry for you, but I'd have you remember that I'm not responsible for the text-books."

"Some other damned Scotsman was, I'll be bound," snapped Arkwright, to the sound of the closing door.

He turned once more to the report on Binns. The man had suffered from shellshock during the War and was apt to show the effects if he were excited or under the influence of drink. After the incident that so nearly led to his dismissal he had been heard to threaten Anthony by more than one witness. He appeared to be unaware of the fact that he owed his reinstatement to him. He had been on duty at the cinema on the Tuesday, Wednesday and Thursday, and could have slipped round to the stage door at any time during the performance, though, if he had been absent for more than a short time it would undoubtedly have been noticed. Assuming that the man was unbalanced and apt to exaggerate a grievance, the motive was there, and he possessed the necessary knowledge of the locality.

On the other hand, it was difficult to see how he could have found time or opportunity for the crime, and there was no evidence that he had ever been in possession of a hypodermic syringe. According to his wife, he had returned home each night at eleven forty-five and remained there until he left for his work on the following morning.

With an impatient gesture Arkwright shoved the paper aside and pressed the bell on his desk.

Macbane's announcement had completely altered the face of things. Arkwright had interviewed a very chastened Herb Plaskett in his cell that afternoon. In company with two youths older and more experienced than himself, he had commandeered a car on the Wednesday night from outside a private house in the West End, and the three of them had driven out into the country, slept that night in the car, and, by a miracle, escaped arrest until late on Thursday night, when they had been on their way back to London, intending to leave the car in some convenient side-street.

Plaskett was almost tearfully insistent that he had not seen Anthony on the occasion of his visit to his father, and knew nothing of his movements. He was clearly not of the stuff of which hardened criminals are made, but one of his companions had already served a term of imprisonment for larceny, and the other had only escaped arrest by the skin of his teeth at least two occasions. Young Plaskett's choice of associates was against him and Anthony's violin had been found in his father's possession; beyond that it was difficult to see what connection he could have had with the crime.

According to his own account and that of his father he had spent the time between Tuesday night and Wednesday evening in his bed at home and loafing about the streets with various pals, none of whom could be looked upon as reliable witnesses.

On his way home Arkwright called at the Parthenon Playhouse and ascertained that conditions there had been much the same on the Wednesday as on the Thursday afternoon and evening. This, however, did not apply to the morning hours, when the cinema remained closed and untenanted until the arrival, at eleven-thirty, of the cleaners who preceded the general staff. Anthony had last been seen at three-thirty on Wednesday morning, and, according to Macbane, might have been killed any time between then and six-thirty on Thursday night. The chances were that his body had been smuggled into the cinema when the building was deserted either on the Wednesday or Thursday morning.

The room under the stage had been thick with dust, and it was unlikely that the cleaners would have penetrated as far as the cavity in which the body had been found on either of the two mornings in question.

Arkwright made quick work of the cold supper his landlady had put out for him, then got into a heavy frieze overcoat and a tweed cap and faced the blustering wind once more. This time his destination was a small public-house in the neighbourhood of Vauxhall Bridge Road.

The proprietor's wife was serving behind the bar.

"Sam going out to-night?" enquired Arkwright softly, as he paid for the beer he had ordered.

The woman gave a quick glance round the bar and dropped her voice as she answered:

"'E'll go out all right, no matter what the weather. Every Tuesday and Friday 'e goes, regular."

"Leaves you a bit short-handed, doesn't it?" he suggested pleasantly.

Her fat, good-humoured face lit up with a smile.

"The potman's 'andy if there should be trouble, and most of our customers are regulars. I don't stand in the way of 'is goin'. What I say is, they've all got their 'obbies, men 'ave, and the money might as well go this way as on the 'orses. Want to see 'im?"

"I'd like a word with him before he goes."

She raised the flap of the counter.

"If you step behind you'll find 'im. You know your way."

A few minutes later Arkwright was sitting in a musty little parlour, deep in conversation with a man nearly as big as himself, whose huge paunch and thickened features suggested that he had been a mighty man with his hands in the days before his muscle turned to fat.

Arkwright had run across Sam Philbegge during the General Strike, when he had come to the assistance of a constable who had lost his footing and was in danger of being kicked to death, but he had known him for a long time before he realized that he was something more than an ex-pugilist who had turned publican, and he had never yet succeeded in discovering what had first led the man in the direction of his peculiar hobby, as his wife called it. Indeed, he had once gone so far as to ask her whether her husband was religious.

"'Im?" she exclaimed, staring at him. "Why, 'e 'ates religion!"
Upon which Arkwright had given it up as a bad job.

But whatever his motive, Philbegge was doing good work in his own queer way. It was his custom, half an hour before closing time, to go down to the Embankment and get into conversation with the homeless derelicts who, huddled together on the benches, tried to get in a few hours' sleep before they were moved on by the police. How much money he took with him on these occasions Arkwright was never able to find out, but he knew that he never returned until long after it was exhausted, and he suspected that financial reasons alone had obliged him to limit his expeditions to two a week. He was almost morbidly self-conscious on the subject of his charities, and it was only by contriving to meet him one night on his self-imposed beat that Arkwright had managed to get a chance to see him at work. Since then Philbegge had realized that he could rely on his discretion, and had more than once come to him for advice when dealing with cases it was beyond his power to help.

"Tuesday," he ruminated, scratching his head reflectively with a hand like a bit of raw beef. "I was out on Tuesday, but I must have missed the old gentleman. Still, there's a chance. Leave me to do the talkin'. I know 'oo to ask and 'ow to do the askin'."

Accordingly, as they made their halting way along the windswept Embankment, Arkwright stood aside and left him to his work. They had almost reached Waterloo Bridge before Philbegge, who had seated himself on a bench beside an ageless and almost sexless bundle of rags, beckoned to Arkwright.

"This old lady 'ere thinks she may 'ave seen the party you're after," he said, edging his way further up the bench to give Arkwright room.

The inspector squeezed himself in between them, and the bundle, gasping and muttering, inclined itself in his direction.

"What's to-day?" it queried, in a voice as thin and rasping as a bit of rusty wire.

"Friday," answered Arkwright.

The voice mumbled inaudibly for a moment, then:

"That's right. It was Tuesday night, then, I see 'im. Sittin' 'ere, 'e was. I marked 'im 'cos it's my pitch, this is. Come 'ere regular, I do. Old feller, 'e was, with a big black 'at. Give me a tanner and then moved on acrost the bridge. I didn't ask for it, 'e give it to me," she finished sharply, as her beady eyes began to take in Arkwright's soldierly bearing.

"All right, mother, 'e's a friend o' mine," put in Philbegge quickly.

"Well, 'e ain't got nothin' on me, no matter 'oo or what 'e is," she mumbled. "I wasn't beggin', I wasn't."

"What time was this, do you remember?" asked Arkwright.

"I dunno. What's time to me? Big Ben struck, I think, as I come along. Or that might 'a bin' another night. Anyhow, it was after midnight."

"He went across the bridge, you say?"

"That's right. Said 'Good night', 'e did, and went across the bridge there."

Her head drooped forward, and the two men, seeing there was no more to be got out of her, rose and left.

"Walked 'er twenty mile a day, she 'as," said Philbegge gruffly. "'Ad 'er own barrer, too, in 'er time. Likes 'er little drop, that's the trouble. Better try over the other side, I'm thinkin'."

He led the way across the bridge and past the hospital.

"We shan't find many of your friends down here," objected Arkwright.

"Coffee-stalls," grunted Philbegge. "Two of 'em. It's surprisin' what a lot those chaps sees."

The first had seen nothing, and they had passed Waterloo Station before they came on the second. At the sight of Philbegge the proprietor poured out a cup of steaming coffee and pushed it over to him.

"Free, gratis and fer nothin'," he exclaimed cheerfully, "and plenty more where this come from."

Arkwright ordered one for himself and drank it gratefully while Philbegge put his question.

"Old chap with a slouch 'at? I seen 'im," answered the man. "Let me see, to-day's Friday. Last night it rained. It wasn't rainin' the night I see 'im. Tuesday it'd be, or, rather, Wednesday mornin'. 'E come along and 'ad a coffee and a 'am roll. Chatty old feller, 'e was. Told me 'e played in one of them cinema orchestras. Time? Just after six, I should say it was. I'd got me eye on the clock, seein' as I close down at six-thirty."

"Think you'd know him again if you saw him?"

"If 'e'd got the same clothes on, I should, but I didn't take no special note of 'im, and the 'at cast a shadder over 'is face. I get all sorts 'ere, and 'e looked like what 'e said 'e was. What's 'e bin up to?"

"A party wants to trace 'im, that's all," said Philbegge. "Notice which way 'e went?"

The man shook his head.

"Might 'ave gone either way," he said cheerfully. "'E just put down 'is money and 'ooked it."

Arkwright leaned forward.

"Can you remember if he was smoking?" he said.

"Don't think so, and I'll tell you for why. 'E was one of them snuff-takers. Offers the box to me, 'e did, but I wasn't 'avin' any. If my old dad'd been 'ere, 'e'd 'ave been on to it. A terror for snuff, 'e is, as I told the old chap."

"What kind of box was it?"

"Silver, with a kind of pattern on it. I remember thinkin' 'e'd get it pinched if 'e wasn't careful."

"Nothing more you can remember about him?"

"Not a thing. 'E acted quite natural, and there didn't seem anythin' wrong with 'im."

Arkwright thanked him and put down the money for both drinks.

"I don't take no money from Mr. Philbegge and 'e knows it," said the proprietor, pushing half of it back to him. "You're welcome. Sorry I couldn't tell you more."

Arkwright did not part from Philbegge till the small hours of the morning, but their luck had turned and they got no clue as to why it had taken Anthony over two hours and a half to get from the Embankment to Waterloo, or what had happened to him after his visit to the coffee-stall.

"If you ask me," said Philbegge grimly, "there's not much that couldn't 'appen to an old gentleman wanderin' round by 'imself on this side of the river. I'll pass the word round and let you know if I get anythin'. They'll talk to me when they wouldn't say a word to you. There's only one 'ope that I can see, though."

"What's that?"

"That there snuff-box. If it wasn't on 'im when 'e was found somebody's got it. If anybody pinched it off 'im when 'e was alive they'll try to pass it on sooner or later. That's where you get on to 'em."

"Nice easy job you think mine is, don't you?" grinned Arkwright, as he turned wearily towards home.

CHAPTER VII

NEXT MORNING, in accordance with his promise, Constantine called on Betty at Steynes House. He found her out, but the Duchess, very much herself, received him with enthusiasm.

"Marlowe has taken the child into the country in his car," she said. "It seems she's got to attend the inquest this afternoon and she's dreading it, of course. I told him to take her right away into the open air and not bring her back till it's time to start for the Coroner's Court. I told him I expected him to do his best to save her from this."

"It's hardly his fault," explained Constantine. "I was afraid she would have to go unless she were too ill to attend. They'll make it as easy as possible for her."

"Well, I only hope she won't run into Civita. She's gone through enough, poor little thing, as it is, and the sight of him will only upset her."

Constantine looked worried.

"I wish you could persuade her not to take that business so seriously," he said. "It's of very minor importance, in any case. I'm afraid there's no doubt that her grandfather did enter into this transaction with Civita, you know."

"Betty says he didn't, and that's enough for me," announced the Duchess, setting her lips firmly.

"But what object could he have in lying?"

"I don't know, but it stands to reason that Betty knew her own grandfather better than he did, even if they were friends years ago in Paris. Besides, I would take her word against his any day."

"I always thought you liked Civita," ventured Constantine with a boldness born of curiosity.

The Duchess, even when self-deluded, was invariably honest.

"I did," she admitted reluctantly, "until he deliberately began catering for the riff-raff of London society, people whose names I have had to take off my own lists. In the beginning he came to me for advice more than once, and I was glad to give it. Now the place has completely lost caste in my eyes."

"He can hardly refuse to serve people. After all, that's the penalty of keeping a restaurant," expostulated Constantine.

The Duchess snorted.

"My dear Doctor Constantine, you know London as well as I do. It's the easiest thing in the world to exclude the wrong kind of people. They may take up a new place for a short time, but if they don't find their own kind there they'll soon fall away. You must have noticed a change in the tone of the place since you came back."

"I've only dined there once," began Constantine.

"Well, did you see one single person you knew?"

Constantine had seen several, but was aware that they were not of a type that would meet with the approval of the Duchess.

"They did not seem to me to differ from the usual restaurant crowd," he hedged judiciously.

"But that's exactly what I mean! The Trastevere used to be exclusive, in the best sense of the word. Look at it now! When Claudine Malmsey first took to going there I was annoyed, because it's difficult to cold-shoulder your own relations, but it didn't worry me because I knew that she'd soon tire of bringing her own insufferable entourage with her. Claudine likes to get her atmosphere ready-made, so to speak," she conclude, with a shrewdness that surprised Constantine.

"There came a time, I suppose, when they brought themselves," said Constantine. "After all, it was only to be expected."

"Civita's one of the cleverest men in London. Oh, I'm prepared to grant him that, annoyed though I am with him! If he'd wanted to he could have discouraged them so tactfully that they wouldn't have realized what was happening. But he didn't want to."

"You can't expect him to ignore any paying proposition," persisted Constantine.

"My good man, they don't pay!" snapped the Duchess. "We do. We may be taxed to the verge of extinction, and I'm ready to admit that our wine bills bear no comparison with theirs, but what we do order we pay for. Claudine and her crowd, unless they're allowed credit, go elsewhere. I should like to see her account with Civita!"

"Does that set really frequent the Trastevere?" asked Constantine thoughtfully.

"They've made it their headquarters. Go there any night after eleven and you'll see them all. The Clisboroughs, Carol Puyne, and those deplorable half-wits who, I understand, now call themselves 'The Gang', poor Elizabeth Gravesend's two girls, and a collection of young men who would never have found their way into any decent house in my day. Bertie can give you a list. He says they amuse him."

Constantine raised his eyebrows.

"Carol Puyne and Lady Malmsey! Civita's talking his chances!"

"And remember he's got a wine list and doesn't put fancy prices on his drinks, as I understand they do at these night clubs. The man's lost his head."

"And your custom, which is worse!" said Constantine, administering a little oil to the troubled waters.

The Duchess relaxed slightly.

"We may be dull, but we're safe," she conceded. "Is it true that they're going to bring in a verdict of murder this afternoon?"

Constantine shrugged his shoulders.

"I'm not a prophet," he said, "but there seems no doubt that Anthony died of an overdose of morphia. Unless he was a drug addict it seems unlikely that it was self-administered."

"And he was last seen at the Trastevere," added the Duchess with a world of meaning in her voice. "Does that convey nothing to you after what I've told you?"

He laughed in spite of himself.

"My dear Duchess," he said, "isn't that a little far-fetched?"

"Claudine's done some astounding things in her time," retorted the Duchess darkly. "It's no good pretending you don't know what I mean."

Constantine did know, and he was very thoughtful as he made his way down the narrow street that led past the garden of Steynes House to the Trastevere. Fantastic as the Duchess's insinuations had been, he could not dismiss them entirely from his mind. Lady Malmsey had drugged herself into two nursing homes already, and, only six months before, had been concerned in a so-called "ragging" case, in which two of the members of the party had narrowly escaped death. There was a faint possibility that Anthony, after his return to the Trastevere, had somehow fallen in with a party of young degenerates whose perverted sense of humour had been stirred by the sight of the old man, so obviously out of touch with his environment. Constantine knew that there was more than one house in London to which he might have been taken, and it was certainly within the bounds of possibility that, carried away by the exquisite farce of drugging a helpless old man, they had gone further than they intended and had then attempted to conceal the body.

So obsessed did he become with the idea that, on reaching the main road, he signalled to a taxi and had himself driven to New Scotland Yard.

Arkwright had just returned to his room and was in the act of hanging up his coat.

"I've been interviewing a bevy of depressing elderly ladies," he said. "And it's taken me all of an hour to get them to admit that it's six months at least since they swept that room under the stage at the Parthenon. Seemed to think I wanted them to sweep it! I nearly told them that the home of lost clues is the dustbin, only I thought it would be bad for their morals. We've got a step further since I saw you last."

He told Constantine what he had learned the night before.

"Beyond the fact that he was still alive at six a.m., it doesn't tell us much," he finished.

"Do you know if he seemed dazed at all?" asked Constantine.

"From what the coffee-stall keeper said, he seems to have been quite himself and rather chatty than otherwise. The loss of memory theory's gone west, anyhow. He not only knew who he was, but where he lived."

Constantine repeated the gist of his conversation with the Duchess.

"I admit it sounds improbable," he concluded, "but if you know anything of these people you'll realize that it's not impossible."

Arkwright nodded.

"I could tell you one or two things myself," he said. "Some of them are hushed up and some so unprintable that the Press can't touch them. When that lot are out for what they call a 'thrill', the more idiotic and purposeless a thing is the more likely they are to do it. But I fail to see what even they can have got out of this."

"Unless they set out to make a fool of him, managed to get something into his drink and then, later, tried to drug him, in which case they got more than they bargained for," was Constantine's grim comment.

Arkwright rubbed his chin thoughtfully.

"He might have been sleeping off the effects of the drug when he was seen on the Embankment," he mused; "but what happened to him after that? You don't suggest that they got hold of him again?"

"I don't suggest anything," answered Constantine hopelessly. "I've merely put forward a theory. It may not hold water, but you must admit that it goes further towards accounting for his being there at all at that time of night than anything that has cropped up so far."

Arkwright swung round in his swivel-chair and faced him.

"Look here, sir," he said. "Aren't you going to have a finger in this pie? I've been hoping to catch the estimable Manners on the job before now, but it seems to me that, so far, I've been spilling the beans in vain."

"I've done my best to arrange them in a pretty pattern for you," Constantine reminded him. "If you don't like it, it isn't my fault. What do you want Manners to do?"

Arkwright grinned.

"I don't mind, so long as I'm privileged to catch a glimpse of him at work. I shall never forget the spectacle of him blandly bamboozling Goldstein's butler. You haven't got a card or two up your sleeve this time, have you, sir?"

"I can't see a ray of light anywhere," confessed Constantine. "So far as Manners is concerned, he's at your disposal at any time. As a matter of fact, I believe he's beginning to look upon himself as a sort of unofficial member of the Force!"

"I should prefer to feel that you were using him yourself, sir," said Arkwright frankly. "One would have thought that this was a problem after your own heart."

Constantine cocked a reproving eye at him.

"When you've reached my age," he remarked, "you'll find little satisfaction in observing other old gentlemen forcibly re-moved from this earth. The truth is, I'm getting too old for problems of any kind, chess included."

Arkwright, after an anxious glance, decided that he was not serious and let him go without further comment.

But Constantine, as he passed through the gates and out on to the Embankment, found himself drifting back into the mood that had assailed him on his return to London only a few days before. The problem of Julius Anthony's death was beginning to rouse in him the feeling of helpless resentment that had so embittered his defeat at the hands of the lady from the Balkans. Looking back on the chess tournament, and on that game in particular, he could trace, not only the precise move that had been his undoing, but the exact moment at which he had allowed his irritation to obscure his judgment.

He crossed the road and stood leaning on the parapet, looking down on the grey, tempestuous swirl of the river.

"If this goes on," he thought bitterly, "I shall become the kind of old man I particularly detest. Arkwright was talking sense. If I'm going to make a move in this game I'd better begin now."

He stood for a moment staring at the racing tide, glanced at his watch and discovered that it was close on half past one, then, coming to a sudden decision, turned and hailed a passing taxi.

He told the man to drive to the Parthenon. The cheap matinée was in full swing and Constantine, disregarding the well-meant efforts of the attendant, chose a gangway seat only four rows from the front. From here he had an excellent view of the emergency exit on his left and the door into the orchestra, a view which also included the greater part of the back of the conductor, the head and the shoulders of most of the players, and the whole of the upper portion of the double-bass. The cinema screen, on the other hand, could only be seen at the expense of a severe crick in the neck.

Constantine gave his attention to the picture for five minutes, spent another five in analyzing the extraordinary symptoms which immediately manifested themselves in his eyes and neck, and then, having become accustomed to the gloom, contented himself with watching the orchestra. He had only the vaguest notion why he had elected to visit the Parthenon, but at the bottom of his mind had been a desire to see the place in action, as it were, and to observe for himself how possible it would be to reach the back of the stage unobserved.

As he watched he saw one of the musicians slip through the door leading from the orchestra into the auditorium, cross the gangway and go out by the emergency exit. Constantine watched him as he pulled the door open by means of the brass bar that ran across it, heard the click of the latch as the heavy door swung to behind him, and realized that it would be impossible to re-enter from outside.

As he watched, an attendant strolled up to the door and tried it. Evidently his informant had not exaggerated when he said that it was next to impossible for anybody to have entered the cinema that way.

In view of Arkwright's conviction that Anthony's body had been introduced into the cinema by the stage door at a time when the house was empty, the point was of little importance, but, at any rate, he had cleared it up to his own satisfaction. He made himself as comfortable as his seat would allow, and, the screen being denied him, gave his attention idly to the orchestra.

The double-bass player, owing to the fact he was standing, was less hidden by the partition than the other players. Constantine had been watching him for some minutes before he became aware that the man was playing under difficulties. Several times he saw him lift his cumbersome instrument and shift it, as though trying to get it into a more convenient position, and once it slipped and jerked violently as he was in the act of drawing the bow across the strings.

Constantine stared at him, a puzzled frown on his face. He had seen the same thing happen to a 'cellist playing in a room with a parquet floor, but it seemed highly improbable that the flooring of a cinema orchestra would be slippery. It was characteristic of him that, his curiosity once roused, he could not rest till he had found some means of satisfying it, and he gave the matter a consideration quite out of proportion to its importance until he suddenly hit on a probable explanation of the man's movements.

The point once settled to his satisfaction, he was about to dismiss it from his mind when he was struck by another possibility, so amazing that he half rose, then dropped back and sat rigid, his hands clutching the arms of the seat, his eyes fixed on the double-bass player.

He waited till there was a pause in the music, then got up and made his way down the aisle to the barrier in front of the orchestra. Leaning on it, he greeted one of the 'cellists with whom he had spoken on the night of the finding of Anthony's body. The man remembered him well, and soon other members of the orchestra were joining in the conversation, anxious to renew their acquaintance with the old man who had provided a welcome relief on that ghastly evening.

In the course of conversation he told the double-bass player of the problem that had been bothering him, and asked him if his solution had been correct. The man laughed.

"You've got it," he said. "I used to stand further back. It's only since they brought in that blessed harmonium and obliged me to move that it's bothered me. After the first night I got them to put it in front here and I went back to my old place, but the harmonium drowned everything, so we had to change round again."

"When was this?" asked Constantine.

"Which day did that little box of tricks come in, Phil?" demanded the double-bass player.

The pianist, who doubled the part of harmonium player, answered him.

"Tuesday last. Was to have come on Monday, but they failed us."

"Then it was moved on Wednesday?" persisted Constantine.

"Yes. We moved it before the last performance on Wednesday, but it didn't do and we shoved it back again yesterday morning. Bill here has been cursing ever since."

"Any objection to my going through and having another look at that room under the stage?" asked Constantine.

"None. Through the door at the end there. The lights should be on, but if they're not the chap near the door will turn them on for you."

Once in the room it did not take Constantine many minutes to find what he was looking for.

Brushing the dust off his knees, he groped his way down the narrow passage by which he had entered on the night of his first visit and let himself out by the stage door. He found this securely fastened, and noted that the spring lock acted easily as he shut it carefully behind him.

He picked up a taxi and drove to his club. There he rang up Arkwright at the Yard.

"I want to see you," he said briskly. "Will you call on me at the club, or shall I come to you?"

Arkwright's voice sounded dubious.

"I've been to the inquest. Only just back, and up to my ears in work. I don't know that I can manage it."

"I've got something for you, and I'm putting all my cards on the table. You'd better come."

There was a note in the old man's voice that Arkwright knew of old.

"I'll come to you," he said briefly.

He grinned as he turned away from his littered table.

"He's got his nose to the ground at last," he muttered. "I'm glad I chipped him, even at the risk of hurting his feelings."

He found Constantine in an armchair by the fire, gazing with seeming satisfaction at the leaping flames.

"How did the inquest go?" he asked.

"Adjourned, at our request. What's the news, sir?"

"I've got at least one step further in establishing the time of Anthony's death," said Constantine. "His body was placed in the Parthenon, some time before eight o'clock on Wednesday night."

Arkwright's face lit up with satisfaction.

"By Jove, sir, you've got ahead of us there," he exclaimed. "This wipes out Wednesday night and the whole of Thursday. How did you arrive at it?"

"Quite by accident. I'll tell you the whole story later. Meanwhile, the facts are these. The body was crammed face downwards into the cavity where it was found. That cavity, as you know, is under the flooring of the orchestra. Just above where I imagine the head must have rested there's a knot-hole in the wood of the flooring, and that knot-hole was responsible for the apparently motiveless wound in the neck."

For the life of him he could not help pausing at the most dramatic point of his narrative. Arkwright stared at him.

"What caused the wound?"

"The spike, or whatever they call the thing, that you'll find projecting from the bottom of a 'cello or a double-bass. In this case the double-bass was responsible."

"Are you sure of this, sir?" demanded Arkwright.

"Certainly not," responded Constantine equably. "It's your job to prove it, but I'm morally certain that you'll find I'm right. The person responsible, by the way, is quite unaware of what he's done. I should suggest that you have the metal analysed. The blood hadn't coagulated, according to the surgeon."

"How do you fix the time limit?" asked Arkwright.

Constantine told him of the shifting of the harmonium owing to the complaints of the double-bass player.

"Anthony was seen alive at six-thirty on Wednesday morning," he said. "During the whole of Wednesday the double-bass player was standing above the hole. Just before the last performance, that is to say about eight o'clock, he moved to make room for the harmonium, which remained there till after the body had been removed. If my theory is correct, it would have been impossible for the wound to have been inflicted after eight o'clock on Wednesday night."

Arkwright nodded.

"Good enough," he said. "You did not see the body before we moved it out of the recess?"

"No. In fact, till I stumbled on this piece of information this afternoon, I didn't know it was lying face downwards, though the position in which I did see it suggested the possibility."

"It was lying on its side, with the knees drawn up, but the head and shoulders were twisted and the back of the neck was in the position you describe. It looks as if your explanation is the right one. The wound was undoubtedly caused by a round, pointed instrument, such as a spike. I'll get Macbane on to this. You got off the mark pretty quickly, sir," he concluded with a smile.

Constantine's eyes twinkled.

"I've moved a pawn," he conceded, "and I feel ten years younger than when I last saw you. I don't mind admitting that I'm thinking of bringing my bishop into action."

For a moment Arkwright was at a loss, then, with a sudden chuckle, visualized the portly, not unclerical-looking figure of Constantine's faithful retainer.

"Manners?" he queried.

"Manners it is. I see one excellent move for that most useful piece. Meanwhile, having missed my lunch, a sandwich and a glass of sherry seem to be indicated. Whisky for you?"

Arkwright pulled himself out of his chair and pressed the bell.

"We'll drink to the opening of the tournament," he said.

CHAPTER VIII

WHEN CONSTANTINE entered his flat that afternoon, Manners, according to his custom, emerged from the back premises to take his coat. There was a reproachful gleam in his eye.

"Mrs. Carter kept your lunch hot, sir, but I'm afraid the soufflé—"

"Good heavens, man," interrupted Constantine, "it's past three o'clock!"

He became aware of an anxious female countenance framed in the doorway at the end of the passage.

"My fault, I'm afraid, Mrs. Carter," he hastened to apologize. "I ought to have telephoned to say I wasn't coming back. The loss is mine if I missed that soufflé!"

Mrs. Carter disappeared, but he still had Manners to reckon with.

"Have you lunched, sir?" he enquired, with an insistence that, though respectful, was not to be gainsaid.

"That's all right, Manners, I had something at the club," Constantine assured him hastily.

But Manners was not to be put off so easily.

"Excuse me, sir," he continued imperturbably, "but those club sandwiches are very small. Mrs. Carter has kept the soup hot."

There were moments, Constantine reflected irritably, when Manners seemed to be endowed with second sight.

"I don't want any soup," he said firmly; then, with an abrupt change of topic: "The inspector was talking about your work on the Goldstein case. I wish you'd been there, Manners."

Manners was only human. Constantine could see by the faint glow of gratification in his eyes that he had gained a moment's respite.

"I only followed your directions, sir," he murmured.

Impelled by the menace of the hovering soup, Constantine forged ahead.

"We were wondering whether you'd like to try your hand again," he said.

Manners, with difficulty maintaining his pose of imperturbable detachment, intimated that he was at his master's disposal.

"You know what I have in mind, I expect?" said Constantine.

"The death of this Mr. Anthony, sir? I understand that the inspector is in charge of the case."

"You know, of course, that he was Miss Anthony's grandfather?" said Constantine, perfectly aware that there was very little connected with the house of Steynes that Manners did not know.

"Yes, sir. A very sad business, if I may say so."

"You've read the newspaper accounts. Has anything struck you?"

Manners cleared his throat. For the moment he had forgotten that his mission in life was Constantine's welfare.

"Only this, sir," he volunteered. "If Mr. Anthony's body was introduced into the Parthenon after his death, it was not brought in while the performance was going on. I am in the habit of frequenting the Parthenon myself, sir, and, from what I have observed, I feel convinced that such a course would be impossible."

"There's a stage door which you may not have noticed," suggested Constantine. "It gives on to a side alley and isn't overlooked."

"Excuse me, sir," said Manners respectfully, "but there is always more or less of a queue outside the house, with the result that there is always a certain number of people standing at the end of the alley. It would be difficult to get past them. And I understand that the door is invariably kept locked. In fact, I went so far as to stroll past it yesterday evening and ascertained that it could not be opened from the outside. From the information I have been able to acquire, I have come to the conclusion that either Mr. Anthony entered the building of his own accord in the morning, before the commencement of the programme, using his own key, and was killed in the room where he was found, or his body was brought in some time in the early morning, before anybody was about. Of course, sir, I have only the newspaper accounts and what little information I was able to pick up on the spot to go by."

He paused, rendered a little breathless by this unaccustomed eloquence.

"Who told you Mr. Anthony had a key?" asked Constantine.

"One of the door-keepers, sir. A man called Binns. He informed me that Mr. Anthony was in the habit of practising on the organ and had been supplied with a key for that purpose."

"Have you known this man Binns long?"

"I've been in the habit of chatting with him on the occasions on which I have visited the cinema, sir."

"He doesn't belong to your branch of the British Legion, by any chance?"

"No, sir, but he was in the same sector as myself in nineteen sixteen, though we never met out there. We have recollections in common, sir."

Constantine regarded him with amused approbation.

"So far as I can see, Manners," he said, "your job's half done already. I was going to ask you to cultivate this man Binns, and see if there is anything he hasn't told the police. There are one or two facts you had better know about him."

He told Manners of the grudge Binns was supposed to harbour against Anthony.

"My own impression is that the man had nothing to do with the murder," he added, "but he may know more than he has chosen to say. You might see what you can do in that direction. And there's another thing. I gather that the members of the orchestra are in the habit of slipping out occasionally during the performance, and I think we may take it that some of them, at any rate, are also in the habit of frequenting some pub in the neighbourhood. Binns would no doubt help you there. Get into conversation with them if you can and pick up anything, no matter how trivial."

"Very good, sir."

"You understand, Manners, I'm not asking you to trap Binns in any way. In fact, if you'd prefer not to touch that side of it I shall understand."

"I feel no anxiety about Binns, sir," said Manners firmly. "If you'll excuse me, I think your estimate is correct. He hasn't the criminal mind. I take it that I report to you, sir, and not to the police?"

Constantine looked doubtful.

"Anything you tell me will be passed on as I think fit," he warned him.

"If you will excuse me, sir, I am quite content to leave it at that. You would wish me to get to work at once?"

"The quicker the better," agreed Constantine. "Mrs. Carter will carry on in your absence."

Mrs. Carter's name had hardly passed his lips before he realized his mistake. Manners hastened to atone for his lapse from duty.

"As regards the soup, sir?" he began firmly.

Constantine fled into his study.

Arkwright rang up in the evening to say that the expert's report on the metal support of the double-bass had come in.

There were undoubted traces of blood on the spike. He had also been to the Parthenon, and, as the result of a careful inspection, had discovered small traces of blood, both at the edge of the knot-hole and on the flooring of the orchestra. There seemed no room for doubt now as to what had caused the wound in Anthony's neck.

"Thanks to you, sir, we can now take it that he entered the cinema, dead or alive, some time on the Wednesday morning," he concluded.

"It narrows things down, certainly," agreed Constantine, "but we've got our work cut out for us still. Will you do something for me? I warn you that it may lead nowhere and will involve you in a certain amount of extra work."

"I'll do a good deal for the sake of that little word 'we'!" declared Arkwright. "It's something to know that the old combination's at work again. What do you want?"

"Anthony's fingerprints, for one thing. I take it that the corpse is still accessible?"

"At the mortuary. That's easy enough, but why on earth—?"

"A possibility has occurred to me, but it's so fantastic that, at present, I should prefer to keep it to myself. Meanwhile— and you'll curse me now—why not add Howells' fingerprints to your collection at the Yard?"

A low whistle reached his ears.

"Now you're asking! However, there are ways and means, and it's good for the young entry to get a little practice. We can probably accommodate you. Anything else?"

"That will do for the present. Good hunting!"

Constantine replaced the receiver and returned to the study of the little leather-covered notebook that had proved so useful in the Goldstein case. The notes he had made in it were rough, mere jottings of times and dates, but they served as a solid basis for his thoughts.

At the head of the page he had written the date, January the eighteenth, the occasion of Anthony's first unexplained departure. He was beginning to feel more and more certain that there was some connection between this journey and the one that had ended so fatally for the old man. Mrs. Berry had met the police with the utmost frankness, and it seemed highly improbable that there was anything more to be learned from her. Still, seeing that she was the only fount of information on that particular subject, she might be worth tackling.

Accordingly, the following day she was startled out of her Sunday afternoon doze over the fire by the sound of the front door bell.

The Anthonys' rooms were empty since Betty had departed in state for Steynes House; her two other lodgers were away for the week-end, and her own friends invariably came to the basement.

She rose ponderously to her feet and stepped with exaggerated caution into the area. Since "that there piano-tuner" had played such a trick on her she had been nervous about opening the door to anyone.

She peered up at the front doorstep and gave vent to a gusty sigh of relief. Constantine was Miss Anthony's friend, and therefore above suspicion.

"I'm sorry to keep you waiting, sir. I'll be up in a minute."

Constantine turned and came down the steps.

"Miss Anthony's away, sir," she informed him anxiously.

"I know. It was you, Mrs. Berry, that I really hoped to see. If I might come down. Or am I disturbing you?"

He opened the area gate and descended, a pleasing study in black and white, on the bridling Mrs. Berry.

"Not at all. It's a pleasure. But I'd have opened the door, sir."

"This way we both save our legs, and that's a consideration at my age. Could you spare me half an hour of your time?"

Still pleasantly flustered, Mrs. Berry led the way into her comfortable front room.

"I hope Miss Anthony's all right, sir?" she panted.

"She's getting over the shock and being well looked after. You can make yourself quite happy about her, though, of course, it will take her some time to get over this tragic business."

Mrs. Berry, fussily pulling up a chair, paused, her china-blue eyes round with horror.

"The poor old gentleman! Who was it did it? They do say he was poisoned."

"Something of the sort. Who did it is what we should all like to find out."

He sank into the chair.

"This is real comfort. I wish I could get fires to burn like that in my flat. But the kettle's boiling! I'm interrupting you at your tea!"

"Oh, dear me, no, I'm sure. I was just sittin' over the fire, havin' a bit of a rest till the water boiled."

She hesitated, then:

"I suppose I couldn't offer you a cup, sir? It'd be a pleasure."

Twenty minutes later Constantine, over his second cup of coal-black tea, was listening to the entire history of Mrs. Berry's connection with the Anthonys, dating from their first entry into her house six years before.

"And nicer, more considerate lodgers no one could have," she finished. "A bit quiet and old-fashioned the old gentleman was sometimes, but Miss Anthony, she'd a pleasant word and a bit of a joke whenever I see her. And thought a lot of her too."

"You must have been worried when he went off like that, that first time, while she was away," said Constantine.

Mrs. Berry nodded portentously.

"I came very near to sendin' for her. And then, when he come back, I was glad I hadn't. A nice fool I should've looked, bringin' her all that way."

"Can you remember when it was exactly that he told you he was going?"

"As well as if it was yesterday I can. I'd had me tea and just washed up all the tea-things, upstairs and down, when he called to me. I always reckon to get through with me washin'-up by six o'clock. Must've been just after six when his bell went and he called down to me over the banisters to say that he'd got to go away unexpected. I went up, and he was just gettin' out his suitcase from the cupboard on the stairs."

"You don't know if he looked up any train or rang up one of the railway companies?"

"He looked a train up. I was there when he did it."

"I suppose the book isn't lying about anywhere?"

She beamed on him.

"It's in Mr. Anthony's sittin'-room on the shelf."

"Might I fetch it, I wonder? It might give us some clue as to where he went."

"You sit where you are, sir. Them stairs are nothin' to me."

In token of which she bustled up them and returned, panting but triumphant, with the railway guide in her hand.

Constantine went through it carefully, but the book apparently had been very little used, and, when he let it fall open of its own accord, did so at a different page each time. Reluctantly he concluded that there was nothing to be learned from it and laid it aside.

"Do you think anything happened while he was out that might have caused him to go away so suddenly?" he asked.

"He hadn't been out, not since he got back from the cinema at five. The moment he got in I took up his tea as usual, and he wasn't thinkin' of goin' out then, I know, because he asked me to give a message to Miss Anthony in case she wasn't back before he left to go back to the Parthenon. That's what I can't understand."

"What was the message? Do you remember?"

"That I do. I was to say that he'd be callin' in at Gunters', the shop at the corner, on his way to the cinema. So that shows he meant to go back there, doesn't it, sir?"

"Looks like it, certainly," said Constantine thoughtfully. "He didn't get a telephone message, I suppose? Would you know if anyone had rung him up?"

"He couldn't have had, without me knowing. You see, that's an extension that they've got upstairs. It's the same with all my lodgers. The telephone rings down here and I press the bell two or three times, according to which party's wanted. That's what I told the police. The Exchange has got to get on to me first, and I was in all the time. It's different when the lodgers want to ring anyone up. They can get through direct from upstairs."

Constantine nodded.

"That wipes out that then. And yet something must have happened to make him change his mind."

"I know, and I've puzzled over it, that I have. It wasn't anything in the paper, I can tell you that. You see, he generally used to bring home a *Standard* with him when he came in to tea, and when he'd read it he'd hand it over to me. Sometimes, if Miss Anthony was home, I wouldn't get it till later, but that day he give it to me when I took up his tea, so he must have finished with it. And he wasn't meanin' to go out then."

"And no one came to see him?"

"Not without me knowin' it they couldn't."

"What about the other lodgers?"

"All out, every one of 'em. It's a mystery, sir, and a mystery it'll remain."

Constantine stayed on for another quarter of an hour, skillfully drawing out what little she knew about the Anthonys' habits and environment, but it was becoming more and more apparent that he might as well have remained away for all the good he had gained by his visit. In fact, he realized that he had only gone over the ground that Arkwright had already covered.

After he had listened to a voluble and circumstantial account of Anthony's depressingly regular habits, he rose to his feet and held out his hand.

"Thank you for allowing me to victimize you, and for one of the best teas I've had for a long time," he said. "I don't wonder your rooms are never empty."

"It's been a pleasure, I'm sure," the gratified Mrs. Berry assured him. "I wish I could have helped you more, but there it is. There's some things it seems we aren't meant to know."

"It certainly is a puzzle," he agreed with a smile. "But we may solve it yet. You know, I've got a theory that that's what puzzles are made for."

"It's him goin' away so suddenly that time, I can't understand," she insisted. "If he hadn't given me that message for Miss Anthony about the accumulator, there'd be some sense in it."

Constantine, already on his way to the door, halted.

"What's that? An accumulator, did you say? Had Mr. Anthony got a wireless set?"

"Indeed he had. A beauty. One of them portables. Not that he listened in much, him bein' out such a lot and not likin' the dance music. Miss Anthony was a one for that, though. Gunters' used to fill up them things for them, and sometimes Miss Anthony would take them round and sometimes him, accordin' to which was passin' the shop."

"Was he listening-in when you took up the tea?"

"No, but likely he turned it on afterwards. He'd generally listen to the news and weather report at six o'clock."

Constantine extricated himself as quickly as possible and made a dive for the nearest telephone-box. It seemed better, on the whole, not to retail his news within hearing of the excellent but loquacious Mrs. Berry.

Arkwright was out, but he left an urgent message for him.

"Make him understand that it's important," he added, "and that he will find me in any time this evening."

Then he went home to await the information he had demanded. It came as he was sitting over his after-dinner coffee, and Arkwright brought it in person.

"You've done it again, sir!" he exclaimed enthusiastically, as his foot crossed that the threshold of the study. "The information has just come in from the B.B.C. Congratulations. I'm running down to Brighton to-morrow on the strength of it, and, after that, with luck, we ought to get a move on. Look at this!"

He thrust a slip of paper under Constantine's nose, placing a finger on the second of three typewritten SOS messages.

Will Julius Anthony, a musician, believed to be living in London, go at once to the East Sussex Hospital, Brighton, where his daughter, Mrs. Bianchi, is seriously ill and asking for him (read Constantine).

The date at the top of the page was January the eighteenth.

CHAPTER IX

"IT'S EASY to see now why Anthony was so secretive about that first journey," said Constantine, his eyes on the SOS message. "He had kept his grand-daughter in ignorance of the fact that her father had a sister. She's certainly under the impression that he was an only child."

Arkwright nodded.

"The old story, I suppose. The daughter kicked over the traces or married someone he didn't approve of, and he broke off all connection with her."

"It's in keeping with his character as I see it," agreed Constantine. "There was a puritanical streak in him, I should imagine, and once he had made up his mind, he would be difficult to move. But, judging from his grand-daughter's account, he was both kindly and affectionate. The daughter must have hurt him deeply to have made him go to such extreme lengths."

"I may get a line on that at Brighton. If she didn't die, there's your connection between the two disappearances. If she did die, we're no better off than we were before."

"Are you doing anything at this end?"

"Somerset House, you mean? We may as well get all the data we can. I'll send a man down."

"Would you like me to try my luck? I know one or two of the officials there. She may, of course, have married this man Bianchi abroad somewhere, in which case we shall have our work cut out for us."

"I should be grateful if you'd take it over, though, honestly, I don't see where it's likely to lead us. To my mind, the whole thing hangs on whether she's still alive or not."

He hurried away, and ten minutes later Manners returned and handed in his report. He had been to a smoking concert got up by the branch of the British Legion to which Binns belonged, and Binns had got leave from the Parthenon to attend it. Manners had treated him generously, which had caused his tongue to wag with amazing freedom.

"He had nothing to do with it, sir," Manners assured his master. "I have observed him closely, and, if I may put it that way, his personality's against it. A weak character with a grievance against everybody and everything—that's not uncommon, sir, with old soldiers. He might get his own back in little ways, but he'd never bring himself to commit a real crime. I should say he's straight enough in himself, but a bit warped, if you understand me."

"I do," answered Constantine solemnly. "But he'd make a good tool, Manners."

"If you'll excuse me, sir, I think not," objected Manners firmly. "A very unreliable character and apt to let anyone down at the critical moment."

"In that case we're barking up the wrong tree. We'd better drop that line altogether. As a matter of fact, the police have no doubt got him under observation."

But again Manners objected.

"If you don't mind, sir, I should feel inclined to carry on for the present. I don't suspect Binns, but he knows something. Whether it's important or not I can't say, but he's very bitter against the police and is holding back on them from sheer spite. He as good as told me so to-night."

"Get it out of him by all means if you can. He may have seen something that night. We seem to have hit a streak of luck, and I believe in following it up."

But next morning, in the gloomy fastnesses of Somerset House, he began to wonder whether he had not spoken too optimistically.

More than one Bianchi had ventured rashly on the seas of matrimony, but none of them had linked his name with that of Anthony, and only those who have dug in vain among the uninspiring records of other people's official lives know the weariness that ensues after the first fruitless hour. Even Constantine's enthusiasm began to wane at last, and it was with little hope in his heart that he attacked the Anthony side of the problem.

His first discovery was that it was a far commoner name in England than he had supposed, and he almost given up hope when he came on what he was seeking.

For a few minutes he sat starting at his find, hardly able to believe the evidence of his own eyes. Betty had assured him that her father had been Julius Anthony's only child, but, according to the certificate before him, the old man must have had not one daughter but two, one of whom, Margaret had married Sidney Howells on December the thirteenth, nineteen hundred and five!

Constantine was forced to the conclusion that either he had stumbled on the wrong Anthony, in which case the Howells connection was curious, to say the least of it, or Howells had actually married Anthony's daughter and had deliberately withheld the fact from the police.

If Arkwright had been in town he might have pursued the obvious course and passed on to him the information he had acquired, leaving the police to deal with Howells. But Arkwright was at Brighton, and Constantine, impelled partly by his own insatiable curiosity and partly by the irresistible temptation to steal a march on him, decided to tackle the problem himself.

He went back to his flat and from there telephoned to Betty Anthony. Giving her no hint as to what he had discovered, he asked her for Howells' address. She gave it, adding his telephone number.

"You've known him a long time, haven't you?" he asked casually.

"Ever since I can remember. He was a great friend of my grandfather's."

"Can you tell me his Christian name, in case I want to write to him?"

"Sidney. What did you want to ask him? Can I help?"

"An idea has occurred to me in connection with your grand-father's life in Paris, and I thought he might help me," stated Constantine mendaciously.

"I'm afraid you'll find him useless there. I don't think he's ever been out of England."

Howells was at home and in the act of giving a music lesson. Constantine, waiting in the ugly, neatly furnished little dining-room, listened to it and pitied him with all his heart, as the wooden-fingered pupil stumbled uncomprehendingly through the first movement of a Mozart sonata.

Howells had opened the door to him himself, and he had introduced himself as a friend of Betty Anthony's. He had been favourably impressed both by the man's quiet, unassuming manner and his intelligent, rather careworn face, and had asked permission to wait until the lesson was over. If Howells felt any misgiving as to the object of his visit he did not show it, but had merely apologized for the delay, which, he said, would not last more than ten minutes, and gone back to his pupil.

When, later, he ushered Constantine into a slightly larger room, furnished sparsely with a grand piano, a couple of easy-chairs and a littered office desk, he did not waste his breath in useless queries, but sat forward in his chair, his strong, capable hands loosely crossed between his knees.

Constantine, studying him, realized that neither persuasion or intimidation would serve with this man. If he had anything of importance to impart he would speak or not only as he felt inclined. Acting on this impression, he broached his subject with crudeness unlike his usual methods.

"I introduced myself as a friend of Miss Anthony's," he said, "but, to be honest, my acquaintance with her is of very recent date. I am, however, a very old friend of Lord Marlowe's. You've heard rumours of their engagement, I expect?"

"I had the news from Miss Anthony," assented Howells non-committally.

"I should like you to believe that, in coming here to-day, I have done so in the hope of saving, not only my own old friends, but Miss Anthony herself, from the unnecessary publicity of a police investigation."

Howells stiffened.

"I have already placed my services at the disposal of the police," he said shortly.

"I know," agreed Constantine. Then, with an abrupt change of manner that took Howells off his guard:

"I have a feeling that we are walking round each other like dogs about to fight. Why not save time by assuming that we meet as good friends of Miss Anthony's, anxious to spare her as much as possible? May I be as frank with you as I hope you will be with me?"

Seeing that the other man remained silent and on the defensive, he continued:

"I have just come from Somerset House, Mr. Howells. By an accident I got there ahead of the police, but unless I report to them to-night they will start an investigation on their own account to-morrow. I have an idea that you may prefer to speak to me rather than to them. After all, they are concerned only with the death of Mr. Anthony. My object, on the other hand, is to safeguard the interests of Miss Anthony and the family into which I hope she will marry."

The antagonism that had deadened Howells' eyes at the opening of Constantine's little speech did not abate.

"Do you mean to tell me that Lord Marlowe's family is placing no obstacle in the way of the match?" he asked dryly.

"May I answer your question with another?" parried Constantine with his most placating smile. "From your personal knowledge of Miss Anthony, would they be justified in doing so?"

A stain of red appeared on Howells' thin cheek-bones.

"Any man who gets Betty Anthony can count himself lucky," was his curt rejoinder.

Constantine nodded.

"Though you may find it difficult to believe, that is the view of her future husband's people. The engagement will be announced almost immediately, and our object, yours and mine, is to prevent anything interfering with it."

Howells hesitated, then, as if he had come to a sudden decision, spoke.

"I have heard about you from Betty," he said slowly. "If I tell you certain things will you undertake to keep them from her?"

"To the best of my power, I will," said Constantine frankly; "but if they have any bearing on Mr. Anthony's death I shall have to pass them on to the authorities. I think you must see that."

"If they had I should have told the police of them myself," answered Howells decisively. "There can be no connection."

"In that case may I give you a lead? The Margaret Anthony whom you married in nineteen five was Julius Anthony's daughter?"

Howells nodded.

"You traced that at Somerset House, I suppose?" he said. "We were married in London and lived here for eighteen months. Then I followed my father-in-law to Paris, where he was playing in a theatre orchestra, taking my wife with me. I wish to God I'd stayed in England. Before we'd been in Paris six months she left me. I've never seen her since."

There was a moment's silence, then Constantine spoke.

"I'm sorry to have to ask this," he said gently, "but is she still living?"

"I don't know. She went away with an Italian, a fellow called Bianchi, who had a financial interest in a cabaret show in which my wife was appearing. She was a singer, you know. Mr. Anthony followed her and did his best to persuade her to come back. I—I'd have taken her back then, gladly."

He paused, and Constantine, who was engaged in reconstructing his ideas, waited in silence for him to proceed.

"She wouldn't listen to him, and I've never had either a sign or a word from her since. Mr. Anthony went to her again, two years after that, when she was very ill, but she refused to see me, and, from then on, we both lost sight of her altogether."

Constantine pulled himself together. He realized suddenly the depth of the tragedy into which he had blundered.

"I'm afraid this has been very painful for you," he said, "and I must apologize for such a gross intrusion on your privacy. But I had no choice. I hope you will believe that."

He was marking time, trying to gauge how great a shock the news of his wife's illness and possible death would be to the man.

Howells nodded.

"I'm not sorry this has happened," he admitted. "I had hoped the whole thing was dead and buried. Mr. Anthony never alluded to it, and I have tried to forget it. But if, as you say, the police have got wind of it, I am glad to have had the opportunity of putting the facts before you now."

"Did you ever have reason to suppose that Mr. Anthony had had news of his daughter?" asked Constantine.

"I'm sure he hadn't. If she had been in any kind of want I know he would have come to me."

"And yet he not only heard from her, but saw her not so long ago," Constantine informed him gently.

Howells stared at him in astonishment.

"But that's impossible!" he exclaimed incredulously. "I've been in constant touch with him, and he'd no earthly reason for concealing the fact."

"In spite of which there seems every indication that he travelled to Brighton last January and interviewed her in a hospital there."

Again there was silence, then:

"Is she dead?" asked Howells, his voice ominously quiet.

"I'm afraid that's more than I can say," said Constantine, "but by this evening I may be able to set your mind at rest."

He told him briefly of his discovery of the wireless message and hinted at the possible bearing it might have on Anthony's death.

"Inspector Arkwright is at Brighton now," he concluded, "and may have important news for us when he comes back.

There is a possibility that she may have recovered on the first occasion and have sent for him again on Tuesday last."

"But why the secrecy?" exclaimed Howells in bewilderment. "I must have seen him only a few days after his return. It's inconceivable that he should have kept me in the dark."

"From what you say, he seems to have been almost abnormally sensitive about his daughter's behaviour," Constantine pointed out. "Miss Anthony is not a child, and yet he has allowed her to believe that her father had no brothers or sisters. As he grew older the thing might have become an obsession with him."

"Unless he had good reason for keeping silent he would have told me," insisted Howells. "As for Betty, if you had been more thorough in your investigations at Somerset House you would have been able to answer that question for yourself," he finished with a mirthless smile.

Constantine stared at him.

"You mean . . ." he began slowly.

"Julius Anthony never had a son. Margaret was his only child, and Betty is her daughter. Now you see why I kept my marriage from the police."

"But if Betty is your child," said Constantine, groping feebly, "I don't see . . ."

Howells shook his head.

"Not mine, Bianchi's," he answered. "Betty was born a year after her mother left me. Margaret was very ill when Betty was born, and, in any case, she resented her coming. Bianchi, who thought she was going to die, sent for Mr. Anthony. He went, and, realizing the kind of life an unwanted child would lead in that sort of ménage, he brought the baby back with him. Betty has been with him ever since."

"You never divorced your wife?"

"I would have if she'd asked me, but Bianchi was a Roman Catholic and would not have married her if I had."

Constantine nodded.

He knew now why Anthony had been so insistent on an interview with Marlowe.

Howells turned to him, his face white and drawn, an agonized appeal in his eyes.

"You see now why I tried to keep the whole story dark. Will this mean the end of everything for Betty?"

Constantine tried to reassure him.

"Not so far as Lord Marlowe is concerned," he said, "and I believe I can speak for the Duke. The Duchess, alas, is always an unknown quantity, but she has taken a great fancy to the girl, and that goes a long way with her."

A bleak smile illumined Howells' face.

"Rather a case of the pot calling the kettle black, wouldn't it be?" he suggested. "I had a look in the Peerage after Betty told me the news."

Constantine's eyes twinkled.

"Every family has to have its beginnings," he said, "and, in the eyes of the world, I'm afraid there's a difference between the indiscretions of a royal prince and those of Signor Bianchi! But, so far as one can see, there seems no reason why the story should be made public."

"Is there any real reason why it should go any further?" demanded Howells. "I can see that the Duke will have to know, of course, but surely, for his own sake, he'll keep it to himself."

Constantine shook his head.

"The police know too much already, and it's better that they should be told than that they should ferret it out for themselves. I think I can promise that, unless it has any direct bearing on Mr. Anthony's death, it will not be repeated. In fact, for the present, I suggest that we say nothing to Betty."

"As regards Betty," said Howells slowly, "I never quite agreed with Mr. Anthony's policy. It has always struck me as possible that Bianchi might turn up and make things very unpleasant for her."

"I suppose the man's still alive?"

"I have no idea. An old friend of Mr. Anthony's wrote to him about a year ago saying that he had heard a rumour of his death, but it was never substantiated."

"What was the fellow like?"

"A typical Italian. Good-looking in a sort of way. Dark, with a small moustache. I saw very little of him, and had no idea that things had gone so far between him and Margaret till the crash came."

Constantine questioned him further about Anthony's life in Paris, but could glean nothing of any significance.

As regards Anthony's prospective tour, he showed surprise that the old man should not have mentioned it to him, but was of the opinion that he would have jumped at any opportunity to get away from his job at the cinema. He considered Betty's attitude towards the matter unreasonable and partly due to the fact that she had never realized how much her grandfather had loathed the cinema work.

"This influx of syncopated music was a real tragedy to the old man," he said. "Light music he could tolerate, indeed he had to, practically all through his life, but this American stuff maddened him. He would have jumped at the chance to get away from it."

"Did he mention his meeting with Civita to you?"

"No. But that's not surprising. He stayed on in Paris for a long time after I left, and had many friends I never met. No doubt this man Civita was one of them."

Constantine had been favourably impressed with Howells from the beginning, and he left him feeling convinced of his loyalty both to Betty and her grandfather. His information had been disturbing, to say the least of it, and he decided to keep it to himself until he had heard the result of Arkwright's visit to Brighton. Meanwhile there could be no harm in sounding Civita.

He caught him at one of the busiest moments of his day.

"I should have excused myself," he said, "if it had been anyone but you, Doctor Constantine. But I know that with you I am safe. You are like me: you say what you have to say, and then—finish! The others sit and talk—but, oh, how they talk!"

"I'm not even going to talk," Constantine assured him. "I've come to ask questions. But I'll make them as short as I can. First of all, during your time in Paris did you ever come across a man called Bianchi?"

Civita's eyebrows rose whimsically.

"I should not like to have to say how many men called Bianchi I have come across in my lifetime," he said with a smile. "But I think I know the one you mean. This is in connection with Julius Anthony, eh?"

"My enquiries usually are, nowadays," parried Constantine. "Can you tell me anything about him?"

"Only gossip, if that is any use to you. For myself, I think gossip is under-rated. It is very useful, and, in a great many cases, true. Personally, I never met the man, but he was talked about at one time. He had, it seemed, too much money, and he was what we call *mal educati.* You understand?"

"Only too well," said Constantine.

"He was living, I think, at Dinard when I was in Paris, but he would come there sometimes. He had an interest in a theatre or a cabaret, I do not know which. I don't suppose I should have remembered all this, but I was interested for the same reason that you are interested now."

"Julius Anthony?"

"Exactly, Julius Anthony. It was said that Bianchi was living with Anthony's daughter. She never came to Paris and no one ever saw her, but I met people who had known her in the old days, of course."

"How long is it since you last heard of him?"

Civita thrust out his hands.

"Fifteen years. More than that, perhaps. I do not know."

"Anthony never spoke of him?"

"If you knew Anthony you would not ask me that. He was a silent man at all times, and I was told that this had almost broken his heart. No, Anthony never spoke of it."

Constantine threw out a feeler.

"Did you ever know Miss Anthony's father?"

Civita looked at him, a long, scrutinizing glance that revealed nothing.

"No. I understood that he had died some years before, but, as I told you, Julius Anthony did not talk of these things, and, if you knew him, you did not ask questions."

And Constantine, watching the thin, implacable line of the discreet lips, the bland impenetrability of the dark, heavy-lidded eyes, knew that Civita had said all he meant to say on this subject. If he knew the secret of Betty's birth, it was safe with him.

And Constantine felt convinced that he did know.

CHAPTER X

CONSTANTINE RETURNED home to a lunch served by Mrs. Carter. Manners, it would seem, was pursuing the other and more thrilling half of his double life.

He returned early in the afternoon and appeared before his master with such a wild gleam in his eye that, for one incredulous moment, Constantine suspected that he had been drinking.

"I beg your pardon, sir," said Manners in a hushed voice that he tried hard to keep level, "but I have one of the musicians in the hall."

In spite of his efforts there lurked in his eyes the modest triumph of a conjurer who has unexpectedly succeeded in producing a rabbit from a hat.

Constantine's lips twitched.

"What do you propose to do with him, Manners?" he enquired mildly.

"I think, sir, it would be advisable for you to see him," said Manners with a touch of reproof in his voice. "He has informed me that he saw Mr. Anthony on Tuesday night in company with another gentleman. From his account this would be after Mr. Anthony left the Trastevere, sir."

If his object was to make Constantine sit up, he quite literally succeeded.

"Who is this man?" he demanded.

"I understand that his instrument is the piccolo," Manners informed him meticulously. "He was at one time a member of the Parthenon orchestra and is now out of work. Following your directions, I have been making a habit of going to a bar frequented by some of the members of the orchestra, and I've already succeeded in exchanging a few remarks on the weather and so forth with some of them. This man joined them to-night, and, in the course of conversation, mentioned the fact that he had some information and was troubled in his mind as to whether he ought to pass it on to the police. When I overheard what he had to say it struck me as advisable that he should tell his story direct to you, sir, so I took the liberty of mentioning your name. One of the musicians recognized it. I understand that he had some conversation with you on the night Mr. Anthony's body was found, and he supported me in my suggestion that this man, Andrews by name, should come back with me and give his account to you in person. Would you wish me to show him in, sir?"

"Good heavens, yes! And, Manners, drinks."

"Very good, sir."

The piccolo player turned out to be a shabby, red-headed little man with a white, careworn face and a manner whose perkiness seemed due more to pluck than good fortune. Sitting on the edge of his chair, a mild whisky-and-soda in his hand, he told his story.

He had known Anthony when he played in the Parthenon orchestra, and was quite positive that he had seen him walking with another man close to Knightsbridge soon after ten-thirty on the Tuesday night. Becoming more at his ease, he admitted that, times being hard, he had followed the two men in the hope that Anthony might part from his companion and give him a chance of asking him for help. But it soon became obvious that he was not going to get the opportunity he wanted, and he had dropped back and had not even watched the men out of sight. All he could say was that they had been going in the direction of Kensington Gore.

"There's no doubt about it being Mr. Anthony," he declared. "I'd know him anywhere."

"Did his manner strike you as unusual in any way?" asked Constantine.

Andrews shook his head.

"He was just as usual," he said. "He wasn't talking much, so far as I can remember. Just a word here and there. The other man was doing most of the talking."

"You'd never seen this man before, I suppose?"

"Never. I should know him again, though. Owing to me wanting a word with Mr. Anthony I had a good look at him."

"What was he like?"

"About the same height and build as Mr. Anthony, but a good bit younger. Pale face, clean-shaven. Might have been a foreigner."

"I never saw Mr. Anthony when he was alive," said Constantine, "but I take it that medium height and slight in build would describe your man?"

"That's right. It was only when I was discussing the murder with some of the chaps from the Parthenon that I realized that I might have been the last person to see Mr. Anthony alive."

"As a matter of fact, he was seen later by two other people, but he was alone then. The police are anxious to trace the man you saw, and I should advise you to go at once to New Scotland Yard with this story."

Andrews rose to his feet.

"Then I'll get along there now," he said with an energy that seemed a little forced. "My time's my own, and I may as well spend it that way as in hanging round the agencies."

He picked up his shabby hat and stood hesitating, evidently at a loss as to whether to shake hands or not. Constantine solved the difficulty by walking with him to the door.

"Work isn't easy to come by just now, I'm afraid?" he said kindly.

The little man achieved a rather sickly grin.

"That's right," he agreed. "Takes the heart out of you hearing the same answer over and over again. However, I'm not one of the married ones, so I can't complain. Got no one but myself to keep."

"You'll be out of pocket in fares, besides wasting time over this business," said Constantine. "As Mr. Anthony's no longer here, perhaps you'll let me act in his stead. I'm a friend of his daughter's, you know, and I'm sure I'm only doing what she would wish."

He slipped a little packet of notes into the man's hand. Andrews stared at him, a slow flush creeping over his pale skin.

"I wasn't thinking of that when I came here," he stammered.

"I know," Constantine assured him quickly. He placed a hand on his shoulder and thrust him towards the door. "Take it, man," he said. "I should do the same in your place."

Andrews hesitated, then pocketed the money.

"I won't say I don't need it," he admitted. "I hardly know how to thank you, sir."

"Then don't try," was Constantine's cheerful answer. "And let me know how you get on. If you can identify this man, you'll earn the gratitude of the Yard."

Arkwright rang him up late that afternoon.

"I'd like to see you," he said, "but things are getting piled up here. If I can come round about elevenish I will. Meanwhile I've got quite a good bag, though how much it's worth I'm not sure, but it may link up with a good deal that we know already. I've seen the report on that chap Andrews you sent on to us. Bad luck he didn't know the man."

"Come round any time," answered Constantine, "no matter how late you may be. There's just one thing you might tell me. Is Anthony's daughter still living?"

"She died the night he arrived in Brighton. It's an ugly story, I'm afraid, but it'll have to wait till we meet."

"By the way, how about that little commission I gave you?"

Arkwright laughed.

"It's done. Our man called on Howells on some excuse and got the fingerprints. I don't know which of the old dodges he used to get them, but he swears that Howells did not spot him.

He reports that he seemed rattled, though, when he discovered that he'd come from the Yard. I wonder if that chap's got something up his sleeve?"

"I doubt it," answered Constantine softly, adding the word "now," for the benefit of the receiver.

"Anyway, I'll bring the prints to-night if I can make it," Concluded Arkwright.

He did make it, though it was close on midnight before he arrived at Constantine's flat in Westminster and sank gratefully into a chair by the fire.

Constantine waited until Manners had brought in drinks and a generous supply of sandwiches, and then, placing a box of Halva at Arkwright's elbow, settled down to enjoy himself.

"You didn't happen to see Mrs. Bianchi's death certificate, I suppose?" he asked blandly.

Arkwright grinned.

"I left that to you," he retorted, "seeing that you were spending the day at Somerset House! As a matter of fact, Anthony made all the arrangements for the funeral, and my informants, the ward sister and one of the nurses, had nothing to do with that side of the affair. I got quite a lot out of them, though. The whole situation seems to have appealed to their sense of romance and they remembered more than I'd hoped for. Their description of her death would have set your imagination working again!"

Constantine looked up quickly.

"Why, what did she die of?"

"Drugs," said Arkwright slowly. "She'd been at it for years. It's curious, after our conversation anent the Trastevere."

Constantine's eyebrows contracted.

"Did anything come out that might link her with the Trastevere?" he asked.

"Nothing. She told the ward sister that she'd only been in England a month and hadn't lived in London for years. She'd come from France, apparently."

"Was she able to speak to her father before she died?"

"Yes. And that may be significant. They had a long conversation, according to the nurse, who says she was very weak, naturally, but quite clear-headed. If her heart hadn't given out that night she might have pulled through. Anthony seems to have been very much moved and furiously indignant over the state in which he found her. She told the nurse that she had learned the habit from her husband, and that he had deserted her and left her practically without funds several years before. No doubt she said the same to her father, which would account for his anger. Why did you ask if I'd seen the certificate?"

"Because, though she no doubt found it convenient to allude to Bianchi as her husband, she wasn't married to him. Her real name was Howells."

Arkwright's glass stopped half way to his mouth. He replaced it on the tray in silence.

"The devil it was!" he ejaculated softly. "Not our friend?"

Constantine nodded.

"The same. That's what he had up his sleeve."

"Then why on earth did he hold up on us? He'd no object in keeping it dark."

"As a friend of Betty Anthony's he had every object. I may as well tell you I'm holding a brief for Howells. He's a very decent fellow."

He gave Arkwright a brief account of his interview with the man following his visit to Somerset House.

"Betty's mother was old Anthony's only child," he concluded, "and my mind is naturally exercised as to how we can keep the fact from her. Marlowe will have to know, of course."

"Anthony was going to tell him?"

"Exactly. Hence his letter to him."

"Unless all this has a direct bearing on the murder, you can trust us not to give the show away," Arkwright said thoughtfully. "According to what I've been able to learn to-day, Anthony stayed for the funeral and then went straight up to London. He seems to have been in a pretty savage mood."

"And may have tried to get on the track of Bianchi. It's not impossible. Bianchi may even have been the man Andrews saw that night."

Arkwright shrugged his shoulders.

"It's as good a hypothesis as any," he said. "If we could find any sort of motive we might get a move on."

"The motive might lie in something his daughter told him. She seems to have spoken fairly frankly to this nurse. Did she suggest that Bianchi was engaged in any kind of drug traffic?"

"Apparently not. The nurse jumped to the conclusion that he was an addict himself and had passed it on to his wife."

"It's likely," agreed Constantine, "and quite sound as regards the psychology of the drug-taker. My point was that she may have told Anthony something that would give him some hold over this man, and, in his anger, he may have threatened him. The manner of Anthony's death rather bears this out."

"And according to your account, Howell's description of Bianchi would hold good for the fellow Andrews saw. Anthony may have got on his track."

"At the Trastevere?"

Arkwright turned and faced him.

"Look here," he said. "Are you hinting at Civita?"

Constantine was lying back in his chair, his eyes on the dancing flames.

"It seems difficult to believe," he said slowly. "Personally, I like Civita, and I believe he had a sincere regard for Anthony. In his own line he's a great man. But he's an unknown quantity."

"If we're going on the line that he's Bianchi, that's a point that Howells can settle in a moment. If he's not Bianchi, I ask you, Why?"

Constantine shrugged his shoulders.

"I don't know," he admitted, "but I should suggest letting Howells have a look at him. Have you got those fingerprints, by the way?"

Arkwright took an envelope out of his pocket and passed it to him.

"Why Howells' prints?" he asked, drawing the box of Halva towards him and burrowing blissfully into it. He had an inordinate love of the sticky Turkish sweetmeat. "I thought you'd given him a clean sheet."

"So I have," admitted Constantine. "I want these for future reference. There's a point I think you may have overlooked."

"What's that?" demanded Arkwright sharply.

"That's a card I'm not putting on the table just at present," said Constantine with an exasperating twinkle in his eyes. "To go back to Civita. Have you got any data as to his movements on Tuesday night?"

"Plenty. We passed the rule over him as a matter of course. We'd only his word for it that he hadn't seen Anthony. Well, there's nothing doing. Anthony was seen alive and, apparently, in the best of health at six a.m. on the Wednesday, and at six-fifteen Civita rang up the police from his flat to say that his car had been stolen. We even went so far as to verify that call. It was from his flat all right. It's humanly impossible for him to have got from there to Waterloo Road and back in the time."

"The car really was stolen, I suppose?"

Arkwright nodded.

"There's nothing fishy there. Civita was undoubtedly at the Trastevere till about one forty-five on Wednesday morning. He then went home in his car. His story is that he went upstairs to his flat to fetch the key of the lock-up garage in which he keeps the car, and came down five minutes later to find the car gone. This is borne out by the fact that the car was found later on Wednesday morning in Kensington. He then went to bed and rang up the police when he got up at six-fifteen to go Mass. He did go to Mass, by the way. We've ascertained that."

"You're sure it was Civita himself who rang up?"

"No. But he took his milk in and was seen by the milk-boy at six-twenty, so you see we've covered him pretty carefully. His charwoman saw him when he got back from Mass, and he was at the Trastevere literally all day, till late in the evening. I'm afraid you'll have to let him out."

"Well, I'm not sorry," said Constantine with a smile. "'Frankly, I should regret to see Civita languishing behind bars. He's too picturesque a figure in my life to be spared easily. Has it occurred to you that the descriptions of Bianchi and the man Anthony was seen with apply also to the bogus piano-tuner who ransacked the Anthonys' room's?"

"What did the old woman say? Shortish, with a little dark moustache, wasn't it? Andrews's man was clean-shaven, but that's not significant. It might be the same man," agreed Arkwright. "I'd give something to know what was in that diary of Anthony's. It's the most infernal bad luck that Miss Anthony did not think of reading the part relating to his journey to Brighton when she looked at it."

"Whatever it was, it was worth stealing, and it could only have described his last interview with his daughter. The clue to this little problem is Bianchi and again Bianchi!"

"Where is Bianchi, who is he?'" misquoted Arkwright. "I'm afraid I shall have to ask you and Manners to produce him!"

Constantine chuckled.

"We may yet," he said reassuringly. "We've only just started on the job, you know."

Arkwright stretched his long legs out to their full extent and sat staring at the tips of his boots.

"Does Howells know about his wife's death?" he asked suddenly.

"I wrote a line to him by to-night's post," answered Constantine. "It seemed only decent. I'm afraid he'll share her father's feelings when he hears the details. It's a tragic business."

Arkwright nodded.

"Bianchi must be a nasty piece of work, according to what she told the nurse," he said. "I'd like to get my hands on him."

"Well, you haven't done badly, considering you were only called in on Thursday night."

"Might be worse," conceded Arkwright. "To-day's Monday, and we've already whittled down our time schedule to the hours between six a.m. and eight p.m. on Wednesday. We've solved the question of Anthony's first disappearance and raked up a pretty little scandal that, from Miss Anthony's point of view, might very well have been left to rot in its grave. In fact, we've done everything but what we're paid for, which is to catch the chap who murdered Anthony. And, incidentally, we've got you to thank for a good part of what's been done."

He was tired, mentally and physically, and in no mood to see the bright side of things. He dragged himself wearily to his feet.

"I'm for bed," he said. "When you've done playing with those fingerprints, sir, you might let me know the result."

He cocked his head on one side, listening.

"That's your front door bell," he exclaimed. "Do people generally call on you in the small hours?"

Constantine rose to his feet.

"I'd better see to it," he said. "I told Manners to go to bed."

But Arkwright was already at the door.

"I'll go, sir," he called over his shoulder. "You never know, this may be a policeman's job."

He was gone so long that Constantine followed him, to find him in low-voiced conversation with a man in the doorway. He turned at the sound of Constantine's footsteps.

"It's for me," he said. "I told them where to find me in case anything cropped up. Something has, with a vengeance!"

"Not Bianchi?"

"Lord knows! Our people were called up just after I left the yard by the local police. Case of suicide. Chap had thrown himself out of a third-floor window. They've just emptied his pockets preparatory to moving him to the mortuary and found a snuff-box that answers to the description of Anthony's. Knowing I was interested, they took the opportunity of cheating me out my night's rest."

Constantine looked sceptical.

"There's more than one tula-work box in London. It's a pity they didn't leave you in peace."

Arkwright gave him a queer glance.

"I'd be inclined to agree with you," he said, "if it wasn't for one thing. Where do you suppose this fellow jumped from?"

"Not one of the windows at the Trastevere?" demanded Constantine, his mind reverting to the Duchess's insinuations.

"Nearer home even than that," answered Arkwright. "Civita's flat."

CHAPTER XI

THE TWO MEN started at each other.

"Is this another link to our chain?" murmured Constantine softly. "Or just a side issue?"

"Anyway, it's good-bye to any sleep for me for another hour or two," was Arkwright's grim rejoinder.

Constantine silently shrugged himself into a heavy overcoat, seized his hat, scribbled a few words on a pad lying on the hall table, and followed Arkwright on to the landing.

"Manners is in bed," he remarked, a mischievous twinkle in his eye. "If he wakes up he will find that."

Closing the front door gently behind him, he followed Arkwright downstairs to the police car.

A plain-clothes detective met them at the entrance to the block of flats which housed Civita.

"We've moved the body into an empty flat on the ground floor, sir," he informed Arkwright.

"Doctor there?" demanded Arkwright.

"Just leaving, sir."

The man led the way through an open door on the right of the main entrance, down a narrow passage and into a room, on the floor of which was the body of the unfortunate man. He was lying on his back, and an attempt had been made to straighten the limbs into a semblance of normality, but, though the face was peaceful enough and unmarked except for a slight smear of blood on the temple, the fantastic angles of the twisted arms and legs lent a strangely boneless aspect to the body, and Constantine, at his first horrified glance, was reminded of a marionette that had fallen from its wire on to the stage.

He bent over the man and tried to reconstruct his appearance when alive. Judging from the dense blackness of the hair, his skin had been probably only a shade less sallow than it was at present. Not a pleasant face at the best of times, with its narrow forehead, thin, hooked nose, and overfull, fleshy lips.

Macbane was speaking.

"Went out head first, and must have turned over as he fell. Neck, both legs, and one arm broken, and Lord knows what injuries there may be internally. Probably the pelvis broken. Must have died at once. Pretty complete job, poor devil."

Arkwright turned to the station sergeant who had just joined them.

"Anybody see it happen?" he asked.

"Mr. Carroll, friend of the owner of the flat. He was just entering the room at the time and saw the deceased pitch out of the window. Says he ran forward, but was too late to do anything. We've detained him upstairs."

"Civita up there?"

"Yes, sir. He was in the flat at the time, in another room. According to his account, the deceased had been drinking heavily all day. He's of the opinion that he lost his balance and fell."

"What about this box?"

The sergeant handed him a silver snuff-box, inlaid with strips of darker metal. Arkwright opened it and discovered that it was half full of snuff.

"May as well have this analysed," he said with a glance at Constantine, "as soon as Miss Anthony's seen it."

"It was in the deceased's trouser pocket," the sergeant informed him. "According to Mr. Civita, he was not a snuff-taker, and he has never seen the box in his possession."

"What's his name?"

"Nicholas Merger. His permanent address is in Brussels, and he was spending a couple of nights with Mr. Civita before returning there. Has no relatives in England, apparently."

Arkwright was watching Constantine, who was stooping over the corpse examining the front of the coat.

"Seen anything, sir?" he asked.

Constantine detached a couple of silky black threads from the second button of the coat, ran his eye over them and handed them to Arkwright.

"Extraneous matter," he said, "and probably of no importance. Silk where one would naturally expect to find thread. From the little bunch of fluff at the end I should say that it was velvet. The button must have caught on it."

Arkwright tucked it away in an envelope and thrust it into his pocket.

"Exhibit number one," he remarked with a smile, "and, as you say, probably of no importance. Still, we'll keep it. What about a little chat with Mr. Civita?"

They followed the sergeant to the lift, and were taken up to the fourth floor by the night porter.

"Are you usually on duty after twelve?" asked Arkwright.

"No, sir. I go off at eleven-thirty. After that the tenants have to let themselves in with their latch-keys and use the stairs. I was up when this happened, though. Got the fright of my life when the wife yelled out for me. Thought she was bein' murdered, I did."

"The body landed in the well behind the house, just outside her bedroom window," explained the sergeant. "Must have given her a bit of a shake-up."

"I'll wager she won't sleep to-night," agreed the lift-man morosely. "And she'll see to it that I don't."

Civita himself met them on the threshold of the flat. His eyebrows rose at the sight of Constantine, who hastened to explain himself.

"Inspector Arkwright was with me when the message came," he said. "I hope this is not an instruction."

"But of course not," Civita assured him. "You would like to see the room where the tragedy occurred, Inspector?"

They followed him into a fair-sized room, furnished as a bedroom and looking out on to the back of the house.

"This was originally intended for the dining-room." he explained, "but it was inconvenient for the kitchen, and I use it as a spare bedroom. Poor Meger was sleeping here while he was with me."

The lower half of the window was pushed up to its full height, and Arkwright leaned out of it and looked down into the dark abyss below.

"I understand that you were not in the room when the accident occurred, Mr. Civita?" he said.

Civita shook his head.

"I was in my sitting-room upstairs," he answered.

"Upstairs?"

"The top floor here consists of two-story flats," he explained. "As I have so few meals at home I did away with the big kitchen on this floor and remodelled the flat accordingly. The bedrooms are now on this floor and the living-rooms upstairs."

Arkwright nodded.

"Your statement has already been taken, I believe," he said, "but I should be obliged if you would tell me, from your own point of view, what happened."

Civita passed his hand over his forehead. His face was as inscrutable as ever, but the dark circles round his heavy-lidded eyes, and the unwonted lines on his smooth forehead, indicated that he had been more shocked than he cared to admit.

"I will try to be as exact as possible," he said wearily. "I had just made some coffee in my sitting-room, and I asked a friend who was with me, Mr. Carroll, to take a cup to Mr. Meger, who was in his bedroom here. He left my room upstairs with the coffee and I heard him go downstairs. Very shortly afterwards I heard a sound, as of something falling, followed by a cry. It seemed to come from outside, and I got up to go to the window, but before I could reach it Mr. Carroll called to me from the bottom of the stairs. I cannot remember his exact words, but he asked me to come at once as something had happened. When I got to the top of the stairs he said: 'He's gone out of the window. I couldn't stop him!' We ran downstairs to the basement and out into the yard. The porter had already got there. There was nothing to be done. Poor Merger was dead."

"What time was this?"

"Carroll was to call for me at ten-thirty, and I think he was a few minutes late. I made the coffee after he arrived and he went down at once with it, as soon as it was made. It must have been about a quarter or ten minutes to eleven."

"Had Mr. Meger ever threatened to do any such thing?"

Civita hesitated.

"No," he said at last; "and I am convinced that the thought of suicide was never in his mind. But he had been drinking heavily for a week and was hardly responsible for his actions. Myself, I am positive that he lost his balance and fell. Mr. Carroll will tell you that he was learning out of the window when he entered the room. His impression is that he fell. He could not have jumped, from the position he was in."

Arkwright frowned.

"The case was reported to me as suicide," he said. "Have you any idea why?"

"The sergeant, who came in answer to my telephone call, took that view at first. This window looks on to the air-shaft, not on to the street, and he could see no reason why Meger should have been looking out of it. I think he has now come round to my opinion that he felt unwell and went to the window for air."

"Did he open it himself?"

Civita shrugged his shoulders.

"It was shut when I looked into my room on my return from the Trastevere at about nine o' clock," he said.

"Was he drunk then?"

"I am afraid he was. And not in a pleasant mood. I left him, hoping he would sleep it off, and as he did not join me upstairs I thought that was what was probably happening. Frankly, I did not want him to come to the Trastevere with me in that condition."

"And you sent down the coffee, hoping it would pull him round, I suppose?"

Civita nodded.

"That was my idea. He was a bad subject, I am afraid, and had reached a point at which he could not pull himself together. To-morrow he would have gone back to Belgium, and I am afraid I should not have been sorry," he finished with a wry smile.

"I'd like to ask you a few questions about him later, when I've seen this Mr. Carroll," said Arkwright. "Where is he?"

"In my room upstairs. He went to pieces completely after it happened, and he is in a bad way still, but he will tell you more than I can."

Carroll turned out to be a tall, very slim young man, with what Arkwright was apt to stigmatize brutally as a "film face". Under normal circumstances one felt he would have lounged and drawled to perfection, but at the present moment he was little more than a writhing mass of nerves. His affectations, if he had any, had fallen from him and left him a second-rate, ineffectual boy of about twenty, badly in need of the glass of brandy that he was trying to keep steady in his shaking hands.

At Arkwright's first question he shrank, almost whimpering, into the corner of the sofa on which he was lying.

"Don't ask me to go over it again!" he moaned. "I can't! I can see him now, falling!"

But Arkwright, though gentle, was inexorable, and, bit by bit, got the story out of him. It tallied with Civita's, and by the time it was finished both he and Constantine were inclined to endorse his opinion that it was a case rather of accident than suicide. One feature in the halting narrative seemed to point specially towards this explanation. Carroll had found the room in darkness when he opened the door and had just switched on the light when the accident happened.

"Looks as if he had been lying on the bed in the dark," said Arkwright, "and, as Mr. Civita suggests, had felt ill and gone to the window. The crumpled condition of the bed bears out the assumption that he had been lying on it."

"He was leaning right out of the window when I saw him," said Carroll, a shudder running through his whole body. "It was horrible!"

He buried his face in his hands.

"What was your own impression, Mr. Carroll?" pursued Arkwright insistently. "Did he appear to assist himself in any way or did he just lose his balance."

Carroll stared at him with haggard eyes.

"I hardly saw him. When I first put the light on I looked for him on the bed. It seemed the natural place. It was a minute before I saw him. Then it seemed as if his feet slipped and he was gone in a second."

"That's probably what happened. The best thing you can do is to go to bed, Mr. Carroll. If you'll leave your address, there's nothing to prevent your getting off now. After a good night's sleep you'll forget this."

He left his victim murmuring "Sleep!" shudderingly to himself.

Outside in the passage the two men's eyes met.

"He'll sleep all right," said Arkwright significantly.

Constantine nodded.

"Yes, poor boy. We may be doing him an injustice, but it looks like a case of dope to me. Curious how we run up against it in this affair!"

"I wish I'd an excuse to let Macbane run his hands over him. Now for another word with Mr. Civita."

Civita was chatting urbanely with the sergeant the hall.

"Just a few questions about this Mr. Meger," said Arkwright cheerfully, "and then we'll leave you in peace. Do I take it that he's an old friend of yours?"

Civita shook his head vigorously.

"He was an employee of mine in Cannes," he answered. "For some years I had seen nothing of him, then, when I was in Brussels on some business four or five months ago, he called on me and asked me if I could not give him work. It was enough to look at him to know why he had fallen on bad times, but he had been first-rate at his job when I employed him before, and there was, as a matter of fact, a way in which I could use him, so I gave him the chance."

"What was his job?" asked Arkwright quickly.

"It is difficult to specify. An agent, I suppose one would call him. In Cannes he used to attend the big sales of wine, for instance, and buy for me. He had a real knowledge of vintages. One of the reasons I was in Brussels was to attend the Chavier sale. Doctor Constantine here will remember it," he finished with a smile.

"I do," agreed Constantine. "In fact, I was fortunate enough to get some of the pickings myself! Chavier was a gouty old gentleman of fabulous age, whose one regret, when he did at last die, must have been that he could not take his cellar with him. The first act of his heirs was to dispose of it, and I wonder he didn't turn in his grave!"

"As you may imagine," went on Civita, "I was only too glad to make use of Meger. I was in that way able to come home and leave the matter in his hands. And I must confess he carried it through admirably. After that I lost sight of him again until he came to the Trastevere the night before last."

Civita paused.

"His story to me," he continued slowly, "was that he had come to London a week ago, hoping to get commissions from the restaurant proprietors here, and that he had purposely kept away from me as he did not wish to take advantage of my kindness. I should like to believe that it was true, but my own impression is that he began to drink again as soon as he arrived and had been incapable of taking any steps until his money ran out and he could no longer afford to drink. He was penniless when he came to me. Could not even settle the bill for his lodging. As it turned out, I found I could again use him. There were certain firms in Belgium I wished to keep in touch with, and we arranged that he was to return there to-morrow, and in the meanwhile, I promised to try to get him other commissions. I had an idea that the man might pull himself together if he had work, and, with that in view, I told him that he could come here for his last two nights in London. As it turned out, it was a disaster from the beginning."

"You advanced him money, I suppose?"

Civita threw out his hands in an expressive gesture.

"It was a stupidity! But the man was penniless, and I believed that for two days he would go straight. He began to drink again this morning while I was away at the Trastevere, and by this evening he was almost helpless and in no mood to listen to anything I could say."

"Do you know anything of his family?"

"Nothing. From something he once said I do not believe he was a Belgian, but I have no idea what country he belonged to. His passport should be here with his things. No doubt that will tell you. Meanwhile, his permanent address was in Brussels. That I can give you."

"Once we've got that, it's up to the Belgian police to find his relations if he's got any. One other thing. This young fellow Carroll. What about him?"

Civita looked at him. There was a slight tightening of the corners of his thin, mobile lips, a hardly perceptible movement of his nostrils, otherwise his face remained impassive, but his opinion of Carroll was as clearly indicated as if he had spoken.

"Not a very nice piece of work?" queried Arkwright.

"You have seen him," said Civita. "Unfortunately, where there is dancing there are gigolos, and he is a very good gigolo. I cannot afford to let him go. I rang him up to ask him here tonight to talk business before going on to the restaurant. After this, he will be ill for a week."

"His account of the affair can be depended on, I suppose?"

"He has not the brains to invent. I do not want to seem heartless, but these types, they are hardly human. I do not like them."

Arkwright thrust his notebook into his pocket.

"That's about all, I think," he said. "Just one thing more, though. Have you ever seen this before?"

He held out Anthony's snuff-box. Civita bent over it.

"Never," he declared emphatically.

"Meger never used it?"

"Certainly never in my presence."

"Have you any reason to think that he was ever known by the name of Bianchi?"

"I have always known him as Meger—Nicholas Meger. And, for another thing, I am sure he was not Italian."

"This time it really is good night. We're moving the body at once. Meanwhile, I must ask you to lock this room and hand the sergeant the key. No inconvenience, I hope?"

"None at all. You will drink something before you go? I think I can even find some of M. Chavier's cognac, if you can wait."

But Arkwright was conscious of only one desire, to get home to bed, and even Constantine was beginning to realize that he was no longer young and that nearly half the night was over. They excused themselves, and left the sergeant to put a seal on the door and await the ambulance.

Arkwright was engaged in giving him his instructions when Constantine became aware of Civita at his elbow.

"That question about Bianchi," he said in a low voice, "came really from you? The inspector did not ask me, but if he had I could have told him that Merger, so far as I am aware, could have had no connection with the Bianchi I used to see in Paris."

He broke off as Arkwright turned and joined them.

He and Constantine descended the stairs in silence.

"Well, we've found Bianchi," said Arkwright with a sigh of sheer weariness, as they turned their backs on the block of flats.

Constantine glanced at him.

"Isn't that a little premature?" he asked. "I've just had Civita's word for it that Meger is not Bianchi. He knew Bianchi well by sight in Paris."

Arkwright came to an abrupt standstill.

"The devil!" he exclaimed. "Is Civita speaking the truth?"

Constantine shrugged his shoulders.

"I see no reason why he shouldn't," he said, "but I don't profess to understand the inner workings of Civita's mind! You're going on the evidence of the snuff-box?"

"And the description. Meger answers to it. And you must admit that the whole story hangs together. The man comes to London, doesn't go near Civita, whom he knows would help him, drinks himself blind in some unknown lodging, and then, when he hasn't got the funds to get out of the country, is driven to appealing to the only person he knows. It fits in all right."

"If the snuff-box is Anthony's snuff-box and Meger is Bianchi. It all hangs on those two facts."

Arkwright caught sight of a prowling taxi and hailed it.

"Civita or no Civita," he said as they got in, "I'm willing to bet not only that Howells identifies this man as Bianchi, but that Andrews recognizes him as the chap he saw with Anthony! Will that satisfy you?"

"It won't," retorted Constantine briskly. "Civita is in as good a position to recognize Bianchi as Howells, and has no better reason to mislead us! However I'll go so far as to call at the Yard to-morrow and give you an opportunity to flap your wings! I'm not by any means of Civita's opinion that Meger was not connected with Bianchi in some way."

He was as good as his word. Arkwright, who had been attending a conference, did not seem in the best of spirits.

"Well," demanded Constantine, settling himself comfortably in his chair, "do I bite the dust?"

Arkwright ran his fingers through his hair.

"You do and you don't," he said with a rather rueful smile. "This business is getting me down, as our old cook used to say. Andrews has identified Meger. He's certain that he's the man he saw with Anthony that night. I had a word with Miss Anthony myself, and she is quite positive about the snuff-box. Says she knows it is her grandfather's. I don't mind telling you that's good enough for me, though I admit that I shouldn't like to take it to a jury. It's purely circumstantial evidence, of course, but given the man's subsequent behaviour, you must admit it is fairly convincing."

"Meger was seen with Anthony, Anthony was found murdered and his snuff-box was found in Meger's pocket," recited Constantine blandly. "I suppose men have been hanged on less than that, but, as the solution of a problem, I find it a little childish. And why this official reticence on the subject of Bianchi?"

Arkwright managed to achieve a rather mirthless grin.

"This is where you begin to enjoy yourself," he said resignedly. "Howells has viewed the corpse. He states emphatically that it is not that of Bianchi. So our most cherished theory goes west."

CHAPTER XII

CONSTANTINE FOUND his case, abstracted a cigarette, and lit it.

"So Meger's just Meger," he said. "Plain Meger. Have you found out anything more about him? Even Megers have a history, I suppose?"

"This one has." Arkwright's voice was grim. "I'll tell you about that presently. Meanwhile, I've scored one more point which I should like to emphasize. Mrs. Berry, the landlady, has seen him."

"Has she identified him?"

"She says that, save for the fact that he's clean-shaven, he's the 'living spit' of the man who ransacked Anthony's room. We stuck a moustache on him and tried her again, and there's no doubt that she thinks it's the same man. She's not a very reliable witness, of course, owing to her natural vagueness. Went all of a dither at the sight of the body, and it was all we could do to get her to look at it. And she admits that she didn't pay much attention to the piano-tuner. All the same, I think she did recognize him. We went through his luggage, by the way. Nothing there. But, if he did take those pages out of the diary, he probably destroyed them."

"Why should he take them if he's not Bianchi?"

"We don't know what passed between Anthony and his daughter," Arkwright reminded him. "The conversation may not have related to Bianchi at all."

"That's true," admitted Constantine. "So far as we know, she may have lost touch with Bianchi some time ago. The fact remains that she was taking drugs and must have been getting them somewhere. If we take that as our starting point we shan't go far wrong."

Arkwright leaned forward, his elbows on the table.

"Exactly. And how about this for an item of interest?" he said. "We got on to the Brussels police this morning, and it appears that they've had their eye on Meger for some time as being concerned in the traffic of drugs, but so far they've failed to get anything on him. It seems that he did work as an agent when he could get a commission, but owing to his drinking habits most of his old customers had dropped him. That side of the business was genuine enough, but, of course, it gave him unlimited opportunities for the other thing. They searched his rooms to-day, and we heard from them again about an hour ago. They'd got what they were looking for."

"Drugs?"

"Cocaine. Twelve packets, each containing four hundred and sixteen grains. Just a nice size for smuggling. Also a useful list of addresses, unfortunately all on the other side of the Channel. Not much help to us, it's true, but remember, Anthony's daughter hadn't been long in England."

"Your theory being that she gave Meger away to her father and he tackled him, with fatal results to himself?"

"Well, that covers it, doesn't it?" retorted Arkwright. "Combined with his possession of the snuff-box. If Merger didn't kill Anthony, I'll eat my hat!"

"And, which seems incredible, probably digest it," said Constantine. "Does that mean that you are ringing down the curtain on the Anthony case?"

"I don't say that," admitted Arkwright reluctantly. "We've got some more spadework yet to do, but we can see ahead pretty clearly now. The Brussels people may stumble on something interesting in the course of rounding up his associates there. He wasn't in England for nothing, you may be sure, and what we're after are the agents over here. Once we get on to them we may get a line as to his movements during the past week."

"In that case you haven't completely lost interest in Binns?"

Arkwright eyed him suspiciously. There was an undercurrent he did not like in Constantine's voice.

"Binns? I've been inclined to wipe him out from the beginning. Our man reports that he's behaving quite normally. Why, specially, Binns?"

"It's gratifying, at any rate, to find that Manner isn't known to the police," said Constantine complacently. "There are times when I've felt that he almost too good to be true!"

Arkwright grinned uncertainly. He distrusted Constantine in this mood.

"So Manners is on that job! He hasn't stolen a march on us, has he?"

"At least you'll be gratified to hear that his verdict is the same as your own. He believes Binns had nothing to do with the murder. All the same, he's made one interesting discovery. Binns has got Anthony's key to the stage door."

Arkwright whistled softly under his breath.

"He has, has he! And he's kept it under his hat all this time! What's his explanation?"

"None, so far. He let drop the fact that he'd got it, and Manners thought it better not to press the matter then. Give him time and he'll get the rest of the story, I've no doubt."

"What was the man's object in keeping it dark?"

Constantine's eyes twinkled.

"I'm afraid he's got an unreasoning prejudice against the police," he said demurely.

Arkwright groaned.

"Another little spot of bother," he sighed. "And the probability is that the man's not involved at all. He wouldn't have told Manners even that if he were. Still, we shall have to follow it up."

"In fact, thank you for nothing," Constantine remarked plaintively. "Our services don't seem to be appreciated."

Arkwright laughed.

"Sorry, sir. But you don't honestly believe that a chap like Binns is capable of drugging Anthony, administering the injection and disposing of the body, do you? This is a carefully planned job, and the fellow who did it was actuated by something a good deal stronger than a fancied grievance. What *is* your opinion of Binns?"

"That he had nothing to do with it wittingly. But it doesn't follow that he hasn't been made use of. I confess I should like to know how he got that key. Shall Manners carry on or will you tackle Binns yourself?"

"I'd better see him. I won't give Manners away to him. We can't ignore the fact that the murderer probably used that key when he brought in Anthony's body. By the way, I turned the snuff-box over to the analyst. The snuff hadn't been tampered with, so that wasn't the way they got the old man."

"It's more likely he was given a drink somewhere and absorbed the chloral in that."

"We've practically established the fact that he drank nothing at the Trastevere. Certainly he gave no order to any of the waiters, and, in any case, if he was given the knock-out drops immediately before the injection, it must have been after he was seen at the coffee-stall. Philbegge vouches for the coffee-stall proprietor, says he has known him for years, and Philbegge knows what he's talking about. There was no one else at the stall at the time, otherwise it would be only reasonable to suppose that he was given the drug there."

"The fact remains that, if your theory about Meger is right, he met him at the Trastevere. Did Meger go there more than once, I wonder?"

"According to Civita's report to the sergeant, which you may like to see, by the way, he went there twice with him the day before he died. He doesn't believe he would have shown up there during the week he was in London, seeing that he didn't look him up, but he admits that he might have been there without his knowledge."

"If there's anything in what the Duchess says, he could hardly find a better market for his drugs than the Trastevere. That sort of thing may be going on without Civita's knowledge, which would account for its popularity with a certain section of the public."

Arkwright nodded.

"We're keeping a pretty close eye on the Trastevere," he said, "but so far we've no grounds for suspicion. I've got that Carroll boy under observation too. If he doesn't lead us somewhere I shall be surprised, and, as I said, we may get a hint from the Brussels police."

When Constantine left him Arkwright went straight to the Parthenon. He had a short interview with the manager in his office, and then Binns was sent for.

At the sight of Arkwright his head jerked nervously, then he stiffened and stood rigidly to attention.

"The inspector here's enquiring into a purse that was lost on Saturday night," said the manager. "Do you know anything about it?"

Binns shook him head.

"There's no purse been found to my knowledge, sir," he answered. "If one of the cleaners had picked it up she'd 'ave taken it to the office."

"Did you go the round as usual on Saturday?" demanded the manager.

Binns met his eye with a rather glassy stare.

"Yes, sir. There wasn't nothin', beyond the usual odd gloves and handkerchiefs and such-like. They're all in the office, except those that have been called for. There wasn't no purse. I'll stake my oath on that."

"The purse was dropped somewhere in the back row of stalls. That's right, isn't it, Inspector?"

Arkwright nodded.

"I flashed my torch under those seats. There wasn't no purse there," persisted Binns.

The manager turned to Arkwright.

"That good enough for you, Inspector?" he asked.

Arkwright learned back in his chair and fixed a genial eye on Binns.

"Mind letting us have a look at your pockets?" he said cheerfully. "I'm not accusing you, and, as you probably know, I can't force you to empty them, but it would be more satisfactory for you as well as for us if we can say you submitted to being searched."

Binns reddened.

"If you think I'm a thief . . ." he began hotly.

"I don't," said Arkwright, "but I understand you nearly got the sack some time ago for behaviour which, to put it mildly, didn't err on the side of honesty. You'll be doing a good turn to yourself if you take this sensibly now."

Binns hesitated. He had nothing to fear on the score of the purse, and he knew his record was against him.

"How do you know I 'aven't got rid of it?" he demanded, with a surly frown.

"All the worse for you if you have," was Arkwright's rejoinder. "And all the easier for us. The notes are marked."

"Well, I ain't got them, see?" flashed the man, unbuttoning his coat and turning out the contents of his trouser pockets.

Arkwright watched the pile of miscellaneous articles on the table grow as Binns emptied one pocket after another. He was drawing a bow at a venture, in the hope that man carried the key to the stage door on his person. With an observant wife at home, the chances were that he did, but, so far, only two enormous keys tied together with a dirty piece of tape had materialized, and he began to think that his ruse had failed.

Leaning forward, he picked a shabby leather purse from the heap and opened it.

"You'll find little enough in that," grunted Binns. "And what there is was earned honestly, which is more than some can say."

There was a wealth of innuendo in his voice. In his opinion the police subsisted entirely on the enormous bribes with which the undeserving rich bought their immunity.

Arkwright tipped the contents of the purse into his palm and added the little pile of silver to the heap on the table. Then he opened the inner compartment and took out a Yale key. For the space of a second his eye met that of the manager.

"This the lot?" he demanded.

The manager leaned forward, peering at the key.

"What's that?" he exclaimed, sharply. "Looks like the key of the stage door. Wait a second."

He thrust a hand into his pocket and took out a bunch of keys. Selecting one, he compared it with the key in Arkwright's hand. He swung round on Binns.

"Where did you get that?" he demanded.

Binns' eyes were wide and staring now, like those of a frightened child. Little beads of sweat stood out on his forehead. He stuttered:

"I—I picked it up."

Arkwright took up the interrogation.

"When?" he snapped.

"On Saturday night," confessed the miserable Binns.

"Where?"

"Back row of the three-and-sixpennies. It was on the floor under the seat."

"What time was this?"

"'Alf past eleven, just about. After the last 'ouse."

"Did you recognize it?"

Binns' overworked brain made an effort to choose, against time, between the relative merits of truth and duplicity, and failed. In desperation he blurted out the truth.

"Not at first I didn't. Only afterwards, when I come to look at it before turnin' it over to the office."

"Why didn't you turn it over?"

"I—I was afraid it'd get me into trouble," the man confessed huskily. "There'd been all that talk about that door and Mr. Anthony's key. As soon as I 'ad time to think of it I knew it must be 'is. There was only my word for it that I'd found it there."

"There's only your word for it now," said Arkwright dryly. "You've done yourself no good by this. Why did you think you were in danger of being disbelieved?"

For the first time Binns looked him straight in the face.

"Because of that bit o' trouble I 'ad," he said, speaking now with a certain rough dignity. "There's more than one 'ere 'eard me say what I thought of Mr. Anthony. Threatening, I suppose they'd call it, but I didn't mean nothin'. There's times when my tongue gets the better of me."

He passed his hand with a bewildered gesture across him forehead. Arkwright was conscious of an odd conviction that the man was speaking the truth.

"Sure this account's correct?" he demanded, indicating his notebook.

"On my oath it is," Binns assured him earnestly. "Someone dropped it in those seats on Saturday night. I ran my torch over them last thing on the Friday, and I'll swear there wasn't nothin' there then."

"That's likely enough," said Arkwright. "My men went over the building pretty thoroughly on Friday morning. I'll take charge of this. Meanwhile, keep it to yourself, and in future don't try those sort of games with the police. You can go now."

"He deserves the sack for this," said the manager, as the door closed behind him.

Arkwright shook his head.

"Give him another chance," he advised. "Once a fellow's got in a bit of a mess he thinks every man's hand is against him. He'd evidently got the wind up thoroughly over this key, and, after all, he'd some excuse from his point of view."

"You think he's speaking the truth?"

"I do. And we'll catch him out if he isn't. We've looked up his Army record and it's a good one. And he had a nasty gruelling in the War. My advice is, let him carry on. He's had his lesson."

On leaving the cinema he went down the side alley and tried the key in the lock of the stage door. It turned easily and the door swung open. Arkwright hesitated a moment and then passed quietly down the passage, and equally quietly opened the door of the room under the stage. As he did so, two men who had been sitting on the table, smoking, turned and stared at him. With a muttered excuse he withdrew and went out the way he had come, but by the time he had reached the end of the alley leading to the stage door, Binns, majestic in his frogged uniform, was waiting for him.

Arkwright stifled a smile as he saw the man's truculence subside abruptly at the sight of his face.

"Got a message through from the orchestra that there was someone 'angin' round the stage door," Binns explained grudgingly. "We got order to keep an eye on this 'ere alley."

"Quite right too," agreed Arkwright cheerfully. "I was only having a look round. Has that order always been in force, or is it only since the murder?"

"Oh no, we've always been on the quee-vee like, on account of the boys. The management don't like *anyone* 'angin' round 'ere."

His voice was venomous, but Arkwright, ignoring the implication, wished him a cheerful "Good evening" and strode off, a broad grin on his face. Walking, though he did not know it, in the footsteps of Constantine, he had established the fact that it would be practically impossible for anyone to have introduced the corpse into the Parthenon during any of the performances.

In the meantime, the attendant on duty in the Insect Department of the Natural History Museum was observing with interest, not unmixed with disapproval, the behaviour of an elderly gentleman who had hurried into the building about an hour before, cast an intelligent but unenthusiastic glance at the House Fly, recoiled before the realistic and greatly magnified reproduction of the *Anopheles Maculipennis* or Mosquito, and eventually come to rest opposite the *Pediculus Corporis* or Body Louse.

The gentleman's absorbed interest in this unmentionable insect had not at first struck the keeper as unusual, but when, after a patrol of about twenty minutes, he returned to find him still riveted in front of the glass case, his eyes fixed in a glassy stare on its revolting occupant, he had begun to observe him more closely. Though quietly, even sombrely, dressed, his clothes, from his well-chosen and obviously expensive tie to his gleaming, rather square-toed shoes, spoke of Bond Street and Savile Row, and were worn in a manner that suggested the services of a valet.

Now it was not unusual for certain eccentrically clothed individuals, both male and female, to linger somewhat shudderingly over the less pleasing contents of certain of the glass cases, and on one occasion he had even surprised a member of the public furtively extracting a small object from an envelope and comparing it with the exhibit; but this old gentleman was not of the type that rents cheap flats in "converted" houses, only to depart hurriedly, leaving a trail of Keatings behind, neither did he bear the remotest resemblance to those erudite specialists to whom the *Cimex Lectularius* is a beautiful and absorbing manifestation of Nature.

The attendant, mildly perturbed, took another turn, only to find when he came back that the gentleman was still a fixture. He had taken off his hat and revealed a formidable crop of thick white hair. His hands being occupied with a pencil and notebook, he had placed his headgear irreverently on the top of the case, and was occupied in alternately consulting the book and tabulating its contents on the back of an old envelope.

The attendant was just coming reluctantly to the conclusion that he belonged to the noble fraternity of scientists after all, when the object of his attention, with a low exclamation, seemingly of triumph, pocketed his pencil, snapped the rubber band round his book, seized his hat and hurried from the building.

If the attendant could have followed him in his rapid transit across the road to the telephone-box in South Kensington Station and seen the number he dialled, his mystification would have been complete.

It is doubtful whether Constantine was even aware of the character of the highly educational exhibit at which he had been staring for so long. He had gone from New Scotland Yard to call on a friend in Queen's Gate, and, finding him out, had been on his way to South Kensington Station when a sudden shower of rain drove him into the Museum.

Once inside, his mind had drifted back to the problem of Anthony's death and certain perplexities that had been troubling him in connection with it. In spite of Arkwright's assurance, he could not bring himself to believe that the case had solved itself so neatly. The utter meaninglessness of the whole affair bothered him, and there were certain discrepancies that had already cost him more than one sleepless hour and had actuated his strange request to Arkwright for the fingerprints of Anthony and Howells.

He brought out his notebook and studied the timetables it contained in a vain attempt to make them conform with the so far unjustifiable suspicion that had been gnawing persistently at his brain.

It was just at the moment when he had come reluctantly to the conclusion that it had no earthly foundation, that the possible solution of at least one of his difficulties came to him. Five minutes later he was telephoning to New Scotland Yard, and within ten minutes was in a taxi on his way to Westminster Embankment.

Arkwright was not at the Yard, but Constantine was well enough known and liked there to get what he wanted. Five minutes' conversation with the constable who had seen Anthony on the Wednesday morning was all he asked, and, as it turned out, he had timed his visit to perfection. The man had just come off his beat, and unless he had already gone home, could be sent for immediately.

Constantine's luck held, and he had hardly time to run through the copy of the constable's report before he appeared in person.

"I won't keep you a moment," said Constantine, "but if you could go through this report with me I should be grateful. How plainly could you really see this man?"

The constable hesitated.

"Not any too well," he admitted; "the bench on which he was lying was some way from the street lamp and it was a dark night, but he answered to the description all right. He gave his name and address too."

"I know," said Constantine. "I'm not questioning your report, but there are one or two details I wanted to verify. I see he was wearing a dark overcoat, broad-brimmed hat, black shoes and socks, with rubber heels to the shoes. In spite of the bad light, you can vouch for these?"

"Yes, sir. I'm certain the hat was black, but I'm not so sure about the overcoat. It might have been a very dark blue or even grey."

"And the socks and shoes?"

"The socks I didn't see so well. They might have been some very dark colour like the coat, but I can testify as to the shoes. He was lying on the bench when I came up to him, and the soles of the shoes were the first thing I saw. I'd gauged him by them before he spoke, seeing as the soles were almost new. I could tell he wasn't one of the usual lot."

"What sort of shoes?" persisted Constantine.

"Narrow and pointed, with thin soles and circular rubber heels attached."

"You're sure of this?"

"Couldn't be mistaken, sir. They were the one thing I did see really plain."

"Now, about his voice. It was that of an old man?"

"Yes, sir. There was no doubt about it. And he was a gentleman."

"I see he showed you some money. Did you notice his hands at all?"

The constable shook his head.

"I didn't take any special note of them. There wasn't anything unusual about them, so far as I can remember."

"There's no other little point you can think of, I suppose? Anything that has occurred to you since?"

"Nothing, sir. I included everything in the report at the time. If the light had been better it'd have been fuller, of course."

"Considering the circumstances it does you credit. I'm sorry to have kept you."

There was a chink, as coins changed hands.

Constantine's next request was for permission to use the telephone. He rang up Steynes House and found that luck was still with him. Betty Anthony was in and kept him waiting only a moment.

Constantine read her the constable's description of her grandfather.

"Is there anything in this that strikes you as unusual or curious?" he concluded. "Will you think carefully, please."

"Will you read the account of his clothes again?" she said, with an odd note of excitement in her voice.

He did so and waited.

"It *is* wrong!" she exclaimed breathlessly. "My grandfather's shoes were broad, with rather square toes. And he'd never worn rubber heels in his life. He hated them!"

CHAPTER XIII

THE PROPRIETOR of the coffee-stall in Guelph Street, just off Waterloo Road, had barely got his urn going and pulled up the flap over the counter when his first customer's head and shoulders materialized out of the damp gloom of the February night.

Casting him an appraising glance, as he turned off the tap of the urn and pushed a steaming cup of coffee across the counter, he perceived a spruce, elderly gentleman regarding him with an unusually bright pair of dark eyes.

"A nasty night," said his customer, with a singularly charming smile.

"That's right," agreed the proprietor. "Not but what it might be worse."

Mindful of another old gentleman who had involved him in a journey across the river to New Scotland Yard, he proceeded to take more careful stock of this one. That he should be a good deal better dressed than most of his customers did not disturb him; he was accustomed to all sorts of clients at this job, but he was vaguely relieved to see that this one looked uncommonly well able to take care of himself. The other, seemingly, had got himself into trouble on that Tuesday night.

Almost as though he had read his thoughts the old gentleman spoke again.

"I'm afraid you've been rather worried with questions about a friend of mine whom you served just over a week ago," he remarked apologetically. "A very distressing case."

The proprietor eyed him with added interest.

"Friend of yours, was 'e?" he said. "'E's caused me more than a bit of thought 'e 'as. Missin' from 'is 'ome, so they said at the Yard, but, putting two and two together, it's struck me it wasn't 'alf likely as 'e was the old gent in the cinema case. Glad to see you. I've bin wantin' to ask that question."

"Well, the police have their own way of doing things," answered the elderly gentleman, "and I don't suppose they want it broadcast, but, as you've guessed so much, I don't see any harm in telling you that you're right."

The proprietor propped himself comfortably on his elbows on the counter and settled down to a pleasant chat. Nothing stand-offish about this chap, anyway.

"I thought as much," he said in a husky undertone. "'Oo done 'im in? Do they know?"

The customer shook his head.

"Not yet, I'm afraid. He seemed all right, I suppose, when you saw him?"

"In the pink. There wasn't nothin' wrong with 'im then. Drunk 'is coffee, took a pinch of that there snuff of 'is, and off 'e went. 'E 'adn't come to no 'arm then."

The customer lifted the thick china cup and sipped his own coffee with every symptom of enjoyment. Manners, if he had been present, would have been shocked to the core, but Constantine, alas, was well out of the radius of his watchful solicitude. He pursued his interrogation with the most convincing mendacity.

"There's some talk of my poor friend having hurt his hand earlier in the evening," he said thoughtfully. "I suppose you didn't notice anything of the kind?"

"There wasn't nothin' wrong with 'is 'ands when 'e come 'ere," asserted the proprietor with conviction.

"You saw them plainly?"

"As plain as I see yours. I see 'is nails even. Noticed them too. You don't often see them that long, unless it's some of them foreigners."

Constantine smiled.

"Yes, he did wear them long. Funny you should have noticed it, but it is unusual, I suppose. He used to cut them in points."

"That's right," agreed the man. "Long, pointed *and* polished. There's no accountin' for taste."

"You didn't happen to notice his left hand, I suppose?" pursued his interlocutor. "That's the one they think was injured."

"That I did, seein' as 'e 'eld that there snuff-box right under my nose. There wasn't nothing wrong with it."

"Nothing wrong with the nails?"

"Not a thing. It was that 'and I noticed them on."

Constantine drew a long breath. The possibility that had seemed so fantastic that afternoon was rapidly becoming solid fact.

His first impulse when he got home was to telephone to the Yard, but Arkwright forestalled him by ringing up before he had had time to get rid of his hat and coat.

"Sorry to disturb you at such an unearthly hour." he said, "but I thought you'd like to hear the latest development. We've caught Carroll with the goods on him. He's badly frightened, but he won't say more than that he got the stuff at the Trastevere. We've been keeping an eye on the place since you dropped me that hint the other day, and there seems no doubt that the traffic's been going on there for some time. Whether Civita's involved or not is an open question, but we've managed to collect enough evidence to warrant a search. If we find anything I'm afraid your friend Civita will be for it!"

"If you can get him and hold him for a few hours I shall be delighted," answered Constantine equably. "I'll explain why when I see you to-morrow. You may expect me early."

"We've a conference at twelve, and I'm afraid I've got my hands full till then," said Arkwright, his voice sounding harassed.

"Better see me before the conference," insisted Constantine. "It will save you both time and trouble."

He heard Arkwright's familiar low whistle.

"As urgent as that, is it? I say, sir, what's up?"

"You'll know when we meet. How early shall I find you?"

Arkwright chuckled.

"If it's like that, we'll say nine o'clock," he said.

"Excellent. Meanwhile, will you have that card that was found in Anthony's pocket-book tested for fingerprints?"

"What the dickens?" exclaimed Arkwright. "All right, I won't waste time asking questions. The report shall be waiting for you."

When Constantine arrived next morning he found him waiting for him, the report in his hand, astonishment on his face.

"Good God, sir, how did you get on to this?" he exclaimed.

Constantine's eyes narrowed.

"Only one set of prints, eh?"

"A thumb and forefinger. Very clear and both unknown. That's all! It's a good surface too. I rang up Howells just now. He declares that neither he nor Anthony were wearing gloves when they handled the card. Do you realize what this means?"

"We shall know that better when we've traced the prints that are on it, but I fancy it's a foregone conclusion."

Arkwright nodded.

"Only one person could have had any object in substituting this card for the original one," he declared, "and that's the person who identified it as the one he had written. Civita must have known all along that this is not the one he sent to Anthony."

Constantine confronted him, his hands folder on the handle of his stick, his dark eyes gleaming.

"If I remember rightly," he said, "the original card was enclosed in an envelope addressed to Anthony, and given by Civita to a waiter, who handed it to a page. The page gave it to Anthony. Is that right?"

"Yes. But I don't see what you're driving at."

"Only this. Unless the page told him the message came from Civita, Anthony would have been unaware of the fact. It's possible, even, that the page didn't know who had sent it. We know, now, that this card is not the one that Anthony received. The question is, why was substituted?"

"Because the original card was too incriminating for our eyes. I think we may take it that it bore the message that sent Anthony to his death."

"And Civita," pursued Constantine, "deliberately concealed the substitution. There's very little doubt now in my mind that he wrote the original card and was certainly responsible for the production of this one. My own opinion is that Anthony did not connect the first message with Civita at all."

Arkwright stared at him, a puzzled frown on his face.

"I don't quite see what you're driving at," he said. "Granted that the message was making an appointment for some place outside the Trastevere, there seems no reason why Civita should conceal his identity. After all, Anthony had come to the Trastevere to see him."

"My impression is that, while Anthony would have been quite ready to meet Civita at the restaurant, he would have flatly refused to go to his private address. If Civita wished to get him there he would have to employ subterfuge."

"You're implying now that Civita's story of his loan to Anthony was a fabrication?"

"Why not? If you remember, Miss Anthony scouted the suggestion from the beginning. I'm ready to believe that Anthony went to the Trastevere to see Civita, probably at Civita's invitation, but it was not for business reasons. Go back to your own theory as to his reactions after his last interview with his daughter."

"We agreed that he'd naturally have his knife into Bianchi."

He paused, then:

"Bianchi," he repeated softly. "Good lord! Bianchi and Civita!"

"Why not? Howells, the only person who could identify Bianchi, has never, so far as we know, seen Civita. It was your own suggestion that Anthony, in his anger, may have sought out Bianchi and threatened him with disclosure. And, after his interview with his daughter, Anthony knew too much."

Arkwright did not answer immediately. His hands deep in his pockets, his eyes on the ground, he took a couple of turns through the room. Then he faced Constantine.

"It's no good," he said flatly. "It doesn't hold water. We've gone into Civita's movements on the night in question pretty thoroughly, and he couldn't possibly have been with Anthony at the time he was murdered. His time's accounted for from six in the morning till eight o'clock that night, and we've agreed that that's the limit we can give to the time of the crime."

"That was my stumbling-block till yesterday afternoon," answered Constantine. "Then I grasped where we'd gone astray. In our preoccupation with his murderer we'd forgotten Anthony. Do you realize why Anthony's snuff-box was found on Meger's body?"

In spite of himself Arkwright smiled. For once Constantine's imagination had run away with him.

"According to your theory, it was no doubt planted there by Civita. It won't do, sir. I'm sorry."

"You'll be more sorry by the time I've finished," retorted Constantine with a flash of impatience. "Meger was in possession of the box because it was an important factor in his impersonation of Anthony."

He leaned comfortably back in his chair to enjoy the effect of his last words.

He was rewarded. Arkwright did and said all the things he had hoped for, and more. He finished on a high note of incredulity.

"But, good heavens, sir, do you realize what you're saying? Anthony was seen by three witnesses, two of whom, at least, are perfectly reliable!"

Constantine straightened himself.

"Sit down," he said, "and pull yourself together. I know what you're thinking, and you're probably right. I'm getting old and possibly senile, but, in spite of that, the facts are on my side. I've only two points to put before you, but they're damning. The man your first witness saw on the Embankment was wearing Anthony's coat and Anthony's hat. As we know now he even had Anthony's snuff-box in his pocket, but he was not wearing Anthony's shoes, for the simple reason that they probably wouldn't fit him. I have his granddaughter's authority for saying that Anthony never wore pointed shoes or rubber heels in his life, and this man was wearing both."

Arkwright shot out of the chair into which he had reluctantly subsided.

"Is this true, sir?"

"Ask the constable who saw him and then look through Anthony's effects. Now for my other point. The proprietor of the coffee-stall who saw him later is ready to swear that he had unusually long, polished nails *on both hands*. And Anthony was a violinist! I'll challenge you to get together fifty violinists and find one among them whose nails haven't been cut almost to the quick on the left hand."

Arkwright was already mumbling to himself, thinking aloud.

"It's true that not one of them saw him in a decent light. Fantastic as it is, it could have been done. God, what a mess, though!" He stopped clawing at his hair and looked up. "This knocks our time-table all to blazes! He could have been killed any time after Andrews saw him. You're not going to kick the bottom out of his evidence too, sir?"

"No, he's the only one of the lot who really had a good look at him. I'll leave you Andrews, if that's any comfort to you. What are you going to do?"

"I shall know that better after the conference, but the obvious step is to get hold of Howells. If Civita's at the Trastevere today we can no doubt manage to let Howells have a sight of him. If not, we must get him down here on some excuse."

"He mustn't see Howells," said Constantine.

"Trust us for that. He mustn't be allowed to get the wind up in any way," agreed Arkwright. "We can't act yet, we've got nothing to go on, even if Howells does identify him. But you're most damnably convincing, sir. What they'll say at the conference, I don't know."

"He'd have some difficulty in explaining that card, even now, in the witness-box," pointed out Constantine; "but I quite agree, as regards the murder, you'll have to go warily. You'll be able to get Civita's finger-prints, I suppose?"

Arkwright nodded.

"That's easy enough. As a matter of fact, we've had a man in the Trastevere for the past few days. He got himself taken on as a temporary waiter. He'll be able to lay his hands on a glass or something out of Civita's office. He's been in touch with the officer who's watching Carroll, and between them they've unearthed some rather interesting facts. It appears that certain of the people who frequent the restaurant are in the habit of running up accounts with Civita. There's nothing unusual in that, but there is in their method of payment. Instead of settling with him in the usual way by cheque, they go to his office, men and women alike, and pay him there. They certainly do come away with receipted accounts—our man has managed to see one or two—but he's convinced that it's a blind. If we could get enough evidence to justify a raid, we might be able to hold Civita for twenty-four hours on suspicion while we search his flat. I'll put it to the Assistant Commissioner this morning at the conference, but I doubt if it will lead to anything. He's too wily a bird to leave any loose threads lying about. Beyond that, it seems to me we're stymied unless something fresh crops up."

Constantine agreed with him.

"Now that Meger's dead we're helpless," he said. "The snuff-box was found on him and he was probably responsible for the impersonation of Anthony, and neither of those two things can be brought home to Civita. We can't even prove that he saw Anthony that night. As regards the cards, I agree with you that we should only put him on his guard by questioning him about them at this juncture. But I'm morally certain that he, not Meger, was responsible for Anthony's death. That alibi of his has been altogether too good from the beginning."

Arkwright sat staring disconsolately at the floor.

"What set you on Civita's track in the beginning?" he asked suddenly.

"Betty Anthony's conviction that the story of the projected loan was a fabrication, to begin with. She knew her grandfather too well to be mistaken as to the strength of his prejudice against debt of any kind, and besides, she's no fool. I tried to persuade myself that her attitude was due to the shock of his death, but it bothered me. Then I was struck by the fact that Civita's alibi covered the times at which we believed, and, as we know now, were meant to believe, the murder had been committed, whereas he had practically no alibi for the two following nights. Mac-bane's first estimate as to the time of death must have been a shock to him. He hadn't, of course, taken into account the effect of the drug on the body and had omitted to cover that period. Mind you, I was only playing vaguely with the theory, but it was Betty Anthony's insistence that made me wonder whether that message of Civita's to Anthony hadn't been juggled with. It was really as a feeler that I got you to take those fingerprints. Then, as you know, I decided yesterday to test those reputed appearances of Anthony and stumbled on the truth."

"There's a faint chance," said Arkwright slowly, "that if Binns' story is true we may get hold of someone who saw either Meger or Civita at the Parthenon on Saturday night. One or other of them must have dropped that key."

"It's a chance in a hundred, but it's worth trying. Meanwhile, if you can get Civita out of the way for a few hours it'll be all to the good. I want to see his flat again."

"There'll be nothing, you may be sure. He'd know better than to take a chance there."

"All the same, I should like to take a look round. Has it struck you that, if our suspicions are correct, Meger timed his suicide singularly aptly, from Civita's point of view?"

Arkwright, who was lighting his pipe, snatched it from his mouth.

"You're surely not suggesting that he engineered that!" he exclaimed. "Carroll's account was pretty convincing, and he's too much of a rabbit to lie convincingly. I'll swear he saw the man throw himself out. What's your idea?"

"I haven't got one," admitted Constantine frankly. "And I'm inclined to agree with you about Carroll. All the same, Meger's sudden death bothers me, and I should like to be with you if you search the flat."

"There's no earthly reason why you shouldn't," agreed Arkwright. "But if you're going to produce any more bombshells, for heaven's sake let it be soon! I've had more surprises this morning than are good for me. I'll ring you up if we get a move on to-day."

He was as good as his word. Constantine, who had cancelled an engagement at his club on the chance of hearing from him, was sitting reading in a chair by the fire when Manners announced that Arkwright was on the telephone.

"It's all right. Very much all right!" came his voice. "We got him absolutely unawares. He didn't even know that we'd taken Carroll. And the stuff was there! Over a thousand grains of cocaine, according to the analyst, diluted and done up, all neat and tidy, in packets. And a bottle containing about seven ounces. They were in a cupboard behind that big desk of his, and we had a bit of a job finding it. He came in just as the fun was over, and he's been busy explaining himself ever since. He's had his solicitor down and he'll be out on bail to-morrow, so now's your chance if you want to take a look at that flat. I'll call for you on my way and be with you in twenty minutes. That right?"

"Very much all right. Congratulations! The conference was satisfactory, I gather?"

"They gave me a free hand, which was all I wanted. With reservations, of course!"

What those reservations were he explained to Constantine as the police car slid smoothly through the lamp-lit streets. Certain people were to be dealt with lightly, should any kind of list of Civita's clients materialize. Lady Malmsey in particular.

"I gather that she's a relation of the Duchess of Steynes," explained Arkwright innocently, and was surprised at Constantine's chuckle of sheer delight.

CHAPTER XIV

CIVITA'S FLAT was in darkness when the porter opened the door for them with his pass-key.

Arkwright led the way, switching the lights on as he went, and swung to the right into the bedroom from which the unfortunate Meger had gone to his death. It looked bare and ungarnished, the only trace of its late occupant being the closed suitcase containing his clothes which stood on a chair near the bed.

"Nothing of any interest here," said Arkwright. "We'd better go upstairs."

Constantine strolled over to the window and peered out, but it was too dark to see into the well below.

"Is this room overlooked from the outside?" he asked.

"The staircase windows opposite look on to it," answered Arkwright, "but, apart from that, this is the only portion of the building that has any living-rooms giving on to the air-shaft. As a matter of fact, we did try to find out if anyone opposite could substantiate Carroll's story, but all the tenants use the lifts, and there was no one on the staircase at the time."

"What room's above this?"

"Civita's sitting-room. Want to have a look at it?"

Constantine nodded, and together they went up the short staircase that led to the upper floor.

Civita's sitting-room was typical of the mind of the man who owned it. The furniture was not only costly, but comfortable, and, while in excellent taste, was faintly reminiscent of a writing-room in the best type of hotel. A french window, with the two smaller windows on either side of it, opened on to the air-shaft, and Constantine, unlatching it, stepped out on to a long, narrow balcony that ran along the whole width of the room.

Arkwright, meanwhile, was engaged in running through the contents of the drawers of the huge, ornate writing-table that stood in one corner of the room. He very soon found that it contained nothing but receipted bills, business papers, and a few private letters, mostly in Italian. There was nothing that could be connected in any way with the secret traffic at the Trastevere. He took out the drawers and ran his fingers over the dusty cavities that had held them, but could discover nothing. Then he turned his attention to the rest of the room, exploring every possible receptacle. Every now and then he glanced towards the window, to see the light of Constantine's electric torch flickering like a will-o'-the-wisp on the balcony outside.

At last he joined him, brushing the dust off his fingers as he did so.

"Nothing doing," he said, "though you might run through a couple of letters from Italy that I've got here. I'll have a squint at the other rooms, but I'm afraid we're wasting our time. If he kept an incriminating list of any sort it wasn't here or at the Trastevere. Any special attraction out here, or are you just trying to catch cold?"

Constantine stepped back into the room.

"Neither," he said cheerfully, "but there's something very suggestive about that balcony."

Arkwright stood leaning against the side of the window, his eyes raking the darkness. The velvety blackness of the air-shaft was broken at intervals by the subdued lights from the staircase windows opposite. To his left and right the narrow walls were blank and lost in gloom. Looking down, he could see a finger of light streaming from between the curtains of the bedroom below, and made a mental note to switch it off on his way out. Beyond that he found the balcony uninspiring, and said so.

Constantine did not answer, but there was a subdued elation in his eyes that made Arkwright suspicious.

Together they examined the bedroom and were mildly astonished at Civita's prodigality in the matter of clothes. His pyjamas could only have graced the figure of a middle-class Latin, and were in amusing contrast to his usual restrained sartorial sobriety. But beyond these revelations of character there was nothing of interest in the bedroom or anywhere else in the flat. Arkwright, grimy and, by now, thoroughly bored with the whole proceeding, decided to go home.

He looked round for Constantine, missed him, and eventually ran him to earth in a small room that Civita had evidently used as a lumber-room. Arkwright had already reluctantly gone through the two built-in cupboards that stood on each side of the fireplace and found them filled with old rugs, curtains, broken electric fittings and discarded pictures, the usual debris that accumulates in the best-ordered flats.

He found Constantine on his knees, examining two pairs of long black velvet curtains that had probably once been used to drape the windows in the sitting-room. They were badly crumpled and torn in places, and had evidently seen a good deal of wear. Beyond that there seemed no reason why they should have attracted his notice.

"Have you discovered any paper or string in the course of your wanderings?" enquired Constantine, rising stiffly to his feet.

"There's a drawerful in the hall," answered Arkwright. "But if you're thinking of taking anything away with you, you can't, you know. This isn't a jumble sale!"

"All the same, I'm going to have these curtains," Constantine assured him blandly. "Get me something to wrap them up in, there's a good fellow."

Arkwright stared at him aghast.

"I say, sir, you can't do that!" he exclaimed. "Civita will be out on bail to-morrow, and if he misses anything here, woe betide us. He'll have his solicitor on to us like a terrier on a rat. We can't plead that a pair of curtains is evidence of drug traffic!"

"All the same, I'm taking these," insisted Constantine calmly, "and it'll look a great deal worse if you oblige me to carry them down in the lift in my arms."

He was folding them as he spoke and piling them in a bulky heap on the carpetless floor.

"Honestly, sir, you can't do it," remonstrated Arkwright. "If he can prove that we've taken anything that isn't admissible as evidence, he can have the coat off my back. It's all very well for you, but the police can't afford to risk a scandal of that sort. The public's a bit touchy already on the subject."

Constantine picked up the curtains and clasped them to his bosom.

"You're quite at liberty to say that you left me alone for a few minutes and were not aware that I had taken anything until the complaint reached you," he said, his muffled voice coming from behind the mass of velvet. "And I'm quite prepared to languish in gaol if necessary, but I'm not going away without my curtains."

Constantine was not a large man and the curtains were voluminous, to put it mildly. Arkwright gave one look at him and subsided into helpless mirth.

"Go ahead, sir," he said when he recovered, "and, if necessary, I'll give my popular performance of the three monkeys. But I hope you realize what you're doing."

He took the bundle from Constantine, who relinquished it with a sigh of relief.

"I shall probably sneeze for the rest of the night," he said, "and Manners will jump to the conclusion that I've got a cold and make my life a burden to me. It seems incredible that they could have got so dusty in so short a time."

Arkwright, the huge bundle tucked comfortably under one arm, stared at him in astonishment.

"They've been there for years, by the look of them," he exclaimed.

"In spite of which I'll take my oath that they were adorning Civita's sitting-room windows not so many days ago," answered Constantine. "Ask his charwoman if I'm not right! Meanwhile, you'll have to trust me till this evening, but I assure you I know what I'm doing. And, just to annoy you, on the way out I'll show you another item of interest you've missed!"

He led the way into Civita's bedroom and pointed to a framed photograph that hung over the mantelpiece.

Arkwright examined it in silence. Then he turned to Constantine, amusement struggling with annoyance, and spoke.

"Except that it shows our friend Civita in a new light, I fail to see its significance. He looks a hefty chap enough, but I shouldn't have put him down as an athlete."

The photograph showed Civita standing in the front line of a group of men dressed, apparently, in running kit. That it had been taken some years ago was evident. Civita was noticeably younger and a good deal thinner, but the likeness was unmistakable.

"The interesting point about the group, to me, is the nationality of most of the members," said Constantine.

Arkwright nodded.

"They're Japs, most of them. I'm only a wretched policeman, I know, but I'm not blind!" he said plaintively. "Looks like one of those ju-jitsu conventions. You don't want to take this, too, do you? It's about the first thing Civita would miss when he came back to the flat, but don't let that deter you!"

Constantine gave vent to a low chuckle. Arkwright, looking at him, realized that he was in one of his most impish moods, his dark eyes alight with a secret glee that, while it spurred Arkwright's curiosity almost to frenzy, warned him that any questions were fruitless at this juncture. He had worked often enough with Constantine by now to recognize these manifestations and to know that, tantalizing though they were, they invariably meant that the old man had stumbled on something of real importance. Even so, he was hardly prepared for his final pronouncement, delivered casually as they tied up the parcel of curtains in the hall.

"You'll never get Civita for the Anthony murder," he said, "though I'm absolutely convinced in my own mind that he's guilty. You can prove that he's Bianchi. I don't think Howells will disappoint us there. And you can prove that he lied about the cards and deliberately misled you, but he's a clever devil, and his explanation, when he does give it, will be a good one. With Meger dead it will be difficult to pin him, even as an accessory. And a term of imprisonment for drug traffic seems sinfully inadequate for the murderer of a decent, harmless old fellow like Anthony. All the same, whenever you drag me into one of your unsavoury messes there comes a moment when I realize that the problem is not a chess problem after all, and that the pieces are not chessmen, but human beings. I wish, then, that I'd stuck to my own game and left you to play yours."

Arkwright tied the last knot and tucked the parcel under his arm. He was puzzled. Constantine's elation seemed to have left him, and he sounded tired and disheartened.

"If you played my game a bit oftener," he said, "you'd soon learn to take set-backs of this sort philosophically. If the public knew of the times we have to hold our hands through lack of sufficient evidence when we're morally certain that we've got our man, perhaps they wouldn't blame us so much. But you're right. Civita will get away with this, though we'll do our best to get him a stiff sentence for the drug racket. All the same, I'm disappointed. I thought, when you were so devilish mysterious over those curtains, that you were going to deliver him into our hands."

"I'm afraid I am," admitted Constantine, with a regret that the astonished Arkwright realized was perfectly genuine. "But not for the murder of Anthony. If you'll come to my flat to-morrow I think it'll be worth your while, but, extraordinary as it may seem, having reached the point towards which I've been working, I'm conscious only of hating the whole business so much that, if it wasn't for the thought of old Anthony and that girl, I should step out altogether and leave things to take their course. I've drunk Civita's wine and spent more than one pleasant hour in his company."

"I'll come to you any hour you like to name," said Arkwright, watching him closely.

He recognized Constantine's mood now. The pursuit of the criminal would always be a game to the old man, in the excitement of which he was apt to forget the inevitable end should he be successful, and it was only when within sight of his goal that the reaction would set in and he would swear never again to get involved in one of Arkwright's cases. He looked old now and tired, and Arkwright made up his mind to get him home and deliver him into the capable hands of Manners as soon as possible. Not for worlds would he have put his thoughts into words, though. Instead, he said:

"Unless you'd rather I came along to-night, sir?"

But Constantine shook his head.

"I'm not ready for you yet," he said. "In fact, unless I can get hold of the person I have in mind, I may have to ask you to wait, after all. If you drop me and my parcel at the flat on your way, I'll see what I can do."

Constantine's first act on reaching home was to write a note. This he handed to Manners when he called him next morning.

"Get off with this as soon as you can," he said. "If the gentleman has moved from this address, find out where he's gone, and, if possible, get hold of him. If he's left England, ring me up here from the nearest call-box. It's urgent."

But the call did not come. Instead, less than an hour later Manners arrived, accompanied by a small, squat, sallow personage, with polished black hair, who greeted Constantine with many bows and frequent dazzling displays of white teeth, and who departed half an hour later still smiling and genuflecting.

Early in the afternoon he returned, bringing with him a companion, slightly taller but in every other respect so like him as to be almost indistinguishable.

When Arkwright arrived he found Constantine in close conversation with the two little men, who had taken off their coats and revealed immaculate, sleeveless white sweaters. Civita's black curtains lay on the table beside them.

"May I introduce Mr. O. Nakano and Mr. Naito," said Constantine. "Mr. Nakano, whom you no doubt recognize, is one of the finest exponents of ju-jitsu in England to-day."

Arkwright, who, far from recognizing Mr. Nakano, felt convinced that, should he ever meet him again in the company of any of his compatriots, he would be totally unable to distinguish him, took warning from the twinkle in Constantine's eye and contented himself with polite but inaudible mumblings.

Bows ensued, in which he manfully did his part, then the party reseated itself. Constantine came to the point at once.

"We agreed yesterday," he said, "that we should never succeed in bringing a certain friend of ours to justice for a crime we are morally certain he has committed. Unfortunately, or, I suppose, fortunately for us, one murder is apt to lead to another, if the murderer is to keep his secret intact. I am convinced that that is what happened in this case, and I think I can prove it to you."

Arkwright glanced from the pile of velvet on the table of Constantine.

"Meger?" he queried, his voice frankly incredulous.

"Meger knew too much and he paid the penalty," agreed Constantine. "As regards the exact details of his murder we shall remain in ignorance, I suppose, but I can tell you more or less how it was engineered. I think we may take it that he was almost helplessly drunk at the time. We know that that was his failing, and he had probably been plied purposely with drink all day. When he was picked up, after his fall, he was so badly injured that it would be difficult to say precisely what had been the exact cause of his death. But one of those injuries, at least, had been inflicted before the accident, and the man Carroll saw pitch out of the window was already dead."

Arkwright opened his mouth to speak, but Constantine stopped him with a gesture.

"Wait till I've finished, then put any questions you like. I believe I can answer them satisfactorily. Briefly, what happened would seem to be this: the murderer, who was alone in the flat with his victim, first of all broke his neck. No, don't interrupt;

given a man helpless with drink, it's not so fantastic an assumption as you may suppose. He then set his scene. Exactly how he went to work I don't know, but I should imagine it was something like this: he went up to his sitting-room, which, as you know, is immediately above the murdered man's room, knotted together the four velvet curtains on the table there, making an enormous loop. The two ends of the loop he tied to the rail of the balcony outside the sitting-room window, arranging them so that the bottom of the noose hung just outside the window of the room below. Then he went downstairs, arranged the dead man, half in, half out of the window, with the loop of the curtains round his body, just under the armpits, being careful to adjust the body so that the greater part of the weight was *outside* the window. Then he left the room, turning out the light. This is an important point to remember, and was essential to the success of his scheme. It was a dark night, and, with the lights out, anyone entering the room would see merely the dark figure of Meger, apparently leaning far out of the window.

"At the precise moment that the witness switched on the light, Meger fell. The chances were a thousand to one against his seeing the black velvet as it was drawn swiftly upwards, the man upstairs having cut one end of the improvised rope at the point at which it was attached to the balcony, thus freeing the noose and releasing the body, which would pitch forward of its own accord into the well below, the light from the window below giving him the signal to act. After that, he would simply leave the curtains on the balcony until he had an opportunity to retrieve them.

"Carroll, as we know, collapsed completely as the result of what he had seen, and there would have been plenty of opportunity to get rid of the curtains before the police came on the scene, though, again, the chances were a thousand to one against their going out on to the balcony of the sitting-room. Certainly we didn't do so, though, of course, we can't answer for the local people when they first arrived. In any case, it's immaterial whether the curtains were on the balcony then or already in the cupboard in which we found them. The point is that they had been used, and, if you look at them carefully, you will see the marks made by the knots, and the jagged edge where the piece is missing that was cut to release them. Added to that, I found these, caught in the ornamental ironwork of the balcony."

He took an envelope from his pocket and shook three tiny fragments of velvet fringe on to the palm of his hand.

"I think," he said, "if you compare these with that bit of fringe that was entangled in Meger's coat-button you will find they match. It seemed insignificant when I found it, but, the moment I saw the curtains and noticed their condition, it took on a new aspect. I'm afraid I bundled them up rather hastily! I wasn't anxious, then, for you to examine them more closely. If you had, you'd have realized, as I did, that the rings on them showed no sign of dirt or rust—in fact, they were practically new. It seemed incredible that anyone would have put new rings on curtains in that state, and I was forced to the conclusion that they'd been reduced to that condition since the rings were put on. Remembering the piece of fringe we found on Meger's body, I began to ask myself how."

Arkwright was already examining the curtains. The fringe undoubtedly tallied with the fragments Constantine had found on the balcony.

"It's a brilliant piece of reconstruction, sir," he said reluctantly, "but the idea's so fantastic that I can't bring myself to accept it yet. If it's true, Civita took a colossal risk in carrying it out."

Constantine turned on him impatiently.

"Risk? Nonsense!" he exclaimed. "That unfortunate creature, Carroll, was in no condition to observe details at the best of times, and I assure you that black velvet is practically invisible on a dark ground. And you must remember that Carroll's attention was focused on the man the moment he saw him beginning to fall."

The two Japanese had been sitting motionless and impassive as a couple of idols while their host had been engaged in his little dissertation. With the natural courtesy of their race they had given their attention to what he was saying, but had shown no emotion save that of polite interest until now. At Constantine's last words, however, the smaller of the two rose to his feet and approached the table.

"You excuse me, yess?" he enquired blandly, as he swept one of the curtains over his arm.

Motioning to his companion to help him, he picked up a chair and carried it to the window, which he opened wide. Before the two men realized what he was doing he was outside, standing precariously on the ledge. He moved sideways, still carrying the curtain. There was a moment's pause, then:

"He says, can you see anything?" volunteered the other Japanese, turning to Arkwright with a flashing smile.

Slipping a hand into his pocket he produced an automatic lighter, snapped it into flame and held it to the window.

The light flickered and wavered in the draught, but it revealed, swaying gently in the breeze, the velvet curtain that his companion was holding suspended at arm's length outside the window.

"By Jove, it could be done!" exclaimed Arkwright.

He made for the window.

"For goodness' sake come in!" he called out. "One smash up of that sort's enough for one week!"

There was a low laugh, and the figure of the little Japanese slithered through the opening, trailing the curtain after him.

"I thought I show you," he smiled, "but that is not what I come for."

He turned to Constantine.

"Shall we begin, yess?"

"If you please," answered Constantine.

With the help of the two Japanese he cleared a space in the middle of the floor.

"Watch this," he said to Arkwright in a low voice. "I've a very shrewd suspicion that this is how Civita worked the thing."

The taller of the Japanese took up his position near the door, then lurched into the middle of the cleared space in a grotesque imitation of a drunken man. His companion approached him, slipped an arm through his as though in support.

Then, with a movement swift and smooth as running water, he swung the other man behind him till he had him with his chest pressed against his back between the shoulders. In the course of the movement he had brought his victim's arms over his shoulders from behind, and was supporting him by holding his wrists together with his left hand on a level with his chest, the recognized position for carrying a wounded or otherwise helpless man.

Thus burdened, he advanced a few steps, then, with a lightning movement, bent suddenly from the waist, holding the man's wrists in a firm grip as he did so. The taller Japanese shot over his head, turned a complete somersault, and landed neatly on his feet.

Both men stood beaming at their audience.

"But I did not hold his head," remarked the smaller of the two. "Oh no!"

"That's a recognized way of disposing of an assailant who comes on you from behind and gets his arms round your neck," explained Constantine. "I don't know whether your men are taught ju-jitsu, but, if they are, you'll recognize the throw. The interesting point, to us, about it is that, if you catch the back of your man's head as he comes over and hold it, you cannot fail to break his neck. When I saw that photograph I recognized Mr. Nakano, whom I have known ever since he first came to England and whose performances I've often watched with interest. I got in touch with him this morning, and discovered not only that he knew Civita but that he had been one of Mr. Nakano's star pupils. Isn't that so?" he concluded, turning to the Japanese.

Mr. Nakano executed a series of little bows.

"Very fine performer, Mr. Civita," he agreed. "He knows all the holds. Fine, big man, very strong. That throw we show you, he can do that any time."

"There's no doubt about it's being possible to kill a man that way, I suppose?" demanded Arkwright.

The little man's eyes shone with gleeful mirth.

"Not possible, easy," he assured him. "With that throw you must be very, very careful. If you touch your man's head, he die, like that—crack!"

He snapped his fingers joyfully.

Arkwright's lips twitched.

"There seem possibilities about this game that I've never realized," he remarked. "Don't you find chess rather tame in comparison, sir?"

"If I were ten years younger I might," agreed Constantine. "It would be a pleasant experience, for instance, to feel you as wax in my hands."

Mr. Nakano ran an appraising eye over Arkwright's huge form.

"Very great, strong man," he said, "but Doctor Constantine he would throw you if he had the training. I am a little man, smaller than Doctor Constantine, but I will demonstrate, if you like, yess?"

Arkwright, with surprising lightness and agility, placed the table between him and the Japanese.

"No, thank you," he assured him. "But I'm very grateful to you for your exhibition. You're positive that Mr. Civita is capable of executing that throw?"

The Japanese bowed.

"I taught him to do it," he said simply, "and I have watched him, not once, but many times."

"Good enough," agreed Arkwright.

He picked up the curtains.

"I'll take these exhibits," he said, "and see what the Assistant Commissioner has got to say about them, but I think we've got a case. Civita came out on bail this morning, by the way."

"Let's hope he doesn't miss his property," remarked Constantine with a smile as he turned to accompany his two other guests to the door.

"We'll have to gamble on that," said Arkwright. "I've put the fear of God into that porter, and I think he'll keep his mouth shut about our visit to the flat. In any case, if, as I hope, I get the warrant this afternoon, we should have him under lock and key before he has a chance to smell a rat."

"A very clever man, Mr. Civita," came in the silky voice of Nakano. "It is possible he may come for his curtains. You will put a policeman here, yess?"

Constantine laughed.

"Nonsense, my dear fellow," he exclaimed. "As Arkwright says, the porter won't give us away, and, without him, Civita will never trace the things to this flat. In addition to that, they won't be here if he does trace them. In half an hour's time they'll be on their way to the Yard. Meanwhile, a thousand thanks to you and your friend for the help you've given us to-day. If Arkwright here had any sense he'd go to you for some lessons!"

"Very glad to see him at any time," smiled Nakano as the two Japanese bowed their way out.

"We can rely on their discretion, I suppose?" said Arkwright when they had gone.

"Absolutely," was Constantine's answer. "Nakano's one of the best little fellows in the world, and I've a strong suspicion that he doesn't like Civita. But I agree with him that you'll do well to act quickly."

"You're right there. Before I go, here's something that may interest you. I've been through Meger's effects and I've found a key. It was in the inner compartment of his purse, and, from the look of it, it belongs to a safe-deposit. If the deposit's in England we'll soon trace it, though, of course, it may belong to some Belgian firm. There's just a chance that we may find further evidence relating to the drug business if we do."

"There's also a chance he may have put what he knew about Civita into writing," suggested Constantine. "It would strengthen his hold against him. There's no doubt in my mind now that Meger impersonated Anthony and afterwards ransacked his room, and I think we may take it that he got out of hand in some way and became a menace to Civita. Either he became dangerously garrulous in his cups, or he deliberately threatened him. In any case, Civita's motive for getting rid of him is clear enough now."

"And his motive for the Anthony murder," added Arkwright. "Anthony's daughter must have known all about the traffic in drugs, and she, no doubt, told her father that he had changed his name and was carrying it on in London. If the old man had exposed him it would have meant the end of everything for Civita."

Constantine nodded.

"And from what one knows of Anthony," he said, "his first impulse on reaching London would be to see Civita and threaten him with exposure. That is the only thing that puzzles me. Why he waited so long after his daughter's death before taking action. He must have returned from Brighton determined to put an end to the man's activities once for all. Why did he delay until now?"

"I think I can explain that," said Arkwright. "We've been looking up Civita's movements for the past year, in the hope of tracing his agents over here. So far as I can remember, he was in Italy from the middle of January to somewhere about the twentieth of February. Anthony, if he had tried to see him on his return from Brighton, would have found him away. He may not have learned that he was back until about a couple of weeks ago."

He began to pack up his exhibits.

"I'll take these with me," he concluded, "and see about the warrant. I'll let you know our plans, but we'll arrest him tonight, and at his flat if we can. You deserve a box seat for this, sir."

Constantine shook his head.

"This is where I make my bow," he said firmly. "Good luck to you. Come and see me when it's over, and, above all, be careful of Civita. He'll keep his wits about him till the bitter end, and he'll stick at nothing now."

Arkwright grinned as he made for the door.

"He'll find his activities severely curtailed in future," he retorted.

CHAPTER XV

CONSTANTINE, LEFT ALONE, felt himself drifting slowly but inevitably into that mood of depression that invariably overcame him when the excitement of the pursuit was over and the capture assured. Now, as usual, he recoiled at the thought of the end he had himself helped to bring about. He was filled with an utter distaste for the whole business, and felt nothing but disgust with himself for the part he had taken in it.

The whole thing was over, he told himself, as far as he was concerned, and he wanted only to forget it.

With that end in view he pulled a table in front of the fire and got out the chessmen he had neglected since his return from abroad. There were a dozen people, chess maniacs like himself, from whom he could take his choice and who would come gladly in response to the telephone, but when Manners came in bearing the tea-tray he found his master idly fingering the pieces, his eyes fixed on the dying fire.

"It's turned very chilly, sir," he said with a hint of reproach in his voice as he stirred the coals into life again.

Constantine roused himself.

"Did I let it go out, Manners?" he apologized. "I'm sorry. I suppose the inspector told you that he was getting a warrant for Mr. Civita's arrest?"

No one, looking at Manners, would have suspected that he was consumed with an almost unbearable curiosity as to the turn events were taking, but Constantine knew that only a life's training prevented him from asking the question that was trembling on his lips.

"He did say that he was arresting Mr. Anthony's murderer to-night, sir," he admitted.

"Didn't he tell you his name?"

"He omitted to mention it, sir," said Manners demurely.

"And you didn't ask?"

Manners's back stiffened slightly.

"It wasn't my place, sir."

Constantine pulled himself upright in his chair and stared at him.

"You're a marvel, Manners," he said. "After all, you did your share and you're entitled to hear the whole story."

He told him briefly what was taking place.

"You were right about Binns, I think," he concluded. "There's no reason to doubt that he was speaking the truth. Either Civita or Meger must have dropped that key in the stalls some time on the Saturday, though why either of them should have gone to the Parthenon I fail to see."

"A very incriminating thing to have about one, sir, a key like that," suggested Manners, "and not easy to get rid of. A dark cinema would be as convenient a place as any."

"But why the Parthenon?"

"Seeing that he'd staged the murder there, as it were, to begin with, the key would act as another link if it was found. It's very much what I should do myself, sir, in his place," said Manners, his rigidly respectable features lit up with a faint glow, possibly indicative of latent criminal tendencies.

Constantine regarded him with interest.

"Would you, now?" he remarked. "No doubt you're right."

Then, suddenly making up his mind:

"Stoke up the fire well. I'm going out."

Manners opened his mouth, shut it again, hesitated, then blurted out:

"You're not going to the Trastevere, sir?"

Constantine glanced at him quizzically.

"Putting yourself in Civita's place, do you consider the Trastevere dangerous?" he asked.

But Manners took the question in all seriousness.

"I shouldn't allow myself to be taken alive," he announced decisively, "and, if I had a revolver, I should use it. I shouldn't care to be in the inspector's shoes to-night, sir."

The amusement faded from Constantine's face. Manners had voiced his own misgivings.

"You needn't worry, Manners," he said. "Now that I know the use the place has been put to I don't propose to put a foot inside it again."

Manners said nothing, but his relief was evident as he adjusted the silver tray more conveniently at his master's elbow and noiselessly withdrew.

Constantine poured himself out a cup of tea and renewed his contemplation of the fire. Civita, bland and tactful, the perfect host, luxuriating in his own success, he had known, and, in a way, admired, but Civita, cornered, he could only imagine, and he had a very shrewd idea of what he would be like. There had always been a disquieting suggestion of latent power behind the man's suave manner, and he knew him now to be ruthless. Until he heard Arkwright's voice on the telephone he would be unable to rest, and he realized that inaction would only serve to increase his anxiety. There could be no news for at least a couple of hours, and he made up his mind to spend them at his club, where he would be within call if he were needed.

The telephone shrilled loudly in the hall, and he heard the deliberate tread of Manners as he went to answer it.

It was inconceivable that Arkwright should have any news for him yet, but with the inconsistency bred of nervousness, he rose expectantly to his feet and went to the door.

Manners, in the act of putting down the receiver, turned as he opened it.

"A police officer, speaking for Inspector Arkwright, sir," he announced. "There has been a hitch. Will you meet the inspector outside Mr. Civita's flat at seven o'clock?"

Constantine glanced at his watch. It was almost six-thirty.

"Say I will be there," he said.

Manners turned once more to the telephone.

"A police car will call for you at six-thirty, sir," he reported, when he had given the message.

Constantine nodded absently and went back into his room to fill his cigarette-case, his mind at work on Arkwright's rather cryptic message. Why this appointment outside the flat when he had made it clear that he did not wish to be present when Arkwright served his warrant? Had Civita taken the law into his own hands and staged yet another tragedy in his rooms? This possibility had been at the back of Constantine's mind all the evening. Civita, once he realized the seriousness of the charge against him, was not of the type to allow himself to be taken alive. He shrugged his shoulders. He would know soon enough, but he wished this abominable evening were over.

He stepped out of his front door into a gentle drizzle. The sky was black overhead and the street shrouded in darkness. He could make out the shadowy body of the police car behind the dazzling swath of light cut by its headlights.

The driver leaned outwards from his seat and opened the door. Constantine stepped in. The car leaped forward and swung round the corner.

He leaned back and lighted a cigarette, too absorbed in his thoughts to notice more than the inevitable delay as the car was held up in Victoria Street, and he was taken by surprise when it drew up smoothly beside the kerb. The driver climbed out of his seat and opened the door. As he did so Constantine noticed that the cigarette he had been smoking was not yet half consumed, and realized that the car must have travelled at a terrific pace to have reached Civita's flat in the time. There was some advantage to be gained by travelling with the police, he reflected idly, as he gathered himself together and prepared to alight.

"Is the inspector there?" he asked, as he rose to his feet.

Bent almost double to clear the low doorway, he was caught utterly at a disadvantage. Before he could even cry out his wrists had been seized, one arm twisted agonizingly behind him, and he found himself on his knees on the floor of the car, his face rammed suffocatingly into the seat.

He tried to raise his head, only to have it thrust down again with a force that brought his helplessness home to him, and for the next minute or so his whole energy was concentrated on the effort of breathing. By working his head sideways he managed to get a little air into his lungs, but by the time his assailant had finished tying his hands and turned him roughly on to his back his ears were singing and he was in no condition to struggle against the folded handkerchief that was jammed into his mouth and kept in place by a scarf tied behind his head.

His eyes, at least, were free and though in the darkness of the interior of the car he could catch no glimpse of the man's face, he could see, through the open door, the bushes and railings of a square faintly illuminated by the light of the nearest street lamp.

The door slammed and the driver climbed back into his seat.

"A pretty neat job for a man working single-handed," Constantine reflected bitterly as the car started once more with a jerk that threw his weight on to his trussed hands and caused him acute agony until he was able to adjust himself to the motion. He managed to work himself forward and peer out of the window. The driver was keeping to the side streets, and it was difficult in the darkness to recognize the rows of small shops and houses as they flashed by, but the Brompton Road, as they crossed it, was unmistakable, and when they drew up at last before the door of a small garage he knew he was in a mews and not far from Civita's flat.

The driver switched off the lights of the car and rolled back the garage door, then he returned to the car, lifted Constantine as easily as though he were a baby and carried him into the garage.

Dumping him on the floor, he tied his ankles securely together with a thin cord, bent over him for a couple of minutes, then departed, leaving him lying in the empty garage, the door closed, listening to the purr of the retreating car.

Constantine's first instinct was to get his hands free, but he soon discovered that his assailant, though swift, was very thorough. Finding that his efforts to reach his ankles only increased the pain in his wrists, he desisted and gave his mind to the problem of working off the scarf round his mouth. But here again he was baffled, and, realizing at last that his struggles only increased, rather than lessened, the tightness of his bonds, he gave up his efforts and confined himself to rolling painfully across the dirty floor until he had reached a position in which he could prop his back against the wall and get what little comfort was possible.

His arms ached atrociously, and the discomfort of the gag in his mouth made thinking difficult, but as his anger abated his mind became clearer, and slowly the absurdity of the situation began to dawn on him. For a moment he derived a certain bitter amusement from the contemplation of himself, trussed like a chicken, in a building probably barely a stone's throw from the man who had been detailed to watch his captor. That his assailant was Civita himself he had little doubt, though he had barely set eyes on him, so quickly and neatly had he done his job. He knew that he was in the neighbourhood of Civita's flat, and inferred that this was the lock-up garage in which he knew he housed his car. It seemed fairly obvious that he intended him no serious harm, since, had he done so, an easier and far safer way to have attained his purpose would have been to have knocked him out or even killed him. What that purpose was remained a mystery. Before leaving the garage he had run his hands through his victim's pockets, but whether he had taken anything Constantine was not in a position to find out.

He shifted uneasily, trying to find a way to ease the increasing agony of the cramp in his arms, and became aware of a tearing draught coming from underneath the ill-fitting door of the garage, adding his permanent bugbear, the dread of rheumatism, to his already gloomy thoughts. Silently he cursed the inefficiency of the detective who had the Italian under observation. If this was Civita's doing, he must have given the man the slip in some way, and it was beginning to look now as if Arkwright was going to lose his man.

A long shiver ran through his body. The draught from the door had increased wickedly and was now blowing on his unprotected head. Puzzled, he raised his eyes, and for the first time noticed the faint grey oblong of a skylight in the roof of the garage. The draught, he realized, must be coming from this.

As he stared at it a shaft of light shot suddenly from above, blinding him for a second as it rested on his face, then swept the floor of the garage before vanishing as abruptly as it had come. A voice, low and sibilant, reached him from the skylight.

"Doctor Constantine!"

He raised himself as best he could and strained his eyes, but the night outside was too dark for him to see more than a faint shadow against the sky. The light materialized once more, hovered over him, and was switched off.

"It is all right. I am coming," sounded softly from above, followed by a gentle thud on the floor of the garage. The torch shone again, revealing a coil of thin rope, down which a small, thick-set figure slid with the swiftness and neatness of a trained gymnast. It advanced on Constantine, the light of the torch, operated from above, following it unerringly.

Constantine's eyes haggard and staring above the tightly bound scarf, lit up with recognition.

"I will untie these first," said the little man gently.

He bent over Constantine's feet, while their owner, suffering tortures of unassuaged curiosity, watched him in enforced silence. The gag at last removed, he burst into speech.

"Nakano!" he exclaimed. "Bless you for this! But how did you get here?"

Mr. Nakano's lips parted in the inevitable smile.

"The police inspector said that he was going to arrest Mr. Civita to-night. Mr. Civita is a very clever man, cleverer than the inspector thinks. We discuss, my friend and I, and say, supposing Mr. Civita finds that these curtains that were so important have gone and learns that Mr. Constantine has taken them? What will he do? Just for protection I think I will watch till this arrest is over. So I wait to-night outside Doctor Constantine's house."

With the help of the Japanese, Constantine struggled to his feet. He held out his hand.

"I don't know how to thank you, Nakano," he said. "But why on earth didn't you come into the flat?"

Nakano shook his head.

"Should I be here now," he queried, "if I had been with you in your room? It was more useful outside. You must excuse that

I was so long in coming, but I could not open the door and had to telephone for Naito and a ladder."

Constantine stared at him in amazement. Nakano caught his eye and answered with a gleam of white teeth:

"It is very simple. Naito was waiting, in case I need him, and he lodges with a builder. He brought the ladder in his car."

As he spoke the ladder made its rather wavering entrance on the scene, lowered by the other Japanese through the skylight. Nakano received it and steadied it. A few minutes later Constantine, stiff and aching, but otherwise none the worse for this adventure, was standing on the flat roof of the garage.

"We descend now," whispered Nakano. "Wait, I will see."

He peered over the edge.

"Good. It is clear. Quickly now."

He helped Constantine down the ladder into a narrow cul-de-sac which gave on to the mews that ran behind the block of flats in which Civita lived. It formed the shorter angle of the larger-shaped thoroughfare, and contained half a dozen small lock-up garages. Naito's car, an ancient and weather-beaten Ford, awaited them, and, with the end of the ladder projecting like a tail behind, they trundled gingerly round the corner and out through the mews into the street.

"We go now to your flat, yess?" suggested Nakano.

Constantine hesitated.

"I ought to get hold of Arkwright," he said, "and let him know about this new development. I imagine that his man is still under the impression that Civita is in his flat. It was Civita, I suppose?"

"I do not know, but I think so from the size and the way he act. You wish to go to the police?"

"The trouble is that I don't know where Arkwright may be. If we go to the Yard and miss him we shall only have delayed matters."

Naito, who was driving, spoke over his shoulder.

"I believe we should go to doctor's flat," he said.

"You think Civita may have been there?" demanded Constantine. "Whoever attacked me went through my pockets. He may have been after my keys. Wait a moment."

He unbuttoned his coat and investigated.

"They're gone," he exclaimed. "And that's the only thing that's missing. That settles it. I ought to have looked before, but I'd forgotten about it."

Nakano leaned forward.

"We go to the flat," he said briefly.

"There's only one thing that can have taken him there—the curtains. Though how he knew I had taken them is a mystery."

"When did you acquire them?" asked Nakano.

"To-day, then I went with Arkwright to Civita's flat."

"And the porter saw you, yess? That is enough for the intelligent Mr. Civita. He would leave nothing to chance."

"All the same, he'll have his trouble for nothing," said Constantine. "Arkwright took the curtains to New Scotland Yard. The only thing that worries me is Manners. He's alone in the flat."

The policeman who had been holding up the traffic dropped his hand and ramshackle little car sped on its way.

Constantine's flat was above a shop, and was approached by a side door opening on to a narrow flight of stairs. Nakano was the first out of the car. He placed his hand on the door. It swung open at his touch. Naito, who had been watching him eagerly, joined him.

"You allow?" he queried.

Constantine, his finger already on the bell, nodded.

"If Manners is all right he'll answer this," he said, but he spoke to empty air. The two Japanese had already disappeared up the staircase.

He followed more slowly. As he arrived at the top Nakano's head came round the door of the flat.

"I think that Mr. Civita has gone," he said, "and there is no Manners. Everything is very badly upset."

Together they went over the flat. Everything was, as the Japanese had said, "very badly upset". Considering the short time at his disposal Civita had been pretty thorough in his search.

There was no sign of Manners. Constantine looked in his bedroom and found that the coat and hat he usually wore in the street were missing from their accustomed hook on the door.

"It looks as if he had deliberately dressed himself to go out," he said. "I only hope so. I'd better get hold of Arkwright if I can."

He rang up the Yard. Arkwright was not there, but he had left instructions that Constantine was to be informed as to his movements.

"I'm beginning to wonder whether we've been on the wrong scent all the time," he said when he rejoined the two Japanese. "Arkwright received word fifteen minutes ago that Civita was at the Trastevere and he has gone there with the warrant for his arrest. If he's taken fright over the curtains he'll hardly dare to show up there."

Nakano shrugged his shoulders.

"It was Mr. Civita," he insisted. "There has been no thief. All the silver and such valuables are here, you say. Unless, perhaps, you have something else of great worth?"

Constantine glanced round the room.

"Everything's valuable, more or less," he said. "My father was a collector. But there's nothing missing, so far as I can see. It certainly looks as if the curtains were the objective. That being the case, why has he deliberately shown himself at the Trastevere?"

"Perhaps there is something there that he must have," suggested Nakano, "before he can go away for good. It is possible. It would be better if this arrest was made quickly."

Constantine nodded.

"I must see Arkwright," he decided. "But there's Manners. If he's in any trouble…"

Nakano solved the difficulty.

"We wait here," he said. "If the servant comes back we telephone to you at the Trastevere. If not, you will be back soon, yess?"

Reluctantly yielding to necessity, Constantine picked up his hat. Any movement was still painful and he felt utterly weary. As he made his way slowly down the stairs his mind dwelt miserably on Manners. It was Mrs. Carter's afternoon and evening out, and he would have been alone in the flat. Taken by surprise he could have stood no chance against Civita.

The sound of a key turning in the lock of the front door brought him to a halt. He stood waiting.

The door opened and revealed Manners, apparently very much himself, dressed for the street. He looked up, realized his master's presence, and, at the sight of him, cast his habitual pose of decorous imperturbability to the four winds. The blood rushed to his face, then receded, leaving him white with emotion.

"Thank God you're here, sir!" he exclaimed.

Constantine seized him by the arm and pushed him up the stairs.

"Your relief can't be greater than mine," he declared. "Where have you come from?"

"Charing Cross Hospital, sir," said Manners.

Constantine turned on him.

"Are you hurt?" he demanded.

Manners shook his head.

"I'm all right, sir, but they said you wouldn't last through the night."

"That's putting it rather strongly," Constantine assured him with a reminiscent twinkle in his eye, "though I'm willing to admit that another few hours of that infernal garage would have made death seem sweet. Good heavens, Manners, but I'm glad see you!"

"You haven't been in an accident, sir?" enquired Manners doubtfully.

"Not to my knowledge, though so many things have happened to me to-night that an accident would have been almost superfluous!"

They had reached the hall where the two Japanese, who had caught the sound of their voices, were waiting.

Manners eyed them in silence, slowly taking in the situation.

"I've been a fool, sir," he announced at last. "All the way home the plate's been on my mind. I expected to find the place ransacked. But I could have sworn I'd taken every precaution. When I got the message on the 'phone saying you'd been knocked down by a car and taken to Charing Cross Hospital I did smell a rat, but I was so upset and worried I didn't know what to do. They said you were not expected to live through the night and would I go at once. Knowing it to be a favourite trick of burglars, I naturally wasn't going to take any steps until I'd verified the message, so I rang off and called up the hospital. I got them at once and asked whether anyone of your name had been brought in. The porter answered in the affirmative and said you were in a bad way. After that I didn't hesitate. I picked up a taxi and went straight there. I've been wasting my time arguing with them, or I should have been back sooner."

"No one could possibly blame you," said Constantine. "You did everything possible. The explanation's simple enough, of course. Civita held the line at his end, gambling on your ringing up the hospital immediately, and he was still on it when you asked for information. It was easy enough for him to answer your questions. You never got on to the hospital at all, but you couldn't be expected to know that. In any case there's no harm done, and it may comfort you to learn that he caught me even more thoroughly than he got you. Mr. Nakano here came to my rescue. If it hadn't been for him I don't know what might not have happened. Even now I'm rather vague as to precisely how he tracked me."

Nakano beamed.

"Very simple," he purred. "I wait in the doorway opposite and I see you get into a car. I think it may be all right, then again, perhaps not, so, to make certain, I run and leap on to the luggage-rack of the car. Mr. Civita keeps to the dark streets for his own purposes, and when we come to Victoria Street I jump off and run along the pavement. In the dark I jump on again.

When he reaches the garage I am not there, oh no! But I am close at hand!"

"I'm deeply grateful to you and Mr. Naito. If it hadn't been for your suspicious I should be in that abominable garage now. Manners, get some food for these gentlemen, will you, and make them comfortable while I try to get a word with Inspector Arkwright. And ring up the Yard and tell them you've come back. I think, in my anxiety, I gave them the impression that you'd been abducted!"

He was gone before Manners could voice his fears. Nakano reassured him.

"Mr. Civita is at the Trastevere under the watchful eye of the police," he said. "And he has no motive now for harming Doctor Constantine. I think his cleverness is over!"

Constantine, meanwhile, walked to the corner and took a cab from the rank. He had developed a prejudice against prowling motors of any description. He stopped it at the mouth of the side street leading from the Trastevere to Steynes House.

As he alighted, a dark, thick-set figure materialized out of the shadows.

"Good evening, sir," it said "The inspector's inside. There hasn't been any call for us yet. Looks as if everything was going according to schedule."

Constantine recognized a plain-clothes detective he had met before in Arkwright's company.

"Are there many of you on the job?" he asked.

"Enough to keep the exits covered. If you go round to the front you'll find a car with a couple of men in it. We've got instructions not to show ourselves unless we get the signal. Pretty full the place is to-night."

Constantine turned the corner, crossed the road and stopped opposite the Trastevere. From where he stood he could see the reflections on the plate-glass shift and disappear as the swing-doors opened to admit new arrivals. Evidently Civita's arrest the day before had proved an excellent advertisement for the restaurant, and, instead of scaring people off, would seem to have attracted them. He crossed the road once more and stood close to the entrance, his eyes on the gay crowd, his ears on the alert for any suspicious sound from within.

His mind was engaged with the problem of how to get in touch with Arkwright. After what had happened he could not show himself in the restaurant. Whether Civita was aware of the fact that he had escaped from the garage he did not know, but he could not afford to risk being seen by him.

He strolled along the line of waiting motors until he came to the police car. Here his luck was out, as the two men in it were strangers to him, and he had to fetch the detective from his post in the side street before he could convince them that his errand was important. Apart from the fact that they were not in evening dress, they were under strict orders not to show themselves inside the restaurant unless they were summoned. The best they could do was to try to get in touch, through the kitchen staff, with the detective Arkwright had planted among the waiters.

While the detective made his way to the service door, Constantine strolled once more past the main entrance to the restaurant. The porter, magnificent in green and silver, recognized him.

"Coming in, sir?" he asked.

Constantine shook his head.

"I'm waiting for a friend," he said. "Are you full to-night?"

"Fair to middling," answered the man.

He took a step closer.

"A pretty mixed lot, sir, between you and me," he said confidentially.

A car drove up and he turned to open the door.

As he did so the unmistakable sound of a shot came from inside the restaurant, followed by two others in quick succession.

The porter stood transfixed, a look of ludicrous surprise on his face, then he pulled himself together and made a dash for the swing-doors.

But long before he reached them, Constantine, moving as he hadn't moved for years, had hurled himself past him and disappeared into the restaurant.

CHAPTER XVI

ARKWRIGHT, MEANWHILE, had spent an afternoon which, if less physically painful than Constantine's, was, if anything, more exasperating. He had hoped to take Civita at his flat, thus avoiding the publicity of an arrest at the Trastevere, but by the time he had seen the Assistant Commissioner and applied for the warrant it was close on six o'clock, and, realizing that if Civita adhered to his habit of going early to the restaurant there would be little chance of catching him at his flat, he changed into dress clothes before returning to the Yard.

He had not been there more than five minutes when the telephone bell rang. The detective who was keeping Civita under observation was at the other end. From the tone of his voice it might be gathered that, at the moment, he wished he was anywhere else.

"He's given me the slip, sir," he said. "I'm very sorry. He'd left the lights on in his flat and I'd no cause for suspicion. He's got clean away, I'm afraid."

Arkwright smothered an ejaculation.

"When did this happen?" he demanded.

"About ten minutes ago. I'm 'phoning from the hall porter's office at the flats."

Arkwright wasted no time in recrimination.

"I'll come along," he said.

He found a very chastened subordinate awaiting him. Civita's plan of action had been maddening in its simplicity. The detective, after an irksome three hours spent in dodging up and down the street, had thankfully taken refuge in the doorway of a timber yard which closed down at six. It was situated immediately opposite to the entrance to the flats and was an ideal place for his purpose, as, invisible himself in the dark entry, he could keep an eye, not only on the doorway, but on the windows of the flat itself. He declared that he had watched both unremittingly, and Arkwright, for all his wrath, was prepared to believe him. The windows of Civita's sitting-room looked out on to the well at the back of the house, but the light in his bedroom had been turned on shortly before six and was still burning. The curtains were not drawn, and the detective had even seen Civita's form pass and repass the window, evidently in the act of changing his clothes before going to the Trastevere.

About half an hour after the lighting up of the bedroom a string of coal-carts had passed slowly down the street on their way to the depot. They were piled high with empty sacks, and for a short space blocked the watcher's view of the door of the flats. Civita must have been in the hall, waiting his opportunity, and have taken advantage of them, for when they were some distance down the road the detective, from sheer force of habit, cast a reconnoitering glance alone the pavement and spotted the figure of a man just turning the corner of the street. Realizing that he had materialized since his last uninterrupted view of the road, he jumped to the conclusion that he must have come out of one of the houses opposite and strolled across to the flats for a word with the porter.

"Did any of your people go out just now?" he asked, holding out his cigarette-case. "I picked this up on the pavement outside, and I'll swear it wasn't there a couple of minutes ago."

The porter examined it.

"Might belong to Mr. Civita," he said. "He's just gone out. You'd better leave it with me."

But the detective already had him by the arm and was shoving him in the direction of his office.

"Where's your telephone?" he demanded. "Quick! The matter's urgent."

And from then on the porter's normally rather monotonous life took on a new aspect. On the arrival of Arkwright he accompanied him upstairs, opened the door of Civita's flat for him with his pass-key, and was even permitted to stand by while the two detectives went hurriedly through the flat.

Civita's bedroom contributed certain illuminating details. That he had changed was evident, and the clothes he had taken off had been left out in a manner that suggested his intention of using them again that night. On a chair by the bed was an open suitcase, packed as for a journey, and, what was even more significant, an attaché-case containing a bulky packet of French and English notes lay on the bed itself. There seemed little doubt that Civita intended to return for these before he left the flat for good.

Arkwright stared at them, frowning, then turned to the detective.

"You're not new to this game," he said. "Do you suppose he spotted you?"

The man shook his head.

"I don't think so, unless something else happened to rouse his suspicions. I was very careful."

An idea struck Arkwright. Without a word he left the room and ran up the stairs leading to the box-room. The door was open, and from where he stood on the threshold he could see the cupboard in which Constantine had found the curtains. He had closed and latched it carefully on leaving, but now the door swung wide upon its hinges. He turned and went back to the bedroom.

"He's smelt a rat all right," he said. "Our only hope now lies in his coming back. We'll leave these lights as they are. Meanwhile, you'll take charge here on the chance that he turns up. If he does, you're to hold him at all costs. I must get a word with Ferrars at the Trastevere and put him wise to Civita's escape."

"I'll carry on till you get back, sir. I'm sorry for what's happened."

His tone was abject, and at the sight of his face Arkwright's lips twitched involuntarily. He knew how the man felt. He had been through it himself his day.

"It's up to us to get him now if he does come," was all he said, but there was a note of comradeship, in his voice that brought a new light to the detective's eyes.

On his way out Arkwright had a few words with the porter.

"See anything of Mr. Civita this evening?" he asked.

"Not till about half an hour before he went out," answered the man. "He called me up on the house telephone and asked me to up to his flat."

"What did he want?"

The porter looked uncomfortable.

"He wanted to know whether anyone had been here while he was away. While he was in quod, he meant, but he didn't say so! I couldn't help but mention you and the old gentleman. Till this evening I'd kept my mouth shut about it, remembering what you'd said, but when he asked me outright I didn't know rightly what to do."

If Arkwright wondered what Civita had paid for the information he did not say so.

"He hadn't asked you before?" he contented himself with asking.

"I haven't had a word with him till now. Been keeping to himself, he has. Wasn't any too anxious to show himself after what had happened, I should say."

"Did he ask you anything else?"

"He did ask had I noticed whether anything had been removed from the flat, and I told him you'd had a parcel with you. He didn't say anything to that, just thanked me and told me that was all."

"How was he dressed?"

"Evening dress, like he always wears at this time of night. He mostly comes in and changes about this time, before going round to the Trastevere Restaurant."

"What happened after that?"

"I came downstairs, and about half an hour later he rang for the lift and I took him down. He hung about in the hall outside my office for a bit. I thought he was waiting for a taxi, but all of a sudden he seemed to make up his mind and went out. That was just before your man came in with the cigarette-case."

Arkwright picked up a taxi and drove to the Trastevere. It was easy enough to guess what had happened. Something had inspired Civita to go to the cupboard, and, once he missed the curtains, he would realize his danger. His interrogation of the porter had done the rest. After that he would be bound to guess that the flats were being watched. He had shown both resource and ingenuity in making his getaway, but made a slip that looked as though it might prove his undoing in leaving his money behind. There was a faint chance that the mysterious business that had taken him out might be connected with the Trastevere, and that, believing the attention of the police was concentrated on his flat, he had decided to risk a visit to his office at the restaurant. All Arkwright could hope was that, if Civita had gone there, he had not managed to get in and out unnoticed by the three men he had placed on this premises.

The theatre dinners were in full swing when he reached the Trastevere, and already a string of motors was parked beside the kerb. Arkwright went round to the service door and asked for the detective who had been taken on earlier in the week as a temporary waiter. There was some delay before the man could be found, during which he chafed helplessly. At this juncture he did not dare to declare himself, and he tried to quiet his misgivings with the reflection that he had covered the interior of the restaurant to the best of his ability.

Before leaving the Yard he had done his best to block all the obvious channels of escape. Both the air and seaports had been notified, and, counting on the fact that up to this evening Civita had considered himself outside the pale of suspicion and could therefore have made no very elaborate plans for evasion, the chances, even now, were against his getting away. But Arkwright was harassed, to put it mildly, and saw himself in for a very unpleasant quarter of an hour with the powers that be if he failed to bring off the arrest to-night.

His man came at last with the news that nothing had been seen or heard of Civita at the restaurant. He was expected to turn up, as usual, between six and seven, but, so far, he had failed to do so.

"Wace and the girl have come," he reported. "They're in the lounge, and Ferrars is dining in the restaurant. I'm keeping this part of the building pretty well covered, though, of course, I'm on the run most of the time. Do you want me to declare myself? I can answer for a couple of the waiters, I think, but Civita's in pretty close touch with the kitchen staff, and I wouldn't put it past one of them to give him the office."

Arkwright shook his head.

"We can't risk it," he said. "We've got to get him now, and in a place this size you can't answer for anyone. I've taken a chance in coming here now, but I had to see you. Can you put the others wise to what has happened?"

"I'll see Ferrars at once, and he can pass the word on to Wace. Where can we find you, sir?"

Arkwright gave him the telephone number of Civita's flat and told him to ring him up immediately should anything transpire, then made for the nearest Public box and rang up the number himself. The detective he had left at the flat answered him.

"No sign of him, sir." he reported.

"Carry on till I come," Arkwright instructed him "I'm taking that garage of his on the way. I may get a line on to whether he's taken the car out or not."

He got into a taxi and paid it off at the entrance to the mews which contained Civita's lock up garage. He had hardly turned into it when he met a constable pacing slowly over the cobbles, flashing his lamp on the locks of the garage doors.

"What's your trouble?" he asked, guessing that the man was off his beat.

The constable cast a fishlike, disapproving eye on him, which flashed suddenly into alertness at the sound of his name.

"I can't see anything suspicious, sir," he said. "But a car came round the corner five minutes ago with three men and a ladder in it. I didn't get more than a glimpse of them, but they went off mighty quick once they got into the road, and it looked a bit queer to me. I thought there'd be no harm in havin' a look. This place is pretty well deserted at this time in the evening."

He glanced round as he spoke. With the exception of a chauffeur engaged in cleaning a car at the far end of the mews, there was not a soul to be seen.

"Been round the corner here?" asked Arkwright, leading the way into the cul-de-sac in which Civita's garage stood.

"I flashed my lamp down it, sir," answered the man, "but there's no sign of anything."

Arkwright tried the door of the garage, and, with the help of the constable's lantern, examined the lock.

"This hasn't been tampered with," he said, "but I'd give something to know whether the car's still inside."

"There's a chap lives over the garage at the corner there," the constable informed him. "He might have noticed it going out."

He crossed the yard and knocked on one of the side doors. There was a pause, then a window was thrown up overhead and a tousled head appeared.

"Didn't hear you at first," said a voice. "What is it?"

"I want a word with the owner of Number Fifteen," said Arkwright. "Do you happen to know whether he's taken his car out to-night?"

"He came back about half an hour ago," answered the head. "I see 'im pass 'ere and I 'eard 'im open the garage doors. A nasty squeak they've got. Then I 'eard 'im drive off again. Came back for something, I should say."

"He hasn't been back since?"

"Not that I know of, but I've been out and only just come in."

Arkwright thanked him and went on the flat. He found detective still keeping his gloomy vigil.

"Nothing doing, sir. I'm thinking he'll have to be pretty hard pressed before he comes back here," he volunteered morosely.

"We've done our best," said Arkwright. "I'll hang on here for the present. I'm banking on his having no money and finding a difficulty in raising any at this time of night. He must have been badly rattled to have gone without it."

He placed a chair against the wall near the front door and settled himself to wait. Through the open door of the bedroom he could see the attaché-case on which his hopes were based. The minutes passed drearily enough, and, in spite of himself, he found his eyelids drooping.

He was fighting the increasing drowsiness that threatened to overcome him when he was startled into full consciousness by the sound of the telephone. He raced up the stairs and into the sitting-room.

"Hullo," he called, keeping his voice as low as possible till he knew who was at the other end.

A high, rather querulous voice, with a marked foreign accent, answered him.

"Is that the Argentine Embassy? I want the Consulate, please."

"Wrong number," said Arkwright gruffly.

He replaced the receiver and sat back in his chair, a grim smile on his lips. So that was Civita's game. Clever enough, too, if he had not been on the alert for something of the sort. The exaggerated accent had been an inspiration, for, excellent as Civita's English was, he had never quite lost his foreign intonation and could not possibly have concealed it if he had attempted to pose as an Englishman. He did not trouble to trace the call, knowing too well that it would be from a public telephone box. He went back to the hall.

"The fat's in the fire," he said. "He knows the flat's occupied. I wonder what his next move will be?"

The question answered itself about a quarter of an hour later. From his post in the hall become conscious of a movement on the other side of the front door. Stepping lightly as a cat he approached it, noiselessly slipped the catch and threw it open.

A spare, lean-faced, middle-aged man in a dark overcoat stood outside. Behind him hovered the hall porter, with the expression of one who scents interesting developments and proposes to share them.

"A gentleman from Mr. Civita," he said. "Come for a suitcase, he says. I'm to let him in with my key."

Arkwright cast a quick eye over the man. He looked inno-cent enough, standing there with his soft hat in his hand, a look of genuine surprise on his face.

"Mr. Civita didn't say that there would be anyone in the flat," he said. "My instructions were to ask the porter to let me in."

"When did you see Mr. Civita?" demanded Arkwright.

"I haven't seen him," answered the man, evidently puzzled by Arkwright's manner. "He rang up the Trastevere and gave orders that I was to fetch a suitcase that I should find ready packed in the bedroom and meet him with it at Victoria Station."

"When was this?"

"About fifteen minutes ago. I came on here at once."

"What's your connection with the Trastevere?"

"Wine waiter. Beg your pardon, but are you the police, sir?"

Arkwright grinned.

"A bit divided in your mind, weren't you? Thought Mr. Civ-ita was going to jump his bail and weren't sure whether you hadn't better put yourself right with us?" he queried.

The man's face reddened.

"I was in a bit of a difficulty," he admitted reluctantly, "I'm in Mr. Civita's employ, and it didn't seem my place to go behind his back. Am I to take the suitcase, sir?"

Arkwright did some quick thinking. He had no doubt in his mind that the telephone call had come from Civita, and it was obvious to the meanest intelligence that if he knew that the flat was already in the hands of the police he would hardly send openly for his luggage.

"Did he say anything about an attaché-case?" he asked.

The waiter shook his head.

"Only a suitcase was mentioned," he said. "He said it was ready packed."

Arkwright went into the bedroom and came out with the suitcase in his hand. He drew the detective aside and gave him his instructions.

"Go with him," he said. "I'll get on to the Yard at once, but you'll have to carry on by yourself till I can get a couple of men down there. You'll have the station police behind you if he does turn up, but I don't think you'll see him."

He turned to the waiter.

"Got a taxi outside?"

"Yes, sir."

"Right. This officer will go with you, but not a word about him to Mr. Civita, you understand. You'll follow your instructions and hand over the suitcase. We'll see to the rest."

He watched them go, followed by the disappointed porter, then applied himself to the telephone. He arranged for the dispatch of two men to Victoria and ordered another to join him as soon as possible, then made his way slowly back to the empty hall, trying to put himself in Civita's place and fathom the meaning of this new move. He had been forced to cover Victoria Station, but he felt convinced that Civita would not show up there. He had been through the suitcase and knew that there was nothing in it that could be of any value to him at this juncture. The money was in the attaché-case, and it was significant that he had not sent for it. Arkwright could only conclude that he had staged this last little scene in a desperate attempt to draw the police away from the flat, but he did not feel satisfied. Unless Civita's nerve had failed him lamentably he was not acting true to type. The whole thing was clumsy to a degree, and not at all on a par with the man's usual standard of intelligence.

Arkwright settled himself once more in his chair. All desire for sleep had left him, but he was not happy. Civita had put in a useful ten minutes on the public telephone, but with what object he was not yet clear.

When the explanation did come it was a complete surprise to him. The telephone bell broke the silence again, and this time Ferrars, the detective who was among the diners at the Trastevere, was speaking.

"Our man's just come in," he said guardedly. "Everything's all serene so far. He's in the main restaurant. According to Wace, who's in the lounge, he came in quite openly, but he thinks he meant to go straight to his office. He got caught by a party and was pretty well forced to go into the restaurant with them. Any instructions?"

"Before you go back call up Headquarters, report to them and get them to send a second man down here in case of accidents. After that, don't make any move until I come, unless you have to. I'm on my way now," ordered Arkwright.

"Got you, my lad," he murmured, as he made for the stairs.

CHAPTER XVII

ARKWRIGHT'S UNEASINESS had vanished. He could follow the workings of Civita's mind now and give full credit to the cleverness of his attempt to concentrate the attention of the police on the flat while he collected the money he needed from the Trastevere. He had guessed that the police would see through the little comedy over the suitcase, and was no doubt gambling on their having omitted to cover the Trastevere, which, in fact, was the last place he might be expected to visit.

For sheer audacity this move took a lot of beating, reflected Arkwright, as he paid off his taxi and entered the restaurant.

He was hailed boisterously by a couple, a man and a girl, who were sitting in the lounge, facing the wide double doors that led to the main restaurant. He waved to them, went back into the foyer, shot his hat and coat across the counter, and joined them.

Bulky enough in the plain blue serge he habitually wore, he looked enormous in the black and white of his dress clothes, and the girl shot him a mischievous glance as he fitted himself creakingly into a totally inadequate cane chair.

Under the cover of offering him a cigarette the man spoke.

"He's still in the restaurant. Must be feeling like a cat on hot bricks by now, but those people have got him and he hasn't had a chance to break away. Had a positive reception when he went in."

The girl's nose wrinkled expressively.

"Not surprising," she said, "from this crowd. They're the limit!"

"Seen Ferrars?" asked Arkwright.

"He's in the restaurant, waiting to follow him up when he comes out. That's our cue."

They sat chatting idly, their eyes alert. Then the girl rose to her feet.

"This is where I fade out, I suppose?" she suggested rather reluctantly.

Arkwright grinned at her.

"Sorry," he said, "but it's time we cleared the decks. You might pass the word outside that all's going well so far."

She nodded, drew her cloak about her and sauntered to the door, chatting to her companion as she went. He saw her out, then returned to his table. Arkwright had produced an evening paper and retired discreetly behind it.

For a time the two men sat smoking in silence, covertly watching the steady stream of people coming and going through the swing-doors. If Constantine had been there he would have agreed with the Duchess that the tone of the place had hardly improved during the past few months.

The big doors of the main restaurant were open, and through them came the sound of a band, almost drowned by the unceasing babel of the diners.

"If we could get at the facts," said Arkwright in his companion's ear, "I bet we should find that Civita's bled most of this little lot pretty freely."

He jerked his head towards a particularly noisy group that had just come in, half a dozen boys and girls barely out of their teens.

The two men watched them as they stood in the doorway impatiently waiting for the head waiter to find them a table. They were apparently in the highest spirits, but Arkwright noticed that the moment the conversation dropped for a second a curious lassitude fell on them, only to be dispelled by an obvious effort on the part of one of the group. None of them was quite sober, and the glazed eyes and chalk-white faces of at least two members of the party indicated that very little more would be their undoing. He observed, too, that the hand with which one of the girls was incessantly plucking at her heavily smeared lips was dirty, and, as he looked at her, he saw a shudder run through the whole length of her figure. It jerked her restless fingers away from her mouth and caused her to clutch at her companion for support, as, with an effort, she joined once more in the babel of high, incoherent voices.

"It's when one sees the youngsters that one realizes to the full what a filthy traffic it is," murmured Arkwright. "It's easy to see why some of that little lot come here. I wonder where they'll go now that the supply's cut off!"

There was still no sign of Civita. The swing-doors opened again, letting in a chill blast of air, this time to admit another larger party, even more clamorous than the first.

It was headed by a tall, almost incredibly slender woman, whose hair, even apart from the vivid, shimmering green dress in which she was literally sheathed, would have made her conspicuous in any gathering. It was of that rare shade, real auburn, and it crowned her curious, arresting face like a gorgeous halo.

Even Arkwright, whose imagination was not easily stirred, was reminded of a mænad leading her Bacchanalian rout, so untrammelled and exuberant were her gestures, so clamorous her high, incessant voice, screaming witticisms over her shoulder to her companions as she swept them through the lounge and into the restaurant.

"Well, I'm blowed!" murmured Arkwright's companion, almost reverently.

Arkwright's smile was grim.

"That's one of the people we've been advised to deal tenderly with," he said. "Lady Malmsey, the Duchess of Steynes's cousin. According to Doctor Constantine, there's precious little love lost between them, but it's kid gloves for us, all the same."

From where he sat he could see through the doors into the restaurant, and he watched the buoyant progress of Lady Malmsey and her train with an amusement that turned to disgust as he saw her pause opposite the bank of flowers that encircled the orchestra, clutch the sleeve of the negro singer, pulling his head down to hers until she could whisper in his ear.

Apparently what she said was worth hearing, for the man straightened himself with a gleam of white teeth and then doubled up with laughter. She passed on to her table, dropping a word here and there to friends as she went.

Wace, Arkwright's companion, had been on duty at one of the Labour Exchanges that morning. There had been trouble with some of the men waiting for their dole, and for a few minutes it had looked as if the police were going to get the worst of it. Wace, remembering the white-faced, half-starved wretch he had pulled from under the trampling feet of his own comrades, found it in his heart to agree with at least some of the incoherent denunciations that had fallen from his lips as he dragged him to safety.

"There's enough money wasted here in one night to keep an out-of-work family for a month," he said gruffly.

"And most of it goes into Civita's pockets," was Arkwright's comment. "I'd like to know what this place is worth to him, apart from that jolly little sideline of his. Enough to have kept him on the level you'd have thought."

As he spoke one of the diners appeared in the doorway. He hovered for a moment there, then disappeared, but neither of the watching men had missed the almost imperceptible jerk of his head that signalled the approach of Civita.

Arkwright swung round in his chair, so that his back was towards the restaurant; his companion, who was engaged in lighting a cigarette, watched the door through the cloud of smoke that obscured his face.

"Coming down the centre now," he murmured. "Reached the door. Damn it, he's turning right! It'll be the flat after all. I'd better give the office to the chaps outside. No, he's stopped to speak to someone."

He dropped his matchbox on the floor and bent down, fumbling for it.

"He's turned left up the stairs. There's Ferrars."

He straightened himself and watched the other detective make his leisurely way up the stairs.

"Fancies himself in those clothes, Ferrars does," he remarked with a chuckle. "He was quite short with me when I told him I'd taken him for one of the waiters. He's got his hat in the cloak-room upstairs. If Civita's gone to his office, he'll let us know."

The two men summoned the waiter and paid for their drinks. Then they rose and made their way quietly up to the next floor. Ferrars, who was leaning on the counter chatting to the cloak-room attendant, joined them.

"All set," he said, as together they approached a door on their right.

Arkwright turned the handle softly, opened the door and went in, followed by Wace. Ferrars took up his position, leaning negligently against the wall outside.

Civita, who was sitting writing at his desk, with his back to them, turned at the click of the latch.

For the space of a second he was transformed. Rage, brutal and unrestrained, banished the secrecy from his eyes and twisted the corners of his thin lips. Then, as if a hand had passed over his face, it slid back into its accustomed form, and the old Civita was before them, calm, authoritative and impassive.

"You wished to see me, Inspector?" he enquired in his full, rather unctuous voice.

But Arkwright was already by his side, a hand on his shoulder, uttering the usual formula of arrest.

As his lips formed Meger's name he heard the soft hiss of es-caping breath, saw the thick white lids drop for a moment over the inscrutable eyes, and knew that he had indeed taken Civita unawares. He braced himself for action, but the muscles under his hand merely slackened and Civita, that one tense moment over, sank back in his chair and looked up at him, a faint, ironical smile curling his lips.

"Isn't this a little fantastic?" he said. "I was not even in the same room with the unfortunate man when he died."

Arkwright's right hand slipped down to the cut of Civita's dinner-jacket. Wace, he knew, had a working acquaintance with ju-jitsu, but he was taking no risks.

"I've warned you," he said, "but, if you care to make a statement, I'm ready to hear it in the proper place. Meanwhile, I must ask you to come with me."

His fingers closed more tightly on the cuff.

Civita stood up. The two men, facing each other, were well matched. If Civita had increased in bulk during the years of his prosperity, he had gained in weight, and at close quarters might prove a tough proposition for Arkwright for all his fourteen stone of sheer bone and muscle.

But Civita, apparently, was too sure of his position to jeopardize it by resisting the police.

"Certainly I will come with you," he said with a sardonic lift of his eyebrows. "But I think you will have some difficulty in explaining this. Just to satisfy my curiosity, perhaps to you will tell me how I am supposed to have brought about the death of a man who was not even on the same floor as myself?"

And Arkwright, herding his man inexorably towards the door, made the mistake of his life. If he had kept silent then, the evening might have ended very differently.

"We have proof that Meger was dead before he fell from the window," he said briefly.

Once more Civita's breath came, this time in a gasp of utter consternation. He stopped dead, bringing the two men to a halt with him, and the face he turned to Arkwright had changed in that second past all belief. It looked dead in its grey pallor, as if a light had been clicked off behind the lifeless eyes.

When he spoke his voice sounded dry and cracked.

"That is—very interesting," he said.

His free hand went to the pocket of his dinner-jacket, and, as it did so, Wace's fingers closed round the wrist.

Civita's lips jerked into a travesty of a smile.

"It is only a handkerchief. You can take it out, if you insist."

Wace ran his fingers over the outside of the pocket and released his grip, his watchful eyes on the hand that disappeared, to come out with a neatly folded square of clean linen.

Civita shook it out and passed it first over his forehead, then over his lips. Then he straightened himself.

"I am ready," he said.

This time there was nothing strained about his smile, it had even a hint of triumph behind it.

The little procession moved on towards the door, and had almost reached it when Civita reeled suddenly and pitched sideways with a force that almost sent Arkwright to the ground.

Instinctively he tightened his grip, only to feel the man's body heave and arch backwards in a convulsion that loosened his hold. He saw Wace's futile grab as an even more violent contortion followed, and Civita, with a scream that was the more horrible for being strangled, crashed heavily to the ground.

As they bent over him he rolled over on his chest, raised himself on his hands until his face, a grinning, tortured mask, was lifted to Arkwright's.

"I will go—in my own way," he gasped, through the spasms that shook him.

"The doctor, on the 'phone, quick!" jerked out Arkwright, already on his knees beside the agonized body, but he knew as he spoke that he was too late.

Wace was at the desk, the receiver to his ear, dialling rapidly.

Civita's back arched until only his feet and hands were on the floor. It looked as though these were the last supreme convulsion, and Arkwright cursed himself for having allowed the thing to happen.

He knew no more till he found himself writhing and gasping on the ground, floored by what felt like the kick of a horse in his solar plexus.

In the midst of his agony he heard the sound of the opening door, followed by a terrific crash, as Ferrars landed inside the room on his head, blocking the doorway.

He caught a glimpse of flying heels within an inch of his face, as Wace, with a running jump, shot over him, only to land just short of Ferrars, trip over him and come hurtling to the ground.

When he did get to his feet and stand huddled and retching, Civita had vanished, and, with him, Wace.

Ferrars was on his knees, his face a ludicrous mixture of fury and dismayed astonishment. From his temple where he had hit the door-knob in passing, a thread of blood was trickling.

From beyond the door came the sound of a revolver-shot. "Hell!" groaned Arkwright, as he made for the landing, with Ferrars lurching behind him.

He reached the top of the stairs, swerved, and ducked just in time as a bullet whistled past his cheek, took the first four steps in one, ducked again as Civita fired, then leaped once more, vaulted the stair-rail, and dropped on to the thick carpet below.

And all the time he was conscious of two things: Civita's massive figure, etched in black and white against a throng of blanched, staring faces, and the tumultuous sound of Ferrars's descent as he tripped and pitched on his face down the stairs behind him.

He charged round the foot of the stairs into the lounge. The white faces receded, revealing a black mass on the ground that he knew to be Wace, and, bending over it, a figure incongruously dressed in a hat and overcoat.

Of Civita there was no sign.

He brought himself to a slithering stop, dropped on one knee beside Wace, and found himself staring into the face of Constantine.

"Badly hit?" he demanded.

"Thank God!" was Constantine's answer. "I thought it was you."

The face he raised to Arkwright's was white and strained.

A voice, husky but undaunted, came from the ground.

"Got me in the shoulder, sir," it said. "I'm all right. You carry on."

Arkwright cast a look at Constantine, received a reassuring nod and leaped to his feet.

He looked round him. Civita was gone. Wace was gone, and there was not one gleam of helpful intelligence to be found in any of the staring faces that hemmed him in on all sides.

He felt a pull at his sleeve and turned to find the cloakroom attendant at his elbow.

"Through the restaurant," he breathed, "with your man after him."

Before the last word had left his lips Arkwright was off the mark. He raced through the restaurant, his eye taking in two service doors on his right, another, leading to places unknown, on his left. He halted and looked round him.

The restaurant was deserted save for a few people scattered here and there among the tables.

He realized that they were all staring at the Palm Court at the end of the room.

"Which way did they go?" he demanded.

A voice answered him.

"The Palm Court," it said, and he started again.

He reached the short flight of stairs leading to the Palm Court and was half way up them when Ferrars cannoned into his arms.

"He's slipped me, sir!" he panted. "I saw him turn right at the top, but that fall had knocked the wind out of me and I got here too late. He's taken cover somewhere. Must have. There's no way out."

Arkwright, looking down, saw that he was holding a revolver in his hand.

"That's his," Ferrars informed him with a grin. "He chucked it at me and nearly got me on the head too."

Arkwright ran up the steps. The Palm Court was apparently deserted. In front of him rose the blank wall that gave on to the gardens of Steynes House. Tall palms masked it, and in front of them clustered a host of little tables with their attendant chairs.

Behind the banks of flowers a plain, wooded dado skirted the two ends of the Court. Above it, and across the whole of the restaurant side, was glass. Except for the opening at the top of the steps on which he stood, there was not a door anywhere.

"Keep the opening here," snapped Arkwright, "and stop him if he tries to bolt. And for God's sake don't use that thing! He's behind those palms somewhere."

But Civita was not behind the palms, and, beyond a tip-sy-looking chair half on its side and a matchstand on the floor, there was no sign of his passage.

Arkwright stood in the middle of the Court scratching his long chin, while Ferrars babbled meaninglessly of miracles.

It was at this moment that Constantine arrived on the scene, escorted by a straggling procession of the Trastevere's best customers.

"No need to worry about Wace," he announced. "There was a doctor present, fortunately, and he's in his hands. It's nothing but a flesh wound. What's wrong?"

Arkwright indicated the empty Palm Court.

"He's gone! Vanished! And there isn't a door in the damned place! I've muffed this job all right," he said bitterly, "and I shall hear of it!"

Constantine swung round and plunged into the little crowd behind him. Arkwright realized that he was calling to him to follow, and leaped in pursuit.

"Waste of time to try to break through it," Constantine was saying as he reached his side. "We shall have to go round. Get hold of as many of your men as you can."

"Where to?" shouted Arkwright.

"Steynes House. He's gone to earth in the garden. There is a door there, but you wouldn't see it. Behind the big palm, matches the panelling. There's a keyhole, but if you weren't looking for it . . ."

Arkwright suddenly remembered.

"And the Duchess has got the key. Of course he kept one, I ought to have thought of it," he groaned. "Let me get on ahead, sir."

He charged through the crowd in the lounge, Ferrars at his heels, through the swing doors, past the taxi into which a pallid Wace was being helped by the doctor, wasted a precious three minutes in giving the word to his men outside, then pelted, this time in the wake of Ferrars, down the side street that led to Steynes House.

Once there he jabbed a finger on the bell and kept it there. After what seemed an eternity the double doors were flung wide. The butler stood in the opening, and behind him, tall, lean, and mildly surprised, the Duke.

Arkwright was by his side before the butler could intervene.

"Beg your pardon, your Grace," he panted, "but this is urgent. I must ask you to let us search your garden."

The Duke peered at him.

"Inspector Arkwright, isn't it?" he enquired. "The garden is at your disposal, but you'll have your work cut out for you, I'm afraid. Portland, show the inspector the way."

"Is there only the one door, your Grace?" demanded Arkwright.

"That's all. It's at the end of a passage leading from this hall. What are you looking for? A burglar?"

"Bigger fish than that, I'm afraid," said Arkwright. "Civita, the proprietor of the Trastevere."

The Duke's good-humoured face hardened.

"Then you're going the wrong way," he said shortly. "He left this house by the front door at my request a minute or two ago."

Ferrars, standing in the doorway, had the advantage of Arkwright. He was down the steps and had run to meet the police car before the inspector was, over the threshold.

His first glance told Arkwright he was too late. Save for the Duke's car standing at the bottom of the steps, the little group of plain-clothes men straggling round the corner and the police car which had just swung into it, the street was deserted.

"I've no idea which way he went when he left here," said the Duke's voice behind him, "but I've no doubt he picked up a taxi. There's a rank just round the corner."

Arkwright watched the police car turn and tear down the road, saw a couple of his men doing a very creditable sprint in the opposite direction and tasted the bitterness of defeat.

He turned to the Duke.

"If I might use your telephone?" he said wearily.

The Duke led him into the library. While he was ringing up the Yard, Constantine arrived. Out of the tail of his eye he could see him deep in conversation with the Duke.

"I must get back," he said when he had finished.

"We're only wasting time here. I suppose Civita got into the house from the garden."

The two men laughed.

"Tell him," besought Constantine.

"I'm sorry to appear heartless," said the Duke, his lips twitching, "but, not content with being made a fool of, I'm afraid I made a pretty complete fool of myself. The fellow's nerve is amazing! I came out of this room and found him standing in the hall. There was nothing in his appearance to arouse my suspicion. He seemed perfectly cool and collected. To say that I was surprised and annoyed to find him there is putting it mildly, and I was flabbergasted when he told me that he was fresh from an interview with my wife. He admitted frankly that she had written to him concerning his lease of the Trastevere, pointing out to him that, owing to the use to which the restaurant had been put, she must ask him to terminate his agreement with us. He declared that he had come in the hope of persuading her to change her mind, but that he had seen her and been unsuccessful. He accepted her decision and was willing to take any course that we considered suitable."

He caught Constantine's eye and smiled ruefully.

"As a matter of fact, it is not within our power to dictate to him in the matter of the lease. If I had had my wits about me I should have realized that he would hardly give in so easily, but I was so overwhelmed by the fellow's impudence in daring to approach my wife, after what had happened, that I let my indignation get the better of me. This is literally the first time I have ever turned anyone out of my house, but I made it very plain to him that any communication in future must be made through my solicitors, and showed him the door myself. It seemed incredible that my wife should have communicated with him in the first instance, but I knew she felt very strongly on the subject of the Trastevere and might have acted on the impulse of the moment. In any case, as I said, I was too indignant at the man's audacity to have my wits about me."

"Arkwright must have missed him by seconds only," said Constantine.

"I was still in the hall when the inspector arrived," agreed the Duke. "My interview with Civita was shorter than it sounds in the telling. My one object was to get rid of the man, but I had only just succeeded when you arrived. I must admit he took it well. Just picked up his hat and coat and walked out."

Arkwright stared at him.

"One moment," he said.

He went to the front door and opened it. Ferrars was standing on guard outside.

"May as well give it up," he said at the sight of Arkwright. "He's got clean away."

"Look here, how was he dressed when you saw him making for the Palm Court?"

Ferrars stared at him in amazement.

"Same as he was when you last saw him, sir," he said.

"No hat or coat?"

"Good lord, no! He hadn't time to get at them."

Arkwright closed the door and went back to the library.

"Would your Grace come into the hall for a moment?" he asked.

The Duke followed him.

"As regards the hat and coat . . ." began Arkwright.

But the Duke's eyes were already raking the polished surface of the hall table.

"Well, I'm blessed!" was all he said, and then fell silent, his heart too full for words.

Constantine, who had followed him, also contemplated the table, a slow smile spreading over his face.

"Yours?" he murmured appreciatively.

The Duke found his voice.

"I was going out," he said slowly, "and my hat and coat were on that table."

He stepped forward and picked up two limp white objects.

"At any rate, he's left me my gloves," he remarked with a wan smile.

CHAPTER XVIII

INSTINCTIVELY ARKWRIGHT looked round for his own head-gear, only to remember that it was still reposing, with his coat, in the cloakroom at the Trastevere.

The Duke was staring at the gloves dangling from his hand, his wrath gradually giving way to reluctant amusement.

"The fellow's incredible," he murmured with something like awe in his voice.

Constantine stood laughing unashamedly in the background. Arkwright pulled himself together.

"I must get along," he said, his hand on the door. "I'm sorry for this, your Grace, and I'm afraid I'm in a way responsible. We'll do our best to trace the things, of course."

"Trace Civita," jerked out the Duke with surprising vehemence. "I'd like to see the fellow in the dock. Hate being made a fool of, even to amuse Doctor Constantine!"

He was struggling with his own mirth as he spoke, and Arkwright let himself out of the front door to the sound of uncontrollable laughter.

He stood for a moment on the step, the door open behind him. The dark form of Ferrars materialized from the street below and hovered, waiting for release. The Duke's car, long, black and gleaming, blocked his view in front, but to right and left the street was empty, save for the plodding figure of a postman in the middle distance.

Behind him the laughter rang out again. Arkwright grinned, but it was a half-hearted travesty of his usual expansive effort. The really supreme touch would have been for Civita to have taken the car as well, he reflected. Indeed, it was hardly like him to neglect so obvious a way of escape. He'd have had an even chance of reaching the outskirts of London and abandoning the car before a cordon could be formed.

Obeying a sudden impulse, he ran down the steps and opened the door of the car.

As he did so the door on the opposite side swung silently on its hinges, a dark figure slipped from the interior of the car, and, before Arkwright had even realized its presence, was away and racing down the street in the direction of the turning leading to the Trastevere.

There was a shout from Ferrars as he charged down the pavement and swerved into the road. Arkwright, his long legs working like pistons, passed him at his third stride.

Civita had almost reached the side-street, and the two men checked instinctively, ready to take the corner should he turn up it.

It was that moment that a woman, driving a two-seater, and carrying three extra passengers on the side running-board chose to shoot silently from the side-street and swing round the corner with the speedometer needle quivering at fifty.

If Civita had been on suicide bent he could not have timed the thing better. He had just reached the corner, running with his head down and his body well forward, when the car caught him.

One scream, shrill and horrible, came from the hatless, dishevelled woman at the wheel, followed, too late, by the screech of the brakes.

The figures on the running-board shed themselves, at various angles, on to the ground, and Civita's body, impelled by the force of the impact, rose, hurtled through the air and fell, with a smack like the crack of a whip, on the road ahead.

The car skidded at right angles, teetered for a moment on two wheels and crashed on to its side.

In a second Arkwright was at Civita's side. He lay, huddled and motionless, his head bent at a curious and unmistakable angle to his body. As Arkwright lifted him it fell back as the head of no living man can do, and he lowered the body gently to the ground again and retraced his steps to the overturned car.

Ferrars was already there, bent low over a silken heap that moaned as he touched it. A woman stood swaying on her feet beside the car. Three men were picking themselves up dazedly on either side of it.

With one swift glance Arkwright took them in, realized that they were not badly injured, and joined Ferrars, who stared up at him with a question in his eyes.

"Dead," said Arkwright. "Neck broken. What about this?"

Ferrars stood up.

"Back, I'm afraid," he murmured, his lips close to Arkwright's ear. "I don't dare move her."

Arkwright looked down at the woman at his feet. She neither moved nor uttered a sound now, but there was a terrible vitality in the face upturned to his. Her eyes were open and filled with a fear so stark that his throat ached suddenly in pity. He knew now why Ferrars had whispered. Her green dress, wrenched and twisted brutally round the inert body, shimmered in the uncertain light of the street lamp overhead, her glorious hair, elf-locked and bedraggled, crowned a face, grey and wet with anguish, like a halo.

Instinctively his eyes went to Steynes House. The Duke and Constantine had descended the steps and were coming towards him.

With a muttered exclamation he hurried to intercept them.

"Is there anything we can do?" asked the Duke. "Civita much damaged?"

"Dead," answered Arkwright. "And I'm afraid the driver of the car's in a bad way."

The Duke took a step forward, then his lips tightened.

"A woman!" he exclaimed. "Do you know who it is?"

Arkwright moved quickly between him and the figure on the ground.

"Lady Malmsey," he said.

CHAPTER XIX

CONSTANTINE WAS in Arkwright's room at New Scotland Yard, summoned there by an urgent telephone call. Arkwright, at the other end, had been apologetic. He was too busy to come round, but he had a document that might interest him if he could spare half an hour.

He could. Arkwright's message had caught him prowling restlessly round his room, engaged in contemplating a lengthening vista of spare half-hours, and conscious of a blank in his life that even chess, at the moment, seemed inadequate to fill. Arkwright did not have to wait for him long.

The inspector was lying back in his chair, his pipe in his mouth, gazing with a look of infinite complacency at the ceiling. He sprang to his feet at the sight of Constantine.

"If we could clear up all our cases like this," he rejoiced, "life would be one long happy dream! It's all there, thanks to this!"

He burrowed in his pocket and threw a small key on to the table.

Constantine regarded it with interest.

"The safe deposit?" he enquired.

Arkwright sank back into his chair and dragged an untidy pile of papers towards him.

"Meger was asking for it," he said, "Civita being Civita! He blackmailed him, right enough; this stuff here proves it, but the poor fool never realized the risk he was running. He'd got Civita in the palm of his hand and had tucked away the evidence where, even after his death, Civita couldn't lay hands on it. If it hadn't been for that key we should never have got on to it. As it is . . ."

He lifted a sheaf of papers from the top of the pile, crumpled, jagged-edged fragments, covered with neat, angular writing, and pushed them towards Constantine.

"Anthony's diary," he said. "No wonder Civita wanted to get hold of it! The mistake he made was in sending Meger to pinch it. Meger, once he'd read it, knew better than to give it up, and, so long as he had it, Civita was helpless."

Constantine was already running through the pages. There was a tense silence while he skimmed them, then:

"Good heavens!" he exclaimed. "The whole story! We weren't far wrong, either!"

Arkwright, lying back in his chair, his hands clasped behind his head, beamed.

"It's all there," he agreed, "from Anthony's interview with his daughter, right down to the night before he paid his last visit to the Trastevere. As we thought, she told him how Bianchi had made his money and that he was operating under the name of Civita under cover of the Trastevere. Apparently he'd deserted her, left her high and dry two years before, and she'd only just got on his track through one of his agents in Paris."

"To do Anthony justice, he seems to have been actuated as much by his abhorrence of the drug traffic as by revenge. He had every intention of denouncing Civita to the police," said Constantine, raising his eyes for a moment from the papers he was devouring.

Arkwright nodded.

"The pity is that he didn't come to us straight away. It seems that he went to the Trastevere on his return from Brighton, only to find that Civita was in Italy. He did not discover he was back till early in March, and, when he did manage to see him, found that the job he had set himself was not so easy as he'd supposed. Civita retaliated by threatening to approach Miss Anthony, reveal the fact that he was her father, and not only tell her, but make public the story of her mother's disgrace. Anthony seems to have been almost abnormally sensitive on the subject, besides which, he had kept all knowledge of her mother's story from the girl and dreaded the effect on her of Civita's revelations. For the moment he was evidently baffled, but he seems to have been a determined old gentleman, and on March the seventeenth he wrote to Civita warning him that he intended to go to the police. He no doubt hoped to frighten Civita into leaving the country and thus avoid the scandal he dreaded."

"It was then that he decided to see Lord Marlowe, I suppose, and tell him the truth about his granddaughter?" said Constantine.

"Exactly. Only, unfortunately, in his letter to Civita he told him what he was doing, realizing that it would spike his guns should he try to molest his daughter. Civita met him on March the twenty-second outside the Parthenon and asked him to talk the matter over with him that night at the Trastevere. Anthony consented. And that's where this comes in."

He stretched out a long arm and picked up a couple of sheets of flimsy notepaper, closely covered on both sides.

"This," he continued, "is Mr. Meger's little contribution, and very interesting it is! He was one of Civita's most useful agents in Belgium, just as he had been in the South of France. A word from Civita and he would have been in the hands of the Belgian police, who already suspected him of being concerned in drug traffic. After Anthony's letter of March seventeenth Civita sent for Meger. They worked the Anthony murder together, Meger impersonating Anthony, while Civita, at his flat, administered the injection of morphia which killed him. Then he placed the body in his car and took it to the Parthenon, arriving there in the early hours of Wednesday morning."

Constantine looked up quickly.

"You haven't cleared up the mystery of the key, I suppose?" he demanded.

"Anthony, in his diary, speaks of having met Civita just as he was going into the Parthenon. He was probably about to use his key when Civita spoke to him. Civita, seeing it, would be quite clever enough to put his knowledge to good use. Which of them dropped it in the stalls later, I don't know, but there is mention of Binns in Meger's statement, and I think we may take it that he had nothing to do with the crime."

"What induced Anthony to go to Civita's flat? I can imagine his being willing to meet Civita at the Trastevere, but I admit

I'm surprised to hear that he consented to accept his hospitality, apart from the fact that he must have realized that the man was dangerous."

Arkwright turned back to the last page of Meger's statement.

"That's one of the cleverest things Civita did," he said. "You were right in your assumption that Anthony was misled. The card Civita sent him at the Trastevere was not, as you guessed, the one we found. Meger's got the whole thing down here in black and white, in the form of a letter to us. I've no doubt he threatened to clear out of the country and post it to the Yard if Civita did not give in to his demands. The card, making an appointment for ten forty-five at Civita's flat, was signed 'Marlowe', and Anthony was certainly under the impression that he would find Lord Marlowe waiting for him when he got there. You must remember that he was expecting to hear from him and had told Civita so, and that he did not know Civita's private address. Meger had orders to wait for him outside the Trastevere, introduce himself as a friend of Marlowe's, accompany him to the flat, and, if possible, induce him to take the coffee with the knock-out drops in it. He carried out his part of the scheme successfully, and states that Anthony was already asleep when Civita arrived. He then went off and spent part of the night in establishing Anthony's presence on the Embankment and elsewhere."

"Civita then went back to the restaurant, I suppose? He was seen there up to nearly two in the morning."

"He went back about half past eleven, leaving Anthony's body in his flat. He seems to have gone straight to the Parthenon on his return to the flat at two. Having disposed of the body, he abandoned the car where it was found next day, walked home and went to bed. At a quarter past six he rang up the police with his story of the stolen car. Meger had it all pat, so that it looks as if Civita had given him quite a frank account of his movements. As a matter of fact, Meger already knew so much that it was hardly worth while to keep him in ignorance. It must have given Civita shock of his life when he realized that had turned nasty and did not intend to return those pages of the diary."

"That was the one really bad mistake Civita made," agreed Constantine, "but he was in a difficult predicament. He had to get at the diary at all costs, but he was too well known, both to Marlowe and Betty, to risk going to the house. Whoever let him in could not fail to remember and describe him. Did Anthony tell him about the diary, by the way?"

"According to Meger he knew already that the old man had always kept one. Margaret Anthony probably told him in the days when they were living together in France. He may even have gone so far as to ask him point blank whether he still kept up the habit. In any case, he was clever enough to realize his danger if such a thing existed. Meger states that he had orders to tear out the pages and bring them straight to Civita. He was then to leave England for Belgium, and Civita would send him the five hundred pounds he had promised him. Instead, Meger took himself off and wrote to Civita saying that everything had gone according to schedule, but that he proposed to keep the papers until he knew what Civita was prepared to offer for them. He then seems to have embarked on a prolonged drinking bout, during which Civita must have been raking London for him. When he did find him, he was not in a condition to exercise caution. This is only surmise, of course, but I think we may take it that he would never have gone to Civita's flat if he had had his wits about him. Fortunately for us, he wrote this statement and placed it, with the pages from the diary, in the safe deposit before he started on his spree."

Constantine threw the papers he was holding on the table.

"I'd like to read these properly some time," he said.

"Of course. But you've got the gist of the whole thing now. Anything I haven't told you?"

Constantine shook his head.

"It's pretty clear," he answered. "How much of this are you going to give the public? The Duke's naturally anxious."

"I don't think he need worry. There'll be the inquest, of course. Civita was killed in trying to evade arrest for Meger's murder. Anthony's name need not be mentioned. The drug traffic will be a sufficient peg to hang the whole thing on, and Miss Anthony need know only so much as you choose to tell her."

"In fact, it's all very neat and tidy and there's nothing now to prevent at least one young couple from living happily ever after. By the way, I've one piece of news for you. There's rejoicing in the House of Steynes!"

Arkwright smiled.

"The date of the wedding, I suppose," he said.

"No, you'll see that in the *Morning Post* shortly. This concerns both you and the Duke. His hat and coat were found last night by his chauffeur. Civita had left them in the car."

"I can see him now when he realized what had happened!" said Arkwright with a reminiscent chuckle.

Then his face sobered.

"Lady Malmsey's in a bad way, I hear," he added.

"They say she'll never walk again. The Duchess, having ostracized her for years, is kindness itself now and talks of putting her up as soon as she comes out of hospital. The unfortunate creature lives in a kind of elaborated cocktail-bar she calls a flat, with no accommodation for nurses, and she has no friends that are of any use to her at a time like this. She'd reached a pitch at which she was hardly responsible for her actions."

Arkwright, who was absently staring at the papers before him, raised his head.

"If she had been she'd hardly have been driving hell-for-leather through the streets like that," he said. "Civita supplied her with the stuff, and, properly speaking, it was the stuff that killed him. There's a queer kind of justice in things sometimes."

THE END

Made in the USA
Lexington, KY
23 December 2016